The Case Files of Sam Flanagan:
Drowning in Deception

Judith White

World Castle Publishing, LLC
Pensacola, Florida
Copyright © Judith White 2017
Paperback ISBN: 9781629897400
eBook ISBN: 9781629897417
First Edition World Castle Publishing, LLC, August 7, 2017
http://www.worldcastlepublishing.com
Licensing Notes
Cover: Karen Fuller
Editor: Maxine Bringenberg

DEDICATION

To Dennis H. White
One of my biggest supporters and a man I was honored to know.
June 27, 1947 - May 21, 2017

CHAPTER ONE

The world was going to hell in a handbasket. It wasn't the same world I grew up in, and none of it made any sense to me. I could look across the street and see what I'd always seen; the light green two-story home of Vasily and Sarah Petrovich, with its shaded front porch and tall gleaming windows. Flower boxes holding blue morning glories and white asters lined those windows, clinging to life as the summer was ending. Even though nothing on the exterior had changed, I knew that within that structure the lives of the Petrovich family would never be the same again.

The couple had purchased the house shortly after their marriage, and shortly after that, they'd begun to build their family, Sarah giving birth to four daughters within seven years. Mrs. Petrovich was forty-one years of age, and her youngest child was fifteen, when she learned she was in the family way yet again. A much-unplanned surprise, Thomas Vasily Petrovich was born in that home across the street twenty-one years ago this very month...the month of September. He'd grown into a handsome young man, and a year and some months after graduating from high school, he'd enlisted in the United States Army Air Corps, answering the call for good men to be at the ready to push back against Adolf Hitler's maniacal obsession of becoming dictator of the world. At the end of March of this year, word had been sent to his parents from Washington D.C. that he'd parachuted into the Netherlands, and that's the last time the other men in his unit had seen him. Somehow, he and another soldier had gotten separated from them, and the two were now missing in action. Vasily and Sarah had lived the last almost six months not knowing the fate of their son. I could not imagine their anxiety and pain.

These thoughts flooded my mind as Mr. Petrovich climbed into his dark blue 1936 two door Ford Sedan Humpback. He was heading out to work, but before he could put the auto in reverse to roll out of his driveway, his wife came running out of the side door holding up a brown paper bag…his lunch, no doubt. She handed it to him through the open window and leaned down for a perfunctory kiss from him. Sarah Petrovich watched as her husband's automobile crawled down the street, and then caught sight of me, sitting on the steps of my own front porch, holding onto a cup of coffee. I waved to her with my free hand and she waved back, and then disappeared inside through the door from which she'd emerged.

No, the world wasn't the same, and I'd find out just how different it was becoming at the end of the case that was about to come knocking on my door, so to speak.

My name is Sam Flanagan, I'm forty years of age, and I live on St. Aubin in the city of Detroit with my eighty-two-year-old paternal grandmother, Ruby Flanagan. I was married for a whole four years, and employed as a cop for the city for the same amount of time. Neither arrangement worked out, so I opened my own office down on Woodward Avenue. The sign on my door says Flanagan Investigations. Working alone suits me just fine. For the most part, I like what I do. I prefer to think of myself as a problem-solver.

For instance, ten days ago I took a little trip down to Ohio to locate, and bring back, the daughter of Mr. Melvin Kittrel...yes, *that* Mr. Melvin Kittrel, owner of two posh hotels in downtown Detroit and a third in Pittsburgh, Pennsylvania. His only child, a daughter named Leona, was soon to be eighteen and had met a man seven years her senior. After a brief three-week courtship, they'd headed south to find a justice of the peace to perform a quick ceremony of marriage. I was to try to find them before any such ceremony could take place, and to relay her father's message that if she went ahead with this nonsense, he'd change the terms of her inheritance of twenty thousand dollars from the girl's grandfather to the age of twenty-five. Now I wasn't sure if he'd actually carry out his threat, and I was guessing the original plan had been to hand it over to her upon her upcoming birthday.

Well, it just so happened I was successful in tracking them down before this young man, Harry Pearcehouse, could slip the ring on her finger. I had caught them eating breakfast at a roadside diner just inside the city limits of Toledo. I'd panicked a little as I pulled out a chair at their table and sat in it while I signaled to the waitress to bring me a cup of black coffee. Leona was wearing an orchid corsage pinned above her left breast on her soft pink frock, and the young man was wearing a black suit coat that was a tad too large in the shoulders. I had worried that they were enjoying a celebratory post-nuptial meal. But that hadn't been the case, and I inwardly gave a sigh of relief.

They were stunned when I sat down, so I quickly introduced myself to the young couple and told them my reason for being there. I delivered Mr. Kittrel's message, but assured them that he might be persuaded to throw them a proper wedding if she would just return home. That last part was my ingenious idea, and I was hoping it wouldn't come back to haunt me. It didn't.

7

After exclaiming, *"Twenty-five?"* in an incredulous tone, Harry insisted that Leona travel back to Detroit in my auto and he would follow—just to appease her father, of course. After a long hug and a short kiss between the couple, Leona and I got into my '38 Chevy and headed north.

Melvin Kittrel was exceedingly happy that I had returned with his daughter while she was still in a "single" state, and he paid me well for it. Problem solved. As for Harry…he'd either made a wrong turn somewhere along the line and gotten lost, or else he had changed his mind altogether about altering his marital status, because Leona hadn't seen or heard from him since we pulled away from that diner. I imagined that the young woman had been shedding a whole lot of tears since then, but in time she'd be ever so thankful for her narrow escape.

It was Monday, September 13, 1943. I'd been sitting on the front porch with my cup of coffee for the last fifty minutes, where I'd witnessed Vasily Petrovich leave for his job at the Ford Motor Company, and I'd waved to the two boys who lived next door as they passed by on their way to school. Albie and Bobby Randle wore black pants and short-sleeved white shirts, and carried books under their arms. Albie, who was twelve, wore a black tie at the collar of his shirt, while eight-year-old Bobby wore a dark blue and white polka dot bow tie. They were growing up so fast.

The sun warmed my face and the mild breeze that wafted through the neighborhood felt heavenly. It was in the low 70s without a cloud in the sky overhead. I was enjoying these mornings of solitude. Twice a week I drove my grandmother to her place of employment…Augie's Cuchina. She'd started the job almost two months ago, where she stayed in the kitchen and baked peanut butter cookies, and sometimes washed and cut vegetables for salads and pizza toppings. Gran was having the time of her life earning her own money, which was a whole forty

8

cents an hour, but she was also allowed to bring home a couple of dozen cookies per week. So far it was working out quite nicely. Her hours were eight o'clock in the morning until one thirty in the afternoon, taking a half hour break to eat lunch provided by the owner of the establishment, Augustino Consiglio. Augie was a big fellow of about four-hundred pounds and in his late twenties, who I had met back in January when I was working on a case in Chicago. After the job was finished he'd visited one day, and ever since, he and my grandmother had become, and remained, good friends, something I thought was a bit strange. But as long as Gran was happy, who was I to object? Now me...well, the guy got on my nerves to some extent. To all appearances, he was a big dumb lug. He spoke in a monotone that drove me nuts, but I had to admit that as of a couple of months ago, I'd started to see him in a light that was softer and kinder. He'd saved my life, and for that, I would be forever grateful to him.

I continued to sit on the porch steps another ten minutes or so while I smoked a Lucky Strike cigarette, allowing what remained of my coffee to grow colder and untouched. There was nothing better to do. I'd gotten into the habit of not going into the office on the days my grandmother worked...that is, not until I'd picked her up and delivered her back home to the house on St. Aubin. Looking at my watch, I noted that that wouldn't be for another four and a half hours. About to stamp my smoke out under my shoe, I thought I heard the ringing of the telephone. I cocked my head to the side and listened more intently. Yep, that was the phone all right. I grabbed my cup and my pack of Lucky Strikes and hurried inside.

"Is this Sam Flanagan, the detective?" a deep male voice inquired after I'd answered the instrument.

"Yes, it is," I answered.

"I'm sorry to have to bother you at home, Mr. Flanagan,

but I was wondering if you would have some time to look into something for me. I called your office this morning, but of course, there was no answer. I hope you don't mind me telephoning you there."

"Not at all," I assured the man. "What's the nature of the case?"

"Actually, I'd rather explain all of that when we meet. Can you meet me at my club at say twelve this afternoon? We can have lunch together there."

"That isn't going to be possible," I said to him, thinking of my grandmother. "Do you feel you could meet me in my office about three o'clock? I can be there then, Mr...uh...."

"Oh, forgive me. Girard, Victor Girard. Listen, now that's not going to work for me, but I'll tell you what. Why don't you head over to the club at five? We'll have cocktails and then I'll buy you a steak dinner. What do you say?"

"I guess I can do that, Mr. Girard. What club is it that you belong to?"

"The Detroit Club on Cass Avenue. Know where it is?" he asked.

I assured him I knew where it was, although I'd never stepped foot into the prestigious location.

"Just tell the doorman that you're there to see me, and I'll leave word with him that I'm expecting you. I'll be up on the third floor in the main dining room."

I hung up agreeing to meet him at five, and then I scratched my head. Victor Girard...of course I knew the name. He was a Michigan state senator. But there was no way the guy on the phone was *that* Victor Girard.

CHAPTER TWO

Ask anyone who knows me, and they will tell you that when expected to be somewhere at a certain time, I am prompt...well, most of the time. Today I pulled into the rear parking lot of the Detroit Club, the Romanesque Revival building, which was situated at 712 Cass Avenue in downtown Detroit, eight minutes late for my meeting with Mr. Victor Girard. The doorman was right where he was supposed to be, standing guard outside the entrance to the exclusive gentlemen's establishment. I told him my name and who I was there to see. He nodded and opened the door for me to pass through.

Stepping into the reception area, I immediately sank a fraction of an inch into the plush, deep red carpeting. This place was fantastic. Portraits of members long since departed from this earth graced the taupe colored walls...men of distinction, men instrumental in forming this great mid-western city. My eyes scanned the solemn faces staring back at me. I recognized the original two founders, attorney Samuel T. Douglas and banker/broker James Campbell. Russell A. Alger, a former Michigan governor, wore a dour expression, as did real estate magnate James B. Book. The others I didn't know, or couldn't recall their

11

names. But still, I was in awe of their positions in life.

Dark mahogany french doors were situated directly to my left. They opened onto a smoking room where the air was foggy with expensive cigar fumes. I glanced in and caught an elderly gentleman eying me while puffing on an ornate calabash pipe. He nodded and I returned the gesture. My eyes darted to the right, where another set of doors stood open to reveal a library and reading room. Black high-backed leather chairs were strategically situated throughout, a few occupied by gentlemen holding newspapers. Bookshelves covered the walls, holding the classics, no doubt. A staircase with carved mahogany railings was straight ahead and I advanced forward. I remembered that my prospective client had told me I would find him on the third floor in the main dining room.

As if awaiting my arrival at the top of the stairs, another elderly gentleman stood in long black tails, black tuxedo trousers, a white vest, a crisp white shirt, and a white bow tie. He bowed slightly as I reached the top.

"May I help you, sir?"

"Yes, I'm here to see Victor Girard. He's expecting me," I said.

"Very good, sir. Please follow me."

I did just that and he led me to a table in the left front corner of the room. A distinguished gentleman occupied one of the chairs by the window at that table and was looking down onto Cass Avenue. The day was still mild and sunny. As if he could sense our approach, he turned to us just before we reached him. The man shoved his chair back and stood. My eyebrows went up in recognition and surprise as he extended his right hand.

"Mr. Flanagan? Glad you could make it. I'm Victor Girard."

"Hello, Senator," I responded. "It's very nice to meet you."

The Michigan politician was taller than he appeared to be

in the periodicals, standing a full inch above my six-foot-two frame. With my weight at two hundred and eight, I probably had a good ten pounds on him. His chestnut colored hair, worn short and parted on the right, had a minimum of gray strands running through it. A neatly trimmed mustache covered the space between his nose and upper lip, and contrary to the hair on his head, it was almost all gray. The man had eyes a shade of light silver that I'd never seen before.

After performing a handshake, we took our seats across from one another, and he turned to the man who had led me to him. "Davis, bring Mr. Flanagan a drink, and you can bring me another Manhattan if you would."

"Very good, sir," Davis said, and then turned toward me, waiting for my choice in beverages.

"Scotch on the rocks, please."

He bowed slightly and left us.

The senator raised his glass to his lips and took two huge swallows, draining its contents. I used the time to take in my surroundings. Although I couldn't be absolutely sure, I thought I spied Henry Ford sitting with three other men I didn't recognize several tables away from us.

"Ever been inside the club, Flanagan?"

I turned back to the man I was here to meet and shook my head. "It's impressive."

"We members like it," he said, and looked around the room. "A home away from home for some of us. On the second floor we have exercise equipment, a swimming pool, and a sauna, as well as a barber shop and a tailor. They do a very adequate job of taking care of our needs." He extracted a slender cigar from his shirt pocket and was lighting it when Davis returned with our drinks. "Bring us two New York strip steaks, Davis," he instructed the man. The senator then looked to me, asking how

13

I liked mine prepared. "Make them both medium, and bring a couple of green salads."

Davis then bowed and departed without a word. When the elderly man was out of earshot, Victor Girard spoke again. "I assume you've heard of my wife's tragic death six weeks ago," he said, tossing his extinguished match into the clear crystal ashtray that sat on the table.

I nodded, but said nothing.

"I don't like the conclusion the Detroit Police Department has come to. I may be completely wrong, but I can't shake the feeling that something's off, and I want you to look into it for me. The desk sergeant at the precinct mentioned you to me."

"What is his name?" I asked, curious to know who would think of me.

"Can't remember," he said. "They humored me for a bit, saying they were looking deeper into the matter, but I can tell when I'm being patronized, Mr. Flanagan. Just nose around for a week or so and see what you can come up with. I can't help but think that it would have been so improbable for her to have suffered that type of accident, that there must have been more involved here. What's your fee?"

"Twelve dollars a day," I answered him.

Just recently I'd upped the cost of my services by two dollars. I was behind the times. Other private investigators in the area had been charging this amount for quite awhile now. I felt it was the right time to do a little catch-up.

The senator was unmoved by the amount mentioned. He laid his cigar in the ashtray and removed a checkbook and pen from the top pocket of his black suit jacket. He filled out a check and handed it over to me before even asking if I would take on this assignment. But that was all right; he had piqued my curiosity, and I currently wasn't working on a case. I placed the eighty-four-dollar draft in my own suit-coat pocket.

"What bothers you about this?" I asked.

I was actually stalling, trying to wrack my brain about the incident. I knew the senator had lost his wife in a drowning, but I could recall nothing else.

"Several things, I suppose. First of all, she called me that night. I was in D.C., but was scheduled to fly home that evening on a nine-fifteen flight. She said she wanted to talk to me about something, that she'd wait up for me. You see, Flanagan, Sonny was generally in bed early each night…usually around nine thirty or ten o'clock at the latest. But that night she said she wanted to discuss something, and I could feel the anxiety in her voice. Something was troubling her. Unfortunately, I didn't have much time to give her on the telephone, so she said she'd wait up."

"Sonny?"

"Sondra," he said. "She was known as Sonny to those who were closest to her."

"What exactly happened, Senator? Please forgive me, but I can't recall the details. Something about a drowning?"

He nodded while taking a long draw from his cigar. "That's right. My wife was a strict creature of habit…very disciplined. She took a swim every morning before heading into the office to be there by nine, and every night before she ate dinner at eight, when weather permitted. She was an avid swimmer, Flanagan. That's why I can't believe she would be so careless. She wouldn't have been. I know it. She would never have done the things they claim she did. Sonny was always too cautious for that. I cared for her a great deal, and feel I owe it to her to look into this."

He cared for her a great deal and owed it to her to look into this? I thought that certainly was an odd way of speaking about his recently departed wife.

I looked up at Davis as he placed our meals before us. The

aroma ignited the empty feeling in my stomach that I was now aware of. The thick strip steak sat on top of a large leaf of lettuce on the fine solid white china plate. A small bowl of fresh greens, tomato, and onion was set to the side, while decanters of oil and vinegar were placed in the middle of the table. Victor Girard picked up his fork and knife and began to cut a chunk off his meat.

"I hope you don't mind, but I don't like conversation while I eat," he said, without looking at me.

CHAPTER THREE

We continued our conversation when the table was cleared of our empty plates and hot coffee was set before us. Cautiously I took a sip of mine while Senator Girard added a small amount of cream and two lumps of sugar to his own.

"Sonny wasn't my first wife," he said as he stirred his beverage. "Do you remember Judge Thaddeus J. Burke?"

I shook my head as I replaced my cup in its saucer.

"He was a prominent judge in the city. Sat on the bench for thirty-two years, but he died in 1921. I wouldn't be where I am today if it wasn't for him. I guess he saw something in me…paid for my education at the university and groomed me for politics. Anyway, I married his daughter Barbara. We'd gone through school together and married when we were eighteen, right after graduating. She was the love of my life, Flanagan, and when she died of cancer three years ago, I was devastated. Oh, I knew it was coming, but I deluded myself into thinking that a miracle would take place." He paused and lit another cigar, then looked me in the eye with a somber face. "There *are* no miracles. Just empty hopes and dreams."

"I'm sorry for your loss," I said sincerely, but I was getting antsy. I found myself not knowing what to say to him. Inwardly I was asking myself where he was going with all of this, and wondering when he'd get around to telling me about his second wife's death and why he thought there was something fishy about it.

He nodded while he took a long draw on the stogie and then exhaled toward the ceiling. Then the man waved the cigar through the air as he continued.

"The days following her death were like living a nightmare. I'd find myself at the breakfast table drinking coffee, and I'd look down and notice I was wearing my three-piece blue suit and couldn't even remember showering and dressing. I was numb, not really living or noticing anything around me. Yet, I couldn't just *stop*. My work in Washington was too important. I owed it to my constituents to continue. Seven months after burying Barbara, I attended a fundraiser in D. C. There was a little gal there from Asheville, North Carolina. Her father was the editor for a local newspaper down there, and she wanted to get a story on the event for it." He stopped and laughed briefly. "By god she was feisty; asking tough questions…accusing my colleagues and myself of not listening to the people's concerns, not addressing their needs. Her manner and actions were a breath of fresh air to me. I hadn't laughed so much since before my wife had become ill. She amused me and I started seeing her whenever I could get away from Washington. We'd meet for dinner, that sort of thing. She eased some of the pain I was still feeling. So, one night I asked her to marry me. Here I was twenty-six years her senior and she said yes. You could've bowled me over with a feather."

"The reporter at the fundraiser was Sonny?"

He nodded. "That's right. But I never pulled any punches with her. She knew right from the beginning that the love I had for Barbara would never die. After all, Barbara was the mother of my children. We'd grown up together and had fully planned on growing very old together. She was all right with that. We were married four months after that fundraiser, and I had just about two years with her before I flew home that night and found her lying on the bottom of the pool in the backyard. See what you can find out, Flanagan. I owe her that much."

***

After I left him, I stood leaning against the trunk of the Chevy in the parking lot of the Detroit Club, smoking a Lucky Strike cigarette, going over in my mind what the senator had told me. The sun had disappeared for the day just moments ago, and the mild breeze brushing against my face felt refreshing. When I'd pulled out my little notebook back in the main dining room to record the names of those who knew her, the man seemed hesitant to tell me who they were, stating that he was sure they wouldn't know anything or be involved in any way. Finally I was able to jot down a couple of names, but when it came to recording the names of his three children by his first marriage, it was like pulling teeth. "They are certainly *not* involved, Flanagan. They don't know anything," he had said in a stern voice. But I had to convince him that I would have to start *somewhere*, and I would need to talk to all those who knew her. He begrudgingly relented. It would be interesting to find out what his and Barbara's offspring had felt about their father marrying a much younger woman, and relatively soon after the death of their mother. I also could now get a feel for who Sonny Girard was from going to her place of employment and speaking with the people who worked there with her. But my first stop tomorrow was going to be at the precinct where I once was a cop. I wanted to find out exactly what they had found in investigating the death of the senator's wife.

19

CHAPTER FOUR

When I entered the precinct house the next morning, I went straight to the desk sergeant—a young man I didn't recognize—and asked to speak to Detective Bill McPherson, my former partner. He'd walked the beat with me for the four years I was with the department, but had been promoted to homicide detective five years ago. We'd remained friends. Mac, as everyone called him, was in the chief's office at the moment, but the desk sergeant asked if I would like to speak to his current partner, Detective Lawrence Brown. I frowned, thanked him, and told him I would wait for Mac.

Lawrence Brown was a total jerk. He was a goofy-looking know-it-all, and I didn't like him. There were very few who did. Besides having a huge gap between his two top front teeth, he had a thick patch of chestnut curls sitting on the top of his head. The man and his wife had only one child, a married daughter who was expecting her seventh baby…and she wasn't even out of her twenties yet. There was no way I wanted to speak with him. At the time that Mac was bumped up to the Homicide Division, Brown had been promoted too, taking my place as his partner. There were plenty of men in the department that couldn't figure out what the chief actually saw in the guy…why the chief actually *liked* him.

I took a seat on the wooden bench across from the officer's desk and waited. It turned out I only had to sit there ten minutes before the young man nodded in the direction of the chief's office.

"There he is now," he said.

I rose and looked into the squad room, where I caught Mac's eye.

"Hey, Sam," he said, waving me back to his office. "You here to see me?"

I nodded, and at that moment the chief appeared in his doorway holding an empty mug.

"What the hell are *you* doing here, Flanagan? The sight of you is all I need to have a perfectly good Tuesday morning ruined."

"Well, gee whiz, it's nice to see you too, Chief. But I'm sure you'll be disappointed to know I'm not here to talk to *you*."

He smiled. "Now that *is* good news," he said, and then nodded toward Mac. "And don't keep him tied up, either. He has work to do." He then headed toward the coffee pot to get a refill.

My former partner chuckled as I followed him into his inner office. "Some things never change, do they?"

"Apparently not," I replied.

Mac took a seat behind his desk and I sat across from him and told him the exact reason for my visit.

"I didn't work on that case," he said. "Betty and I were up north with the girls on vacation when that happened. You ever get up to Alpena?"

I shook my head and he continued.

"Nice area, Sam. My father-in-law was born and raised there. Life is slow and peaceful, and the fishing is great. Caught some bass. Real whoppers. The girls had a blast swimming in Lake Huron, and Betty seemed to relax. She's been on edge lately

21

for some reason." Mac then returned to the point of my calling on him. "Anyway, as I recollect, Larry took the call on that one. Hang on," he said, and then rose from his chair and left the room. He was gone before I could tell him not to bring Brown back with him. Five minutes later, he reentered the room carrying a file and returned to his seat.

"Here we go," he said, opening the folder and silently reading the pages within it. A few moments later he said, "Seems pretty straight forward to me. Really sad, though. She was only thirty-three. The call came in at twelve-seventeen Saturday morning on the seventh of August. The senator himself had called. Said he found his wife in the pool upon arriving home from the airport. He'd taken a nine-fifteen flight home from D.C. Brown responded to the call, along with Macgregor and some officers. Fergus did the autopsy. Found a mixture of wine and sleeping pills in her system. Accidental death, it was ruled." He looked up from the report with a questioning expression on his face. "What bothers the senator about the findings?" he asked.

"First and foremost, he says his wife was an avid swimmer. She won all sorts of trophies in school for the sport. Claims she was always cautious, never being careless about safety." I paused, looking down at the fedora I held in both hands. I then lifted my gaze to meet Mac's. "Did Macgregor say how many pills she took? Or how much wine she drank?"

Fergus Macgregor was the coroner for Wayne County. A man in his early sixties now, he'd immigrated to the U.S. from his native Scotland, with his parents and ten siblings, in 1889 at the tender age of nine years old. The man was a jovial sort most of the time, and we'd remained on good terms since my departure from the force.

"Well, enough to make her fall asleep in the pool, or at least to get so groggy and relaxed that she went under. Why don't you talk to him? I'm sure he could probably tell you more."

"Tell him more about what, specifically?"

I pivoted in my seat to see Larry Brown with his arms folded across his chest, leaning against the doorjamb to Mac's office. Turning back to my ex-partner, I rolled my eyes and groaned inwardly.

"Sam's looking into the death of Sondra Girard," Mac answered him.

"Why?" Brown asked as he moved farther into the room. He sat on the corner edge of his partner's desk and crossed his arms again, glaring at me. "It's a done deal, Flanagan. Nothing for you to look into...the *professionals* handled it. If you insist, go ahead and play detective, but you won't find anything different." A smirk formed on his lips.

"Well, Brown, it seems the senator doesn't think you did such a *professional* job. He doesn't like the conclusion you came to," I offered, matching his stare.

Larry Brown reddened slightly. "Oh, right! The wine glasses! That's weak, Flanagan. He just doesn't want to *believe* it was an accident. He's got to let go at some point, and sooner rather than later. He'll be doing himself, and this department, a huge favor."

Going back and forth with this idiot wasn't my idea of a good time, so I dropped the subject of his investigation into the drowning death of Senator Victor Girard's wife. Instead I looked down at the hem of his brown trousers, which had risen about an inch or two above the top of his socks — which were white — while he was in a sitting position.

"You always wear your trousers so short?" I asked him.

He looked down, and in a flash jumped off the desk. His face was turning that shade of crimson again. He grabbed the folder, which was laying in front of Mac.

"You done with this?" When Mac responded with a nod, he

said, "I'll put it back then. And don't forget that we have to leave to question the blonde dame in about an hour." Mac nodded again and Lawrence Brown left us.

"I think you hurt his feelings," Mac said with a smile.

"Good."

"What did he mean about the wine glasses?"

"That's one of the things the senator thinks is pretty strange about all of this. When they were married, her parents gave them two wine glasses etched with a gold design for a wedding gift. He says it's real gold and they're very delicate. Anyway, she decided they'd use them only when they were together. No one else can use them, and they would *only* use them when they were enjoying a glass of wine *together*. She kept them tucked away in the cupboard to the right of the sink. They've got a couple of dozen or so other wine glasses for entertaining, but they're kept behind a bar they have in a room they used for throwing parties and casual get-togethers.

"By the pool there's a chaise lounge, with a small table by it, where she would lay and relax after she got done with her before dinner swim. On the table that night was one of the gold etched wine glasses with the smallest bit of wine left in it. He thought that was strange. She had never used one of those when he'd been gone. It was kind of like *their* thing. He says the police took the glass with them to analyze the wine that was left…which, by the way, was exactly what it looked like, a red cabernet. When they returned the glass the next day he washed it, and was putting it back in its spot in the cupboard when he found two of the regular wine glasses sitting next to the other gold etched one. Like I said, those are always kept in a different place, behind the bar, so it seemed strange to him to see them in the cupboard. That strikes him as odd. He says she was such a creature of habit…a place for everything, and everything in its place. I guess it could be nothing, really. I mean, he did say she'd called him earlier in the evening when she got home from work, having something on her mind. She was a bit troubled and wanted to speak to him about something."

"He didn't know what she was upset about?" Mac asked.

I shook my head. "No, he says he didn't have the time to listen to her, and that's when she told him she would wait up for him to get home. I guess normally she would be in bed at an early hour."

"Well, you may be right in saying it might be nothing. If she had something on her mind, she might have just grabbed the first glass that her hand came to," Mac suggested.

"True," I said. "But why take the pills? If she told him she'd wait up for him, why do something like that? And there's something else. He says she not only was a creature of habit, but a clean freak, too. I guess she had a woman come in twice a month to do the heavier cleaning, but he says she was picky about the house and did most of it herself. Well, when he went upstairs to their bedroom that night, there was water on the floor in the adjoining bathroom...like she was in there while wet...and a damp towel was tossed inside the tub. Again, he claims she'd never do that. She would have hung it up neatly on the towel rack to dry. Also, there was a place on the bed that was damp, like she sat down on it with her wet bathing suit on. He says she would never do that, either. Plus, there was a towel on the chaise lounge near the pool. Lots of little things that didn't add up to him."

"Well, I don't know, Sam, but I have to agree with Larry. It all sounds a bit weak to me, too."

Mac shrugged while I twirled my fedora in my hands. I stood, knowing since Mac hadn't handled the case, he wouldn't really be able to help me at all.

25

"I think I will swing by to see Fergus," I said. "He might be able to tell me a bit more. Maybe I can have this whole thing wrapped up just by talking to him. Like you say, she may just have been too preoccupied with her thoughts to have followed her normal routine. If so, she made a very fatal error in judgment that night."

***

I found Fergus Macgregor in his office down on the lower level of the Wayne County Morgue. He was sitting behind his desk eating a peanut butter and jelly sandwich and drinking from a bottle of Vernor's ginger ale. I looked at my watch as I knocked softly on his open door. It was still well before noon. He looked toward the door, saw me, and waved me in.

"Sam, what brings you to this part of town?" he asked after wiping some grape jelly from the corner of his mouth with a paper napkin.

"I wanted to ask you about something," I said, then nodded toward his sandwich. "Early lunch?"

"Yeah, didn't have any breakfast this morning. I woke late and barely had time to wash my face and brush my teeth. You want this half?" He picked up the other part of his sandwich and held it out to me, but I declined.

"I wanted to find out about an autopsy you did some weeks back. Sondra Girard ring a bell?"

He nodded while taking another bite out of his sandwich. "Yep," he said with a mouth full of food. "What about it?"

"The senator called me to look into it further. Says he's not quite sure it was accidental. He thinks there may be more to it."

"Like what?" Fergus took a long swig of his soda pop after asking the question.

I shrugged. "Not sure. He insists everyone liked her, but he feels it's strange she'd been so careless. He says it wasn't like her."

The coroner was nodding. "I can understand that. Senator Girard told us that that was *her* sport; been swimming since she was a wee lass. Let me get my report and we'll see what we can discover," he said, rolling his chair over to his filing cabinet. He opened the drawer labeled with a G. His fingers flew over several manila folders until they rested on the one that held the information on Sondra Girard. He pulled it out and rolled back to his desk with it. Moving the remainder of his sandwich to the side, he laid the file in front of him. "Let's see now," he continued. He read silently and I didn't interrupt him. A few minutes later, he reached for his bottle of ginger ale and took another drink, clearing his throat afterwards.

"The team and I arrived at the senator's residence at 12:31 a.m. Saturday, August 7. We found Senator Girard in the rear yard of the property giving the victim mouth-to-mouth on the concrete by the pool. It was no use; she was gone. He told us that seeing his wife wasn't in the home when he arrived there, he checked out back and found her skimming the bottom of the pool. He jumped in and pulled the body up and out of the water, called the department, and then started administering mouth-to-mouth resuscitation. My attendants took over once we got there, but after twenty minutes of them trying, we knew it was of no use. Victim was five feet six and a half inches tall and weighed one hundred and nineteen pounds. When I did the autopsy, I found water in her lungs, meaning she was alive when she went under. I determined she'd been dead anywhere from maybe two to six hours. The body hadn't been submerged long enough to start developing gases, which would make it surface and float. Besides, her call to her husband earlier in the evening confirms that. Upon examination, we found the stomach virtually empty, except for the wine and sleeping pills. I didn't find any signs of a struggle. No bruising, no scrapes, and no skin cells under her fingernails, which means there were no signs that she fought with an assailant. With no additional information sent to me by Detective Brown, I had to rule it accidental."

"Could she have slipped and fallen into the pool? Maybe hit her head and it knocked her out for a bit?" I asked.

"I suppose she could have walked too close to the edge of the pool and slipped, but she didn't hit her head. There weren't any signs of that. Either way, it would be accidental."

"How much wine did she have in her system? Could you tell, Doc? And what about the number of pills she took?"

He shrugged and ran his hand over his stark white crew cut. "A glass, I suppose. No more than two, that's for sure. As for the pills, I can tell you exactly how many she took. When I told the senator that there was a sleeping draft in her system, he brought down a fairly new prescription of pills. Senator Girard said she'd mentioned to her doctor at her last visit that she'd had a bit of trouble sleeping, and he suggested she take a sleeping aid, which she rebelled against. The doctor finally talked her into at least getting the prescription filled, saying they were low dosage and to just take one for a particularly difficult night. It was a thirty-day supply. I confirmed this with a call to her physician. He told me that, at the time, he highly doubted she would actually take them, seeing as how she hated to take any type of medication at all, but he thought it would be best if she had them on hand. I counted the pills in the bottle and there were six missing. Senator Girard was stunned at that information, stating he knew for a fact she hadn't taken any since filling the prescription."

"Don't you find it odd that she would take six at one time, now knowing that she was averse to the idea of taking any medication at all?" I asked him.

The coroner nodded. "I do. And that's why there's always

another theory to consider."

"I'm considering the same thing, I think. Suicide?"

"Yep, but without any evidence, or at least more information from Brown, which I haven't received, I have nothing to go by. And her husband himself said she wasn't depressed or despondent in any way."

"Not that he knew of," I offered. "She seemed to have something on her mind when she put in that call to Washington D. C. that evening."

"Right," he said. "Not that he knew of. And you want to know what I *really* think?"

I nodded.

"I think she was stupid. Having never taken a sleeping pill in her life before, and then to down six of them with a glass of wine right before taking a leisurely swim in the pool, was downright damn stupid! And if it *wasn't* carelessness, and her aim was to end it all...well, that's damn stupid, too!"

CHAPTER FIVE

It was going on lunchtime when I pulled out of the parking lot of the Wayne County Morgue located on Brush Street. The day was young and I wanted to go on over to the office of The Monthly Patriot, a monthly magazine devoted to our heroes in the fight against Fascism, whether they were stories of the men stationed on the battlefield, or the lives of the mothers and wives they'd left behind on the home front. Sondra Girard had worked there. In fact, she was the owner of the periodical. Its suite was housed in an eight-story building on Michigan Avenue, across the street and down a block from the Michigan Central Depot... the train station. Located in the same eight-story building were the offices of the Detroit News. Across the street, and a few doors down from the train station, sat a little diner called The Boxcar Café, and that was where I would make my first stop. I was hungry.

The Boxcar Café had been in existence for the past twenty-five years, and was owned and operated by Charles and Ruth LePage. In their early seventies now, Ruth stayed mainly in the kitchen preparing dishes to be served to customers, while Charles was the front-of-the-house man. It was rare when one didn't find him with a raw potato and penknife in hand. He'd slice off thin strips of the peeled vegetable and graze on them all day long. And that's how he got the nickname of Spud.

I saw Spud standing behind the counter as I entered. The beanstalk of a man waved to me, penknife in hand. I nodded, thinking of the last time I'd been there three weeks ago. I'd been sitting at the counter, browsing a menu mindlessly. I knew what I wanted...a hot ham and cheese sandwich. Ruth LePage faced no competition in making them, piling high thin layers of shaved ham on a bun with melted cheddar cheese and a slice of tomato topping it. Spud was telling an old war story to the guy sitting on the stool to my left, a regular to the eatery himself. Spud was in his usual form that day, sporting a phony French accent. I was sure somewhere in the old man's lineage early family members had migrated to the United States from someplace in France, but he was pure Michigan born and bred. And I knew for a fact that he'd never been in military service at any point in his life. When the man called him out on it, all hell broke loose.

"Oh, come on, Spud! How many years you gonna go on with this? You ain't French and you ain't seen no action in any war, either. Remember who you're talkin' to. Hell, I lived down the street from you for goin' on twenty years when we were raisin' our kids. Nineteen seventeen came and went, and you stayed right where you always been. Hell, you ain't never even been out of the state of Michigan!" the guy sitting next to me complained.

Spud's face reddened. "You callin' me a liar?" he bellowed, forgetting all about the foreign accent. He did that quite often... forgetting to keep up the charade in mid conversation.

"Well, not exactly," the man said, and then he thought for a moment. "Well, maybe I am. But I don't mean it in no disrespectful way, if that's what you're gettin' at."

"You get outta here!" the restaurant owner yelled even

31

louder. "No one comes in here callin' me a liar!"

"Aw, now come on, Spud. My chili and pancakes are about to come out. Now just settle down. I don't mean nothin' by it."

"No, you just get out and you won't be welcomed back!"

"But what about my food? You can't let that go to waste."

"You get out and don't come back! No one comes in here who calls me a liar!" he hollered. "And you don't have to worry about any food goin' to waste, because *this* guy is gonna eat it!"

Huh? Spud was gesturing with his thumb toward *me*! Chili and pancakes? What kind of meal was *that*? My mouth was watering for a hot ham and cheese sandwich. When I objected, Spud turned on me giving me a hard stare, daring me to go on with the fight. My eyebrows rose and my eyes widened. Well, the fact of the matter was, I liked chili and I liked pancakes, just not together in the same meal. But at that point, seeing as how Spud felt so strongly about the situation, I figured it might not hurt to broaden my horizons. I mean…how bad could it really be? And more importantly, I didn't want to get banned from the café, forgoing Ruth's hot ham and cheese sandwiches for the rest of my life.

Today the place was jammed-packed with area employees on their lunch hour. I was scanning the restaurant for a place to sit when I heard my name. When it was called out a second time, I found its source. Pete "Bulldog" Dixon had his hand in the air, gesturing to me.

"Over here!" he called. "Come sit with me."

I headed toward the booth he was sitting in. He had a cup of caramel colored coffee sitting in front of him with a spoon immersed in it. Pete was a journalist for the Detroit News. Once he sniffed out the hint of a story, he latched on with his teeth until he got every last detail…hence the nickname of Bulldog. Once the dope was totally uncovered, he had an impressive way of transferring it to paper, and his readers always got the straight low-down on what was happening in Detroit. I'd made his acquaintance a few years ago, and we had become casual friends. Trust was always a given with us…he never printed information he'd received from me until I gave him the go-ahead.

"Hey," I said, lowering myself into the booth.

"Hey, yourself," he responded.

I took a good look at him. His dark blond hair was messy, looking like it hadn't been washed or combed in about a week. The collar of his white shirt was standing up on his left side. In fact, the shirt was badly wrinkled under his gray suit jacket.

"You look like hell," I said to him.

"Gee, thanks! I had a rough time last night playing poker with some of the guys. The bottle of bourbon I drank didn't help. I had an even rougher time getting up this morning."

"It shows." I pointed to his coffee. "That all you're having?"

"Nah, I just put my order in," he said, and lifted his cup to take a sip.

Picking up a menu from behind the sugar, salt, and pepper, I scanned the day's specials. The soup of the day was split pea, and I thought a cup of it would be good with my hot ham and cheese sandwich. Returning the menu to its proper place, I noticed a woman making a beeline for what looked like our booth. I was right. She came to a stop at the end of the table and turned to glare at Bulldog. She placed her tightly clenched fists on her hips before speaking.

"Where on earth have you been?" she asked sternly.

She was tall, maybe standing five feet eight inches without heels. Her shade of blonde hair was not unlike Bulldog's, and she wore it down, resting across her shoulders with the sides rolled back and pinned with black barrettes. I was guessing she was in her mid to late twenties. Her large dark brown eyes were shooting bullets at the thirty-two-year-old reporter.

"What's the problem?" he asked.

"I've been waiting for you in the office for over an hour and a half! You're supposed to be going with me to interview…." She stopped in mid-sentence and hesitantly looked at me.

Bulldog waved his hand in the air dismissively. "Eh, you don't have to worry about him. He's not going to steal our lead. Sam, this is Virginia Anscombe. She's new to the News. Just moved down from Grand Rapids," he explained. "I'm showing her around the city of Detroit and trying to teach her how to be a good reporter…if she'll listen, that is." He grinned and took another swig of his coffee.

Instantly I furrowed my eyebrows as she stomped her foot on the wooden flooring. Bulldog held up a hand, stopping any further rush of angry words that were on the tip of her tongue.

"*But,*" he said. "Please refer to Miss Anscombe as Vee. She doesn't like being called Virginia." Then he turned to her. "There, is that better?" he asked in a sarcastic tone. "Furthermore, I am hungry, dear Virginia. We'll do that interview when I get finished with my lunch. Now go back to the office like a good little girl, and stay there until I come and get you."

Her face suffused with color, she looked at me.

"It was nice meeting you, Vee," I said.

"Yeah, right!" she replied, and stomped away in a huff.

I followed Vee's back until she disappeared out of the café, at which point a middle-aged waitress, who should've had the words Wide Load written across her derrière, delivered Bulldog's hamburger. She then pulled out her order pad and a pencil.

"What'll you have, hon?"

I gave her my soup and sandwich order and told her to bring a large glass of milk with it, and she left us. When she was gone, Bulldog smiled broadly.

"You know, Flanagan," he said. "Someday I'm gonna marry that little gal. You just wait and see!"

"The waitress?" I asked with surprise.

He got a look of disgust on his face. "The *waitress*? Are you nuts? No, not the *waitress*. I mean Vee Anscombe. Besides being beautiful, she's one helluva writer. Puts real heart and soul into the words. Real compassion."

"Of course, you know I'm no expert in matters of the heart, but I'm not so sure you scored any points with the way you spoke to her just now. So, I'll believe it when I see it."

"Just you wait and see, my man," he repeated himself. "Just you wait and see."

CHAPTER SIX

From the directory inside the lobby, I found that The Monthly Patriot was located in suite 226 on the second floor. Three elevators were to my left, but I chose to take the stairs. When I reached the office, I discovered the door standing fully opened. Inside, a man was standing at the window with his back to me, looking down onto Michigan Avenue, holding a cup of what I guessed to be either coffee or hot tea. Steam rose from the cup and he raised it to his lips, taking a sip as I knocked lightly.

"Hi," he said after turning toward me.

The man was probably six feet tall. I placed him somewhere in his early sixties. He was lanky and stood fully erect, sprouting a slate colored crew cut and full mustache to match. His dark brown eyes radiated gentle warmth. As I entered the office, he took steps toward me, extending his hand in greeting. I shook it.

"Are you here to answer the ad?" he asked.

I shook my head and told him who I was, explaining the senator's call to me.

"Ah," he said. "That's sad business. We all miss Sonny terribly around here. Still doesn't seem right coming into work and not finding her here. What does the senator think has happened if it wasn't an accident?"

"He's not really sure. It just doesn't seem right to him, the way it occurred. It sounds like she was a pretty experienced swimmer, so it's a bit odd that she would down those pills with a glass of wine right before taking her nightly swim. It doesn't sound like she'd be that careless, from what I've been told so far. What I really want to find out is if anything was bothering her in the days before her death. Would you happen to know?"

He looked at me for some seconds before it dawned on him what I was indicating. He stepped back and gestured me farther into the room.

"Take a seat, Mr. Flanagan," he said while he lowered himself to sit on the edge of the desk that was facing four chairs, one right next to another, lining the wall across from it. I sat down in one of them and waited for his response. He took another sip of whatever was in the mug and then shook his head.

"Are you saying what I think you're saying? That maybe it wasn't accidental, but intentional on Sonny's part?"

"I don't know. I didn't know Sonny Girard. You did. Would you say she would have been the type to do something like this? Was she in that frame of mind? Was she worried or upset by anything that you can recall?"

"First of all," he began, "I knew of Sondra Girard the day she was born. Her father and I go way back. We were both editors of newspapers. He still is. I retired from the Detroit News about four months ago. I needed a break...or at least I thought I did. It took me all of two weeks of just sitting around with nothing to do with myself to find maybe I'd made a mistake. And it took only two weeks for my wife to realize she might kill me if I didn't get out of the house and leave her to her solitude and get out from under foot. I guess Sonny heard of my retirement...I suppose from her father. She paid me a visit and asked if I was up for editing the magazine. I jumped at it. All she really wanted to do was hunt down the stories and write them. And she was darn good at it, too. She had a way of bringing her articles to life, along with the people in them. And I'm doing what I love, but don't have the stress of a daily rag." He paused and took another drink from his mug before continuing. "Now you're asking me if I think she was bothered enough by something to want to end it all? I say no. Why on earth would she? She had a very bright future ahead of her. I didn't know Sonny all that well while she was growing up in North Carolina. Oh, I made the occasional trip down there to visit my friend, and I would see her then, but I didn't really know the girl. But in the months I've been working here, I feel I've gotten to know her pretty well. She wasn't unhappy. She was usually in a good mood. The lady wasn't the type to dwell on the negative."

Something jarred in my memory, and I asked him, "You say you were the editor with the Detroit News? You wouldn't happen to be Ty Carver, would you?"

"That's right," he said while nodding.

I smiled. "Well, I think I met another friend of yours just this past winter. Back in January. Charlie Kuntz with the Chicago Tribune?"

"No kiddin'! It's just a little over a year since I saw old Charlie. How was he when you saw him?"

"I don't know him very well, but he seemed just fine to me," I answered.

Never did I think I'd be sitting there, or anywhere, speaking to Ty Carver! I'd first heard his name when a case which took me to Chicago came knocking on my door back in mid-January. While there, I stayed with an old school chum who happened to be an investigative reporter for the Trib. At my friend's suggestion, we lied to his editor...this man named Charlie Kuntz...telling him I was a reporter for the News in Detroit. We told the whopper just so I could get a press pass and some information from the man. When he asked me how my editor was doing—a man named Ty Carver—I didn't know what to say, but was able to fudge it just enough to get by. How was I to know he was good friends with Ty Carver, the editor in chief at the Detroit News? I thought I'd covered myself pretty well, but in the end, he had seen right through me.

I steered the conversation back to Sonny Girard's state of mind in the days before her death. "How about in her last few days or weeks? Was Sonny bothered by anything that you know of?"

"Now that I can't really tell you. It certainly didn't appear that she was. She died sometime Friday evening, but I didn't come into the office that day. I'd been nursing a toothache for two weeks before that, and my wife finally made me go to the dentist on that Friday morning. I hate those guys! Always poking around with picks and needles. He ended up yanking the tooth out, and I went home and slept the rest of the day. But I saw her here in the office on Thursday and she was her chipper old self. She was eager to do an interview for a story she was working on."

"She interviewed someone on that Thursday?" I asked.

He shook his head. "Nah, the appointment for the interview was on Friday, but she was excited about it on Thursday. She got that way when she was working on something. Just like a kid with a brand new toy. She loved her job."

"Hmm. So, you can't think of anything that would have led to her being despondent in any way? Anything at all?"

"No, I can't," he replied. "And I'll tell you something. If Sonny was despondent in any way over anything, she certainly was a terrific actress in hiding it. But I'll let you know if something surfaces in my mind. And I hate to do this, but I have an appointment across town in about fifteen minutes. You'll have to excuse me, Mr. Flanagan. I trust I can leave you here? You need to talk to Bernie. Bernie will be back anytime now…knew Sonny better than anyone."

I nodded and thanked him for his time. He disappeared behind a door to the right of me. I was assuming it was his personal office at the periodical's headquarters. He reemerged wearing his suit jacket and hat. With a wave of his hand, he was out the door.

It was a good fifteen minutes that I sat in that chair waiting for Bernie. Drowsiness was overtaking me, and I thought it would be a good idea to rise and stretch. I walked over to the window and looked down onto Michigan Avenue. This was a busy section of Detroit, with the train station situated in the block over. Two men in naval uniforms were walking at a quick pace toward Michigan Central Depot, each carrying a large duffle bag, and I wondered if they were going to catch a train that was heading out to some naval base here in the States. Turning back, I was about to pick up last month's issue of the magazine, which was laying on top of a tall table along with a vase full of yellow carnations, when a middle-aged woman walked in. She stopped when she caught sight of me.

"Who are you?" she asked.

"I'm here to speak to Bernie. I'm just waiting for him."

"Speak to Bernie about what?"

"Excuse me?" This woman was a bit nosey. She said nothing, but kept eye contact with me, waiting for my reply. I gave in. "I need to talk to him about Sondra Girard."

"Why?" she persisted.

Now she was really getting on my nerves, but instead of causing a scene, I told her why…that the senator had hired me

40

to find out more about his wife's death. Without responding further, she moved behind the desk, lifted a lightweight black sweater from the back of the chair, and put it on. She then bent to retrieve a purse, which had been on the floor under the piece of furniture, and headed for the door again.

"Well, come on. I haven't eaten lunch and I'm starving. You can keep me company while I eat."

She was out the door before I had time to reply. I didn't move, but called out, "Now why would I want to go with you when I'm waiting for someone?"

The woman stuck her head back in the office. "Because I'm Bernie."

CHAPTER SEVEN

Well, I was back in The Boxcar Café sitting in a booth across from Bernice "Bernie" Dayle. The woman was in her early to mid-fifties, short, and a bit on the fleshy side. Lightly streaked with silver, her dark brown hair was short and worn close to her head in waves. I watched her as she dipped a piece of crusty french bread into a bowl of hot split pea soup. And it was true…she had been closer to Sonny Girard than anyone else.

Sondra's parents had hired Miss Dayle in the spring of 1910 to be the companion and nanny to their only child. The infant was two months of age at the time, and her newly named nanny fell in love with her upon sight.

"In my opinion, I thought it was disgraceful!" she told me. "That woman gallivanting all over the world without a care for her only child being left to home. That's how she was…too busy with her own life even to spend time raising her own daughter. Of course, *she* was the one with all the money. It didn't come from him running that newspaper. She came from a family with big money, and played the part of a Southern Belle to the hilt." Bernie shrugged. "So, I raised the girl myself the best I knew how. I was only twenty-one when they hired me. And I don't

42

mind telling you, I did a pretty doggone good job of it. Sonny was a happy child; she had not a care in the world. I taught her all of her school subjects at home until she was fourteen…then she entered the public school. She wanted to be with the other school children, and I couldn't see anything wrong with that," she said. "Bright, too! She did well in all her subjects while there, and she loved the fact that they had a girl's swimming team. They accepted her right away. Of course, she'd been swimming in the family pool since she was just knee high to a grasshopper. I taught her myself. That's where we spent our exercise time most days, unless the weather was bad." Bernie stopped speaking and seemed to stare off into space. When she spoke again, her voice had lowered. "You know," she said, leaning in a bit closer to me over the table. "I didn't want her to marry him. Of course, I didn't tell her that in so many words, but I asked her if she was sure. You know what she said? She told me that she didn't mind, that she liked him." She straightened. "Now can you imagine that? Using words like *didn't mind* and *liked* to describe how you feel about a man you're about to marry?"

"Why?" I asked.

"Why, what?"

"Why didn't you want her to marry the senator? Were there other issues?"

The woman looked at me as if I didn't have a brain in my head. "Well, that and because of his age is why! He was too old for her. And there weren't any sparks. A woman needs to feel sparks fly, and from what I saw, neither of them felt those sparks. That's *why*! I wanted her to find someone who was madly in love with her…who she was madly in love with. Someone who could give her a family. *He* sure wasn't interested in having any more children. He already has three, you know. They're all grown and on their own."

Making direct contact with Bernie's gaze, I asked, "So, what do you think happened that night?"

She shook her head, as if puzzled. "I don't know, Mr. Flanagan. I honestly don't know. It keeps me up at night wondering what in the world went wrong. Sonny was witty, kind, and energetic. She didn't have an enemy in the world. She wasn't careless; I didn't teach her to be careless. And she wasn't upset about anything, either. It was me who put a bug in his ear about it. If it hadn't been for me, I don't think he would've done a thing. I told Senator Girard that her accident just didn't sit well with me, and there had to be something more to it. But I just can't figure it out."

I looked at my watch and found it to be later than I had thought. I was starting to get a feel for who Sonny Girard had been, but it was evident that her one-time nanny couldn't provide me with any revelations about what happened on the night of her death. And I was well aware that Gran had wanted me to stop at the market to pick up a few things for supper. I needed to get there before they closed up for the day.

"Well, if that's all…," I said as I began to inch out of the booth.

"Where you going?" Bernie asked suddenly. "I want a warm up on my coffee." She looked around, signaling to the waitress with her almost empty cup. "Besides, I want to tell you something." She waited until her mug had been refilled with the steaming black java, and then said, "I wanted to tell you about my great granddaddy. Did you know that my great granddaddy was a second cousin to Jefferson Davis, President of the Confederacy?"

I blinked a couple of times. *This* I hadn't expected, her changing the subject so abruptly.

"No, I didn't," I said, and waited for her to continue while I slid back fully into the booth. Her face then seemed to take on a slight shade of pink, and her expression froze for a moment or two. Without warning, Bernie Dayle lowered her head into

44

the palms of her hands and burst into sobs, without any concern for the people around us who were watching. She went on and on, as if there would be no end to her tears. I reached across the table and gently touched her forearm, allowing her to know I was there for her.

At last she came out from behind her hiding place and sighed heavily as she reached for a paper napkin. She wiped her eyes and blew her nose then she slumped back in the booth, and in a weakened voice said, "I walked right past her that night. I walked right past that pool and didn't even know she was lying at the bottom of it. It's entirely my fault. I might have been able to save her, but I never even looked to my left to see if she was out there. If I had, she might still be with us at this very moment." Bernie's eyes focused on me now. "Oh, Mr. Flanagan! What am I going to do without my Sonny?"

***

That look! It meant that I was in the doghouse. It came as no surprise. When I walked in the back door of the house on St. Aubin empty handed, I knew there would be hell to pay in one form or another. I had stopped by the market, but arrived six minutes after closing time. The aroma of homemade spaghetti sauce that assaulted my nostrils when I entered the kitchen only served to intensify my guilt. And now Gran gave me that look.

"Sorry, but I got held up and didn't make it to the market in time," I said to my grandmother.

"What am I going to do with all this sauce and no spaghetti to spoon it over?" she whined.

"I'll get the spaghetti tomorrow. And to make up for my dastardly sin, I'll make us supper tonight," I offered.

We sat down at the kitchen table to fried bologna sandwiches and Campbell's Chicken Noodle soup. The pot of spaghetti sauce still sat cooling on the stove. During supper, my father's mother

45

asked me about my day and I told her. I asked her about her day and she said nothing, but a few moments later she blurted out that she wanted to play a game of Monopoly after the dishes were washed and the kitchen was cleaned.

"Maybe another night, Gran," I said. "I'm sort of bushed tonight."

There was that look again. She was playing this for all it was worth. I gave in—I had to—and set the board up on the dining room table after our meal was finished. We played for two hours before we called it a night, but not before my father's mother had acquired Boardwalk and three of the four railroads. We left the game right where it was when her eyes became too heavy to keep open. I would have hopes of preventing her from purchasing Park Place and B&O Railroad tomorrow night.

With Gran tucked safely away behind her bedroom door, I slipped into my pajama bottoms, wearing only my sleeveless undershirt to cover my chest. Going into the kitchen, I got a glass down from the cupboard above the sink and poured three fingers of scotch into it, adding a few cubes of ice. I took my drink back to my bedroom, where I sat on the bed with a newly purchased notebook in which I could record information about my current case involving the drowning death of Sonny Girard. With the help of Bernice Dayle, I now had a few more names of those who worked at The Monthly Patriot.

Russell Harwood had been a reporter for the magazine, but was abruptly terminated a couple of weeks before Sonny's death. Bernie said she wasn't sure of all the details, but I somehow had the feeling that she was holding out on me for some reason. A woman named Kay Rewis also was a journalist employed by the periodical, obtaining stories she then penned on a monthly basis. Hildie King acted as a personal assistant to the writers/reporters, hunting down leads on stories to include in the digest. All of the reporters relied on her solely to obtain their appointments for interviews. She also had the duty of scouting and securing the account for the Detroit area businesses that were willing to advertise their goods and services in the monthly magazine.

It was a small publication, usually containing about thirty to thirty-five pages per issue, Bernie had told me, but she also said it had a vast readership in lower Michigan. The assistant and reporters named were the extent of those employed, besides Bernie and Ty Carver, who was the magazine's editor in chief. Bernice Dayle acted as a receptionist, whose duty was mainly answering the telephone. I could now understand why Ty Carver thought I'd shown up at their office to answer an ad. With Sonny Girard dead and Russell Harwood terminated, they were down to one person to fill the pages of the monthly rag.

Of course, I wanted to speak with the senator's children, too. He and Barbara had three children who weren't youngsters anymore. Victoria and Simone lived in the city, married and with families of their own, but their youngest was Steven. He was still single and living in Montana after serving there in one of the camps as a trainer to those who enlisted in the Civilian Conservation Corps.

After entering the names of those I needed to speak to about Sonny, I closed the notebook and set it on my bedside table. I tipped my glass, drained it of its contents, and turned out the light. I was beat and wanted to get some sleep.

CHAPTER EIGHT

Wednesday morning was a bit gray, with fast rolling clouds moving in from the northwest. At Gran's insistence, I made a trip to the market before heading to the office on Woodward Avenue. Not only was the day without sun, but it was windy with warm, humid air. I didn't like the looks of it. This was tornado weather. I was greatly relieved Gran had the day off from the restaurant. Before leaving again, I cautioned her to stay inside, but told her that if the sky took an ugly turn, she needed to run over to the Randle's next door. They had a cellar beneath their home and we didn't.

Approaching Flanagan Investigations, I could hear the young attorney, Irwin Malcolm Wright, dictating something to his secretary from his opened door. My office was directly across from his. Not wanting to disturb them, I inserted my key and went inside. I was met with a strong gust of wind blasting through my half-opened windows, and I quickly crossed the room to lower them, leaving them above the sill a quarter of an inch. I then read the notice that had been shoved under my door from the superintendent of the building, one of many informing the occupants that the hallway walls were scheduled to be given a fresh coat of paint beginning Friday, September 17. Balling up the flyer, I tossed it in the trash. I then put in a call to Bernie Dayle at the office of The Monthly Patriot.

"Hi Bernie," I said when I heard her voice on the line. "This is Sam. Who's coming into the office today?"

"No one that I know of. Mr. Carver is in, and of course, I am, too. But Kay called this morning saying she wouldn't be here, and Hildie called to say she would work from home. I guess because it looks like it's going to storm out. She told us once that she's deathly afraid of storms."

"How about giving me some addresses then, of where can I find these people? And don't forget to include Russell Harwood."

I wrote furiously as she rattled off the home addresses of the employees of the magazine. Thanking her for providing me with the information, I was in the process of laying the receiver across the base of the telephone when I heard her ask, "Can I do anything to help?" But it was too late to answer her. I'd hung up. Grabbing my hat off the filing cabinet, I left, locking up behind me. Hurrying down to the parking lot, which sat behind the building, I had to hold my fedora onto my head to prevent it from blowing out into the city.

Kay Rewis lived in an apartment building on the east side. That would be my first stop today, and maybe my *only* stop if the weather continued to get worse. I found ample parking out on the street in front of the building when I reached her place. The complex was a small single-story wood frame, maybe housing four units. By the entrance, a directory listed the sole name of a K. Rewis, in apartment four. No buzzer was needed to announce myself...the building wasn't locked, and besides, there *were* no buzzers. She lived in the apartment situated at the back right. I knocked when I stood outside of her door. Minutes passed and I gave it a second rap. About to leave, figuring no one was in, I

49

heard a shuffling sound from inside. The door opened an inch and a short, petite gal peeked through the narrow crack.

"Yes?"

"Hi, I'm sorry to disturb you without notice, but I was wondering if I could ask you a few questions about your former boss? I'm Detective Sam Flanagan."

I used the title somewhat often, knowing that I was giving the impression of working for the Detroit Police Department. It gained me entrance and more respect than just explaining that I worked on my own. Yet I wasn't lying. It worked. Her dark brown eyes widened a bit and the door opened farther. She gave a wave of her hand, beckoning me inside. The woman was maybe twenty-five, if that. Her slightly frizzing brown hair was fastened to the sides of her head with bobby pins, the back of it caught up in a short ponytail. She was dressed in a teal, full-length terry cloth robe, tied at the waist. Her eyes were watery and her nose was red. She sneezed twice into an already used tissue. It seemed I had caught her at a bad time.

"I'll do the best I can," she said nasally, "to answer your questions."

"I see you're feeling under the weather," I said as I moved past her into the apartment.

"I've got this lousy cold!" she complained. "Would you like a cup of hot tea? I'm going to have one."

"No, but thanks for the offer. Is that why you called off work today…the cold?"

She nodded. "And yesterday, too. Gee, I hope I'm not going to get reprimanded for taking the time off, but what can I do?" She pointed a finger. "Take a seat," she said.

I sat in one of the two chairs that she'd gestured to at a small kitchen table. While she turned to fill a miniature saucepan with water, I looked around. The place was compact, what one might call a studio apartment, with the living room and kitchen combined. Viewing only two other doors, I figured it was a one-bedroom unit with the other door leading to the bathroom. The furnishings were worn, but the joint was clean. She lit a fire under the small saucepan and waited until the cupful of water came to a boil, then carried her tea with her as she took the seat opposite me.

"So, what do you want to know about her? There's probably not much I can tell you. I wasn't that close to her. Is she in some sort of trouble?"

I frowned. Her question had taken me by surprise and it took me a moment to say, "Trouble? She's dead! She's been dead for over a month."

A hand rose to her chest, where she grasped her robe tighter around her neck. "Dead? Mrs. Keppel is *dead*? Oh, my goodness, what happened?"

I was still frowning. "I may have made a mistake here," I explained. "The name outside on the directory said that Kay Rewis lived here in apartment number four."

"She does, but she isn't in right now. I'm her roommate, Mary Sue Easley." She briefly chuckled, which made her cough. "Now it makes more sense. You're talking about the woman who owned the magazine where Kay works. That was awful! The night it happened, Kay came in about nine-thirty all emotional and upset, and then she had *more* bad news the next day about her boss! What a really rotten couple of days she had!"

"Just what the hell are you doing? And what are you telling this man about me?"

We both jumped at the sound of her voice. Neither of us had heard the door open or close. Mary Sue's face took on a look of alarm and she quickly rose from her chair, knocking the table and splashing her tea onto it.

51

"Kay!" she said. "Nothing; I didn't say a word, honest I didn't!" She began to protest further, but doubled over with a fit of coughing.

Kay Rewis glared at her roommate, tossing the small bag she'd been carrying onto the kitchen counter. "Like hell you didn't!" And then looking in my direction, she asked, "Just who *are* you?"

Before I could answer her, Mary Sue rushed past me and, on the verge of tears, disappeared behind one of the doors leading out of the living area. My gaze returned to the angry woman.

"Now was that necessary?" I asked. Getting no answer, I continued. "I'm Detective Flanagan."

"Detective?" Her stern expression transformed into one of confusion. "What do you want with us?"

"This concerns your former boss, Sondra Girard," I said.

"But that investigation is closed. It was an accident, wasn't it?"

"We're trying to tie up a few loose ends."

"I see," she said, easing herself down into the chair that the other girl had been sitting in just moments before. "I don't know how I can help you with anything."

"Maybe you can tell me what your relationship with her was like."

I wasn't sure where I was going with all of this, but I had to start somewhere. My main concern was to find out if she knew if anything had been bothering the senator's wife in the days leading up to her death. I wanted to know if Kay was close enough to the deceased that the young owner of The Monthly Patriot would confide anything troubling to her employee. In my gut, I knew this could not have been an accident. I kept leaning toward it being more than that. Sondra Girard took those pills and drank that wine with intent. That had to be the case. Otherwise....

"She was my boss," the woman stated in a matter-of-fact tone.

"Did you get along well with her?"

"Of course," she said. "She was my boss and we had no disagreements. If you're wondering if we were friends outside of work, the answer is no. It was all business, but I had no trouble with her on the job at all. Why do you ask?"

"Did you notice if she was troubled in the days, or even weeks, leading up to her death? I'm asking if you were close enough to Mrs. Girard for her to have confided anything that was bothering her."

Kay shrugged. "I never noticed anything. And she never said she was upset about anything, either. Actually, Sondra Girard *had* nothing in her life to be upset about. Everything was just peachy keen. She was young, pretty, smart, and she was married to a U.S. senator. She lived in a huge house and owned her own business. What would there be to be upset about?"

Something in Kay's tone spoke volumes. This woman had been envious of her former boss, maybe even resented her...that much was evident. I suspected she may have worked for the woman and, on the surface, got on fine with her. But she didn't truly *like* her.

"So, taking the pills while drinking wine...would you say that would be something Sondra Girard would do? Do you think she'd be that careless?"

She shrugged again. "How should I know? I think it was a dumb thing to do, myself. Sometimes people make very dumb mistakes and they don't get a second chance. That's life. We only get one chance; one shot at happiness."

I studied her as she spoke. To all outward appearances she was a classy young woman; in her mid-twenties, tall and slender, beautiful blonde hair done up in a twist at the back of her head,

53

large hazel eyes bordered by thick dark brown lashes, and dressed in an attractive, although inexpensive, tailored suit. But her expression and manner were cold and distant, uncaring and guarded. What was the story below the surface? I didn't think she'd be willing to reveal it.

"You worked with a reporter named Russell Harwood. I have been told that he was fired from the magazine a couple of weeks prior to Mrs. Girard's death. Know anything about that? Can you tell me the reason she let him go?"

"You betcha I can," she said with anger. "He stole a story of mine!"

"Stole a story of yours?"

"Yes," she replied, nodding her head. "Back in June I hadn't been feeling so well. One night I doubled over with so much pain I thought I was going to die. It turned out it was a severe gall bladder attack and they admitted me into Harper Hospital for surgery. I had been working on a story of a woman in the city who had lost her son in the war. He was actually the very first casualty for the United States. Obviously, with my attack, surgery, and then recovery, I had to put it on hold. For the most part though, the article was pretty much written. I'd left it in my desk, and when I returned to work I was going to put some finishing touches on it and then submit it for publication. Imagine my surprise when the July issue came out and there was my story on page eight, with Russell Harwood's name attached to it! He'd passed it off as his own! So, I got on the phone immediately and told Sondra what he'd done."

"How did she react?"

"Skeptical. Like I was mistaken or something. I think she was hoping I was. She asked me several times if I was sure! She finally told me that she would talk to Russell about it. I guess he denied it at first, but then ended up admitting what he'd done. I honestly don't know how he ever thought he would get away with it. He said he was in a pinch for a story," Kay said sarcastically. "She had no choice but to fire him. I saw to that!"

"How did he take being let go?" I asked her.

She shrugged and said, "I don't know. I wasn't there. He probably didn't like it, but who cares? I didn't feel sorry for him one bit! When I returned to work, Russell's desk was empty. He was gone, and Sondra and I never discussed it again. In fact, no one in the office spoke of it at all. She never once brought up his name in front of us again. I'm sure some might have wondered where he'd gone, but no one asked...not while I was there, anyway."

I rose and placed my hat on my head, thanking her for seeing me. Kay walked me to the door, but before I took my leave of the apartment, I said one more thing.

"Don't be hard on your roommate. I thought she was you and I'd just arrived. She didn't tell me a thing. Is she a reporter, also?"

"Mary Sue?" She softly let go of a brief laugh. "No, she works behind the accessory counter at J.L. Hudson's."

CHAPTER NINE

Next my intent was to ride over to the residence of Russell Harwood to question the man about his relationship with Sondra Girard while he was employed at the magazine and after he'd been terminated from it. The wind was just as strong and the sky was darkening, but there had yet to be any drops of rainfall. He happened to live at 14409 Dequindre in apartment B, just a couple of doors down from The Double Shot, a neighborhood bar I would sometimes frequent. I drove up and down the street twice, not seeing any apartment building. Traveling the area for a third time, I spotted the matching numbers on a white wood frame two-story home. I pulled up to the curb and parked. Attached to the right side of the house was a covered staircase leading up to an outside entrance to the top level. Maybe this was apartment B? I decided to find out.

Waiting some minutes after knocking twice, no one answered and I heard no noise from within. I descended the stairs and tried the front door of the lower level. Responding to my knock was a woman of about sixty. Her hair was a mixture of blonde and gray, pulled back severely in a bun at the nape of her neck. She wore a black dress that had a crisp white collar. The woman was of medium height, but frail and brittle looking in build. When she opened the door she said nothing, but just stared at me.

"Hello," I greeted her. "I'd heard that Russell Harwood lives here. Is that right?"

She nodded, but said nothing.

"Is his place the one upstairs?"

Silently, she moved her head up and down to indicate yes.

"Well, I knocked upstairs, but there was no answer."

She shrugged.

"Do you happen to know when he'll be back?" I asked, feeling myself getting impatient with her.

Ahh, *this* time she moved her head from side to side to indicate no, while standing on the other side of the screen door. Gee, this was fun! I loved it when it felt like pulling teeth to try to get someone to speak.

"I'll try again some other time. I'm a friend of his and I'm only in town for about a week. I want to surprise him, so I would appreciate it if you didn't mention that I was here," I said, and sincerely doubted I had to worry about that.

True to form, she nodded. I had almost reached the '38 Chevy when I heard her screen door open and she yelled, "If you see him before I do, tell him I need that rent! He's over two weeks late with it now!"

I nodded.

***

It was going on five o'clock when I pulled into the drive on St. Aubin. After leaving the residence on Dequindre, I had stopped at the Stop and Shop, a corner store situated a couple of blocks from the house, and bought two packs of Lucky Strike cigarettes and a six pack of Champagne Velvet beer for Gran. I ended up talking to the owners, Hank and his wife, Rosie for more than a half hour. It seemed that Rosie had recently cut her finger deeply enough to warrant eight stitches, and she proceeded to tell me how it had gotten infected. I heard all the gory details on top of an already empty stomach, and it wasn't pleasant. I made my escape at the soonest possible moment.

Well, it didn't seem as though I'd gotten much accomplished in the way of investigating Sondra Girard's death, but I'd been ready to call it a day. Besides, I didn't want to be out when the sky opened up and released the downpour that we were surely going to get.

As soon as I opened the back door, the aroma of warm spaghetti sauce met me. I could smell heavy doses of oregano and garlic, and my mouth began to water. I hung my fedora on the hook by the telephone and fully entered the kitchen to see that the sauce was being stirred, and not by my grandmother. The woman who turned when I entered and said, "Well, it's about time! We thought we were going to have to eat without you!" was none other than Miss Bernie Dayle.

"Get the table set," she said.

CHAPTER TEN

Conversation around the kitchen table flowed freely as we ate; the only trouble being, I was barely able to get a word in edgewise.

"Well, that's just it, Ruby," Bernie said after shoving a forkful of spaghetti into her mouth. "She was always so happy-go-lucky. Nothing ever seemed to bother her or get her down. Sonny just always figured if a bump appeared in the road, there was a way to go around it."

"I know what you mean, dear," my grandmother replied. "I went to primary school with a girl who was like that. Her name was Lizzie Mae Lydell, and everything was such a joy to her." Gran stopped chewing and stared into space with her eyebrows knit together. "Wait; come to think of it...," she continued, "She giggled all the time and at everything. She was nothing like your Sonny. She was a knucklehead." My grandmother shrugged and resumed twirling her fork in the plate of spaghetti.

"Well, Sonny certainly was no knucklehead. She was full of life. She was a great swimmer and everybody she met loved her. So, what happened? I want to know!"

Both ladies turned their questioning gaze in my direction, as if I could give them a definitive answer right at that very moment.

"Hey, at this point, I'm not sure what happened. It's going to take more than a day or two to find the answer...if there is one. I know you don't want to accept it, Bernie, but she may have just been careless this one time. She certainly wasn't thinking straight when she downed those sleeping pills with that wine. Now, either something was bothering her to the point where she did it deliberately, or else she didn't realize the effect the two mixed together would have and she became so groggy, she slipped and fell into that pool."

Bernice Dayle slammed the tabletop with her clenched fist and said tautly, "And I am telling you that nothing was bothering her, and if it was, I would've known about it. She would have told me. We were close, Sam. She was my baby. My goodness, I raised her. I knew her better than even her parents did. She told me things. She confided in me."

"Like what?" I asked.

"Like all sorts of things. Like female things."

I rolled my eyes. "Okay, skip that and tell me about that last Friday in the office. How was she on that day?" I asked Sonny's one-time nanny, my impatience with her sounding in my voice.

"She was fine!" she all but yelled. Bernie was getting emotional, and I needed to take a gentler tone with her.

"Well, tell me all you remember of that day, and start from when you first saw her."

"She and I caught the bus and were in the office earlier than usual that morning. Sonny always liked to arrive at work a bit earlier on the days she had an appointment for an interview. She was excited to get to that interview. The challenge of writing another piece for the magazine was what she loved. She was like that with each new story. Sonny wanted to tell the personal side of the war. The triumphs and the tragedies, you know?"

60

"The bus? Sonny didn't drive?"

"Oh, yes she did, but...." Bernie covered her mouth with the palm of her hand while she softly giggled. "Really, she wasn't that good at it. She'd had a couple of small accidents, and that was enough to make her a bit nervous at getting behind the wheel of an automobile. Especially in a big city like Detroit. She said she'd rather take buses and taxicabs."

"Oh, that's all right, Bernie," Gran interjected. "My own husband, Paddy, God rest his soul, often said they should have never allowed women to drive. I have to agree with him. Now Mae Randle, next door, well, she drives and she's real good at it. Of course, she *has* to know how to drive because her husband gets drunk a lot and she has had to drive home from family gatherings lots of times. I don't drive, myself. Paddy always said he'd rather walk a good twenty miles in one direction than to get in a car with me driving. Do you drive, dear?"

"Nope," Bernie answered. "That's why we always took the bus to work. Unless the senator wasn't in Washington and was going into the city, that is, and then he would drop us off."

"Now, my best friend...her name is Helen Foster...she drives and—"

I cut Gran off. "Let's get back to that day at the office."

"Well, my goodness, dear. I was only going to tell Bernie that I should have been dead ten years ago with the way Helen drives."

After sending Gran a warning look that said "I'd appreciate it if you would stop interrupting," she took the hint and made a gesture of zipping her lips shut. I then asked Bernie, "Okay, so you get to the office on the morning of August 6 and she seems in good spirits, right?"

Bernie nodded.

"Do you know if Sonny and the senator had been getting

61

along? Do you know if they'd been arguing about anything?"

"Arguing about what?" she asked.

Exasperated, I responded, "*I don't know*! *Anything*! I'm just trying to get into her frame of mind. I'm trying to figure out what was going on in her life at the time."

"Nah," she said, and shrugged. "They never argued...not really. Like I told you, their relationship wasn't hot and it wasn't cold, if you know what I mean. Besides, he'd been in Washington all week and was due home that night, and she was looking forward to seeing him. Come to think of it, I don't know one time that they'd really ever argued about anything."

"Okay, so we can rule out any marital distress. If...." I held my hand up, palm toward Bernie, in an effort to get her to just open her mind a bit. "On the off chance she had anything at all bothering her, it didn't have to do with her relationship with her husband."

"Right, and she wasn't bothered by anything."

I sighed and went on. "Now, about the appointment...what time was it and where was she going?"

"To some Chrysler plant. I think it was in Highland Park, or something like that. Sonny was going to get a taxicab around eleven that morning. She was going to find out about a gun they manufactured there. I guess they figured out a way to make them in a lot less time than they do overseas. I have this all written down in the scheduling book at work," she said.

"Do you know the person she was going to interview there?"

"It's all in the book. I can't recall the name right now. What does all that information have to do with anything, though?"

"I want to get a feel for what her last day was like. I've still got places to go and people to question. This is going to take a bit of time before we figure out what happened. That is, *if* anything happened other than just an accident," I said, shoving my empty plate to the side. I leaned on the table with my forearms, my fingers intertwined. "So, how was she when she came back from her appointment?"

"Well, okay, I guess." Bernie shrugged. "It was about four o'clock, and I'd just gotten off the phone from speaking with Nola. That's Ty Carver's wife. Since moving up here with Sonny, Nola is about the only one I've made friends with. I guess Ty was being a big baby over some dental work he'd had done that morning, and she finally convinced him to lie down and take a nap, but he wouldn't get in the bed. He laid down on the sofa instead, and was snoring up a storm. She said she couldn't take it any longer and just had to get out of the house. She wanted to know if I wanted to go with her to get a sandwich at the lunch counter at Woolworth and then take in a movie. I told her sure, so when Sonny came in, I told her Nola was going to pick me up in a half hour and where we were going. I asked her if she wanted to come along, but she told me no. She seemed sort of preoccupied, but I guess that was because she was thinking of the story she was going to write. She must have been really concentrating on her story, because the last thing she said to me before I left was that she hoped I would enjoy my shopping trip with Nola. I hadn't said anything about shopping. I had told her we were going to the cinema." Bernie shrugged. "Then I asked if she wanted me to wait with her while she closed up the office…I mean, no one else was there; they'd all gone for the day hours ago. The staff would leave early sometimes on a Friday afternoon. But again, she told me no. When I left her, she was in her inner office looking out the window. I left about twenty-five minutes after Sonny had come back from the interview to go out front to wait for Nola."

"The two of you didn't discuss anything else? Not how her appointment went? Nothing like that?"

Bernie shook her head. "The only other thing I can remember

that she said was that she needed to talk to Victor when he got home that night."

"She didn't say what about?" I asked Bernie.

Again, Bernie shook her head.

Rising from the table and stretching, I said, "Well, I think I'll take a ride out to that Chrysler plant within the next few days and see if I can talk to whoever it was she interviewed on that Friday. I'll probably be calling you at the office at some point to get his name."

Bernice Dayle nodded and then turned to my grandmother. "Ruby, you got anything for dessert?"

"I've got some peanut butter cookies. We can have those with a cup of hot tea if you'd like."

At the mention of the cookies, I suddenly felt the urge to take my seat again at the kitchen table.

***

It was just past seven thirty when I headed out in the '38 Chevy with Bernie Dayle as my passenger sitting beside me. Before leaving the house, Gran and the receptionist at The Monthly Patriot gave each other a hug in farewell. Apparently, they'd become fast friends.

"Ruby, are you sure you don't have Southern blood in you?" Bernie asked. "That was the best spaghetti sauce I've eaten in years! And we all know that Southerners make the best cooks."

Gran smiled widely, shrugged, and said, "Not that I know of."

"Well, I sure did enjoy myself tonight; yep, I sure did."

"Come again, dear," Gran said.

"Now isn't that sweet of you?" Bernie responded. "And now that you mention it, you wouldn't happen to be having spaghetti leftovers tomorrow evening, would you?"

***

It just so happened that Bernie Dayle made her home in the guesthouse that sat at the rear of the property behind the senator's home. I pulled up to the curb out front and parked, shutting the engine off. The woman gave me a questioning look.

"It's getting dark, so I'll walk you to your door," I explained, but she just shrugged.

Senator Victor Girard's residence was a traditional three-story white Victorian with a dark green roof. It had a wrap-around porch, and a turret loomed large on the left side of the structure. I opened the door of the vehicle for Bernie, allowing her to exit, and then tipped my head to look at the home while emitting a whistle at its grand appearance. A dimly lit stained-glass window on the second floor, which overlooked the street, told me the politician was at home.

"Impressive," I said.

"Sure is," Bernie replied. "According to the senator, it was built in 1872. And you should see the inside. I know Sonny loved it."

We followed the right side of the house until we came to a wrought-iron gate. Bernie opened it and I followed her as she continued to walk on the cobblestone path leading to the diminutive guest quarters that she now called home. I noted the pool area to the left, and I also noticed that Sonny's one-time nanny avoided looking that way. Once Bernie was tucked safely inside her residence, I made a detour to the pool on my way out to the car. It was rectangular in shape, underwater lights illuminating the clear, clean water. The shallow end was probably three feet deep, while the opposite end looked to be double that, or more, in depth. The thing that struck me as odd was that the area where the two chaise lounges sat, with a small table in between, was at least a good fifteen feet from the closest edge of the water. If Sonny had gotten out of that lounge chair and lost her balance, there was no way she would end up falling into the pool.

My eyes scanned the sky when a loud boom of thunder reverberated through the atmosphere. Suddenly, the heavens that had threatened rain all day long were beginning to shoot huge drops at an angle. I pulled my hat down farther over my face and headed for the Chevy. As I reached the auto, a woman from the house directly across the street shouted "Hey!" while raising her hand in the air. She was standing just outside her door under a wide wooden overhang. I waved back, jumped into the protection of the car, and hurriedly started its engine. I wanted to get home before these splatters became a torrential downpour.

CHAPTER ELEVEN

With quarter-sized drops of rain pelting the rooftop throughout the night, I slept like a baby until almost seven on Thursday morning. I woke to find Gran singing in the bathroom behind a locked door while fresh coffee percolated on the stove. I dressed in my tan suit, which I'd purchased recently, wearing a black shirt and tan tie. Pouring myself some coffee, I sat down at the kitchen table to read the Detroit News that had been delivered to our front porch. It was a bit damp from the drizzle that still moistened the Detroit city streets. The big headline of the day was that Michigan National, the bank on Gratiot Avenue, had been robbed overnight. It was the second time in two months, and the article said the police had no suspects. Back in July, a gunman had severely wounded a security guard who had pulled through the surgery. Last night, no one was injured.

Having dropped off Gran at the door of Augie's Cuchina a few minutes before eight, I headed over to Russell Hardwood's upstairs apartment yet again. I knew it was early, but I wanted to catch him before he escaped his landlord's demands for his unpaid rent. When he opened his door to me, he wore a pair of dark blue boxer shorts and nothing else. The young man, appearing to be in his mid to late twenties, had been roused from sleep by my knock. His light brown hair was completely flat on the left side of his head, while it stuck up on top. Russell peered at me from the slit of his right eye. His left eyelid was a deep shade of purple and was swollen shut.

"Yeah?" His voice was husky with sleep.

"Russell Harwood?"

"Yeah," he answered.

"I wonder if I could speak to you for a moment. I'm Detective Flanagan."

He sighed heavily with resignation and backed up to allow me entrance to his apartment. I stepped into a small kitchen, and he motioned for me to take a seat at the table. The room was outdated, with green and white tiled flooring that appeared not to have been scrubbed in a month of Sundays. A white Hoosier cupboard had one of its doors missing, and I could see inside where an opened box of corn flakes sat next to two cans of Campbell's Chicken Noodle soup. His gas range and icebox were diminutive in size, as was his badly chipped white porcelain sink that sat on the adjacent wall under the only window in the room. It looked out into the back yard and had no curtain covering it. On the table in front of me was a half-eaten apple that had turned brown, along with a partially eaten piece of toast. Mold was overtaking the hard bread. He grabbed the apple and toast, threw them onto the orange enameled countertop, and then sat down in the chair opposite me.

I gestured to his eye. "I hope the other guy is wearing some damage, too."

"I didn't touch her, I swear I didn't, and she's lying if she told you I did! You know what my crime was? Telling her she was a good looking broad. I guess I shouldn't have called her a 'broad.' It would seem she didn't like that. I would have called you, myself, had I known her name. What she did was assault and battery. That dame can sure pack a punch! She should go into boxing." He paused and carefully touched his eyelid. "Does it look really bad?" he asked.

I nodded.

"And how did she even know where to send you? I didn't even tell her my name. We didn't get that far. No introductions were made."

"I didn't come about that," I said. "I'm here to talk to you about your former boss, Mrs. Sondra Girard."

"Sondra? What do you want to know about her?"

"I want to know about your relationship with her. Were the two of you close?"

"That depends on what you mean by close," he said. "I got on well with her. She was A-OK in my book, if you ask me. She had a good sense of humor, and I liked that. When I heard about her death...well, that was a real shocker. I just couldn't believe it. She was so young, you know?"

"Did you still like her even after she fired you?"

"Well...yeah. Oh, sure, I was ticked at first. But then I had to admit that it wasn't really Sondra, it was that bitc...well, it was that louse, Kay Rewis. *She's* the one that pushed for my dismissal from the magazine. That gal sure has a lot of cojones, if you ask me, pushing her weight around like that. I could tell that Sondra wanted to give me another chance, but Kay threatened to quit, herself, if I wasn't fired. And Kay is a really talented writer, I'll give her that. She can pull in stories like there is an endless supply of them. I can see why Sondra didn't want to lose her. But shoot, I thought I was doing Kay a big favor by getting her story out there."

"By putting *your name* on it?" His attempt to justify himself was lame at best. He had the good grace to color slightly.

"Yeah, well, okay...I was in a bind. I needed to submit something and I didn't have anything. I borrowed Kay's article, but I would have made it up to her. I never got the chance, though. But I don't get it. Why all the questions about this?"

"Do you know of anything that might have been deeply bothering Sondra? You know about the wine and the medication she took. Do you feel that she would have taken those deliberately, knowing what effect they would have had?"

He shook his head. "Yeah, I heard through the grapevine about that, but nah, not a chance. Now I don't know if anything was troubling her, because if there was, I doubt she was the type to broadcast it. At least, she never did. I can honestly say that I've never even seen her in a nasty mood. For the most part, she seemed pretty satisfied with life. But, hey, I don't get this...why all the questions?"

When I left Russell Harwood's apartment at ten minutes after nine, he was standing at his stove boiling water that he was going to pour over an already used tea bag. He was still wearing only his boxer shorts.

Since it was still quite early, I drove over to the office of The Monthly Patriot hoping to find Hildie King there, but it wasn't to be. Bernie told me that the woman had called in, stating that she would work from home for a second day.

"But I'm glad you're here," Bernie stated. "Tell me how the case is going. What are you finding out?"

"Not much," I replied. "Everyone says basically the same thing...that they liked her, that she was swell and a happy person, and some think it was rather stupid of her to be so careless about taking the wine and sleeping pills and then jumping in the pool for a swim."

Bernie's gaze focused on the wall beyond me while she tugged at her lower lip. "Nuh uh," she said when her eyes met mine again. "I don't buy that. She didn't mix the wine with those pills deliberately because nothing was troubling her. And besides, she wasn't the sort of person to ever give up even if something *was* on her mind." She pointed an index finger at me. "And don't argue with me because I know! If she accidentally fell into that pool... well, I just can't see how that could have happened. It doesn't make sense to me."

"Me either," I admitted. "I took a look at the pool area after you went inside last night. The lounge chairs are too far away from the edge for her to have fallen in accidentally. She could have tripped over her own two feet and she still would not have landed in the water."

"What do you think happened then, Sam?"

I shook my head. "I don't know, Bernie, but there's only one other alternative, isn't there?"

"You mean she was murdered? Someone did this to my little girl? Jeepers, I don't even like saying that. I guess it's occurred to me fleetingly, but I suppose I pushed the thought right out of my head. I don't want to believe someone did this to her."

Shrugging, I said, "*You're* the one who said everybody loved her. She had no enemies. How do I know that's true? How do I know you didn't just say that because *you* want it to be so? You want everyone to love her because *you* love her so much and can't imagine anyone *not* loving her. You lied to me about Russell Harwood, saying you didn't know why he was fired. You *did* know. Sonny confided in you, remember?"

Bernie said nothing, but looked a bit sheepish. "It's just that I liked him, you know? Sonny did, too. He was fun to have around, always joking and being flirty. I just didn't want to put him in a bad light is all."

"Now I want you to think really hard and tell me if she had a spat with anyone...besides Mr. Harwood, that is. Can you think

71

of *anyone* who would want to do her harm?"

But she just shook her head and didn't utter a word. The last thing Bernie said to me before I took my leave was, "How about picking me up after work? That way I won't have to grab a taxicab to your place for dinner."

I nodded. "What time do you want me here?"

"Make it around three-thirty if you can. I wanna get out of here early today. Sometimes I just can't stand being here without her." She then reached down and grabbed the handles of a paper bag that had been sitting behind the desk by her chair. "Do you think Ruby has some butter, cinnamon, and flour at home? I brought apples, oatmeal, and sugar to make a crumble for dessert tonight."

I shrugged and said, "We'll find out, won't we?"

***

Gran walked out of Augie's Cuchina that afternoon a few minutes after I had arrived to pick her up. In between my visit to Bernie and coming to get my grandmother, I had used the time well. I had finally paid a call on the senator's oldest daughter, Victoria. She lived in an upper-class section of Detroit, with second storied brick homes and well-manicured lawns. She was married to an accountant for the city named Neil Chelton. When I knocked, it wasn't Mrs. Chelton who answered, but her housekeeper. I was ushered into a stylish sitting room, one in which the thirty-seven-year-old woman sat, dressed in a white negligee and matching silk robe, with her feet extended up across the length of the sofa. It hadn't even been noon yet, but she had a tall glass in her hand filled with some sort of amber-colored cocktail, a cherry resting on the bottom. After introductions were made — and I *didn't* think it was wise to give the impression I was with the Detroit Police Department — she asked me what my interest in Sondra's death was.

"I mean, why are *you* looking into it? I don't understand."

This woman was actually quite a looker; long black hair flowing down her back in waves, piercing blue eyes, clear ivory skin adorned by expensive cosmetics expertly applied. Although I couldn't really tell because of her outstretched position, she appeared to be on the tall side, and she was slender.

"Your father contacted me on Monday," I explained. "Apparently, he isn't satisfied with the department's findings. He just wants to clear up the story surrounding her accident...*if* it was an accident."

"*If*? Are you saying it wasn't, Mr. Flanagan?"

"I don't know," I responded. "That's what I'm trying to find out."

What happened next was pure madness, at least in my opinion. A girl of about ten years of age entered the room dressed in solid pale yellow pajamas, and I could tell from the reddened area under her nose that she might have stayed home from school because she was ill. She gingerly held her right forearm in the palm of her left hand, and was on the verge of tears.

"Mommy, Timmy bit me!"

I could see pinpricks of blood forming on a patch of reddened and swollen skin.

"Oh, for heaven's sake! Go knock his block off. In fact, give him a couple of hard belts, and that will teach him not to bite."

The girl began to cry. "But Mommy —"

Victoria raised her voice, calling to the housekeeper. "Millie! Millie, come get her out of here!" Millie appeared and tugged at the girls' injured arm as she resisted.

"Millie," Mrs. Chelton continued. "Timmy bit her and I told her to retaliate. I don't want you stopping her. And I don't want you coddling the boy after he's gotten what's coming to him. Do you understand?"

73

"Yes, ma'am."

Moments later, alarming screams of pain pierced the air. My God, the anguish was coming from a toddler...I was sure! What in the hell was going on here? Before I could bring myself out of the impact of my shock, a tall and stately man entered the room. This was Neil Chelton, Victoria's husband. Loosening his tie, he made a beeline for the bar that sat in the corner of the room and began mixing himself a cocktail.

"I won't be home long, darling. I've got an early meeting this afternoon in the mayor's office. What's wrong with Timmy?" And then he took note of me sitting in the chair across the room from his wife. "Who's this?" he asked, gesturing toward me with his glass.

In the end, I made my escape without finding out too much. Neither of them cared for Sondra Girard one way or the other, but felt it was quite embarrassing of the senator to have taken a wife four years younger than his eldest daughter. And I came to the conclusion that this pair probably didn't care for much of anyone, not even their own children. Millie had shown me to the door, but before taking my leave, I asked the woman what Timmy's age was.

"He's three, sir," she had answered.

The people who lived in the home I'd just been in were nuts... all of them. I made my way to the '38 Chevy and felt as though I could breathe again.

CHAPTER TWELVE

With Gran tucked away inside of the house on St. Aubin, I pulled away from the curb. I wanted to take my chances at seeing the senator's younger daughter, Simone Barnard. Feeling the need to get this over with, I sincerely hoped she wasn't like her sister in character. I cruised down Woodhall Street until I came to the house number that Victor Girard had provided me with. The home was a small brick bungalow that sat two houses from the corner, nestled among others similar in style. Several coats of light gray paint covered the brick. Parking directly in front, I noticed no car in the driveway, but there was a pink tricycle with multi-colored streams of ribbon hanging from the handlebars on the lawn.

After my knocking twice, a woman resembling Victoria Chelton opened the door, but this daughter of the senator wore no elaborate lounging outfit and her face was bare of make-up. A messy bun at the back of her head corralled her charcoal colored hair. It appeared as though the two ladies resided in vastly different worlds. This home was much like what the majority of us had...a home belonging to the average working man. I told her who I was, that her father had hired me, and what I needed to speak to her about. She hesitated.

"My father sent you *here*?" she asked, somewhat astounded.

"Not exactly, but I feel I have to speak to everyone who knew her."

"I don't know anything about her accident," she said.

"I appreciate that, but if I could come in and speak to you for a few moments…."

She hesitated again. "Come to the side entrance. I'm in the kitchen cooking." The woman then shut the heavy wooden door that led into her parlor and I descended the steps.

The kitchen was a cozy room that gave off the feeling of comfort and warmth, with its moss green linoleum flooring and tan wallpaper with dark green leaves scattered across its surface. Something was baking in the oven, and the scent of strawberries traveled its way to my nostrils. As I sat at the square table, Simone had her back to me while she peeled potatoes at the kitchen sink. I was guessing she was maybe an inch or two shorter than her sister. She was not as slender, but she was not overweight by any means.

"I'm not sure what I can tell you," she said over her shoulder.

"I'd like to know if Mrs. Girard had been upset by anything in the weeks or days before her death. Would you happen to know? The accident angle on this seems improbable, but if she intentionally took those sleeping pills with the wine that night—"

Simone Barnard turned abruptly toward me. "*Must* you call her that?" she asked with an edge in her tone.

I said nothing, but continued to look at her.

She returned to working on the potato she held in her hand and emitted a loud sigh. "I'm sorry. I *know* she was my father's wife. I don't have to like it, though."

"I take it you didn't care for her?" I asked.

She turned to me again. "That's putting it mildly! How

would you like it if your father acted like a fool, taking up with a tart a year younger than yourself just a bit over six months after your mother had passed away? How would you like it if he then married her and moved her into your mother's house, slept with her in your mother's bed? No, I guess you could say I didn't welcome her with open arms."

"I'm just trying to find out what exactly happened that night, and as I said, it seems improbable that she would have had that kind of accident."

"So, you want to know if she was depressed. If something was bothering her to the point where she did herself in? I don't know, and I really don't care. But if that was the case, she did us all a big favor, Mr. Flanagan!" She quit talking but kept eye contact with me. Finally, she continued by saying, "Does that seem a bit harsh to you? Do I seem cold? Well, I don't care what I sound like. My father is a fool!" She turned away as a young girl of about four or maybe five entered the room carrying a cutout doll.

"Look, Mommy. I dressed Penny in her pajamas."

Simone lowered herself to be on eye level with the child. "Uh huh, she's pretty. Now go and play, sweetie. Mommy's talking with someone."

The little girl then spotted me and buried her face in her mother's shoulder. Simone gently pushed her daughter away and stood.

"Go on, honey. After dinner, I'll play with you."

When the child was gone, Simone took a seat opposite me at the kitchen table.

"Is that the only reason you didn't care for Sondra? Or was it the woman herself?" I asked.

"Isn't that enough? That and the fact that she tried to worm her way into my father's will? She never said as much, but how

77

dare she think she deserved anything from him…or us! Whatever my father has is *our* inheritance."

"What's this about an inheritance?"

The voice came from just inside the side door to the kitchen. A large man stood there…stocky, not fat. I was guessing his height was around five feet ten. He was solid in build, with dark wavy hair and a clean-shaven face. He wore a one-piece light gray coverall that was spotted with grease or oil or both.

"Nothing, Wes. Mr. Flanagan here is a private detective Daddy hired to look into *her* death. I was just telling him how much we *loved* Daddy's choice in a second wife," she said in a sarcastic tone.

"Daddy! Daddy!" The child was back, running to her father as he stood on the back landing.

Extending his arms, he lifted the child, saying, "How's my princess today? Have you been a good girl?"

Simone was on her feet in an instant. When she reached her husband, she snatched the child out of his grasp. "Wes! How many times have I *told* you to hose off outside before you come in here? Don't touch her! You're filthy! And the smell…I can't stand the smell anymore. I can't stand the taste of it in my throat." He stood there like a scolded child. "And how many did you have today? I can smell it, Wes. You've been drinking again."

The man said nothing, but exited the house. Simone turned to me while holding her daughter's hand.

"That's all I have to say, Mr. Flanagan. There's nothing I can tell you about her, or what happened to her. I'm just glad she's out of our lives. Now, I have to attend to my daughter."

With that statement, I was left alone in the kitchen. I found Wesley Barnard leaning against the side of the house, smoking a cigarette. Pulling out a smoke of my own, I extended my hand while introducing myself. He hesitated in taking it, noting the grease that badly stained his own hand, but finally shook it.

"I'm sorry about that display in there. She wasn't always like this. You'll have to forgive her."

"Not a problem," I said. "She doesn't seem to be too thrilled about her father's remarriage."

"She's not thrilled with a lot of things these days, including me. I can't seem to reach her anymore. It's like I'm living in my own home with a stranger, someone who wants to have nothing to do with me. She yells about my drinking, but I have to have a couple of beers just to face coming home each day. I won't quit trying, though. I love her too much." He hesitated while taking a deep drag on his cigarette. "She spits venom each time Sondra's name is mentioned, but she never even gave the woman a chance. In fact, she never got to know her at all. My father-in-law married the woman down in North Carolina at her parents' estate. We didn't go to the wedding, even though we were invited; neither did her sister or brother. When the senator got back in town, he and Sondra came to visit. Simone was so rude to both of them that they left within fifteen minutes, and we haven't seen them since."

"Not her father, either?"

Wesley Barnard shook his head. "Nope, and it's not for him not trying. She doesn't want to have anything to do with him. I try to talk to her about it for my daughter's sake, but...well, you see how she reacts to me. I can't talk any sense into her. I can't please her. She thinks I'm an idiot without a brain in my head. I do the best I can at providing a stable life for her and the child, but it's not good enough for her. I embarrass her. She feels I wasn't ambitious enough to reach some higher calling. But I'm a mechanic. It's all I know and it's what I love. I don't measure up to her sister's husband, or her father."

As he spoke, I watched him. He was a handsome man, but

a broken man; I could see it in his face, in his eyes. He puffed on his cigarette again.

"Is there some reason the senator wants you to look into her death?"

"He just wants to make sure he knows what happened that night," I answered him.

He nodded, and I once again shook his hand, thanking him for speaking with me.

"Anytime," he told me.

I walked down the drive toward the Chevy. My watch told me it was nearing the time that I needed to pick up Bernie, but first I wanted to swing by the senator's residence and quickly bring him up to speed on who I had spoken to and what I had found out...which wasn't a helluva whole lot.

CHAPTER THIRTEEN

At dinner, my grandmother and Bernie held a non-stop conversation while I was lost in thoughts of my own. As I drowned their chatter out, I pondered that fateful night that was to be Sonny Girard's last. I wasn't willing to believe that this was a random and tragic accident. From what I had learned from the people who knew her best, she was just too serious about taking precautions, so that left out the theory that she took sleeping pills with a glass of wine before diving in for her nightly swim, unaware. She would not have been so stupid as to not give a thought to the effect the two mixed together would have had on her physical well-being. I just couldn't buy that. I just wasn't willing to believe that the woman could be that dumb. If not a very fatal misstep, then what? One alternative was that she did this deliberately to herself, knowing exactly what the outcome would be. Suicide would be an alternative to suffering in agony, mentally and emotionally. But over what? Something was on her mind…that much was clear, given the call to her husband that night. But that still didn't make much sense to me. Everyone I had spoken with so far was quick to claim they were unaware of anything truly important bothering her to such a degree. They claimed she wouldn't be the type of personality to take that course of action. They claimed that she was a happy woman, generally in high spirits. So, that left only one other option... murder. *Murder*? But by who, and *why*?

As much as Bernie wanted to deny it, some people hadn't cared for the young woman she had raised. Kay Rewis had not said it in so many words, but there wasn't a lot of love felt for her employer, of that much I was sure. But to murder the woman because Kay was jealous or envious of the fortunate breaks in life that her boss had received? I highly doubted that. That would be ridiculous. Or was there more to the story of Kay's bitterness? Of course, there was Russell Harwood. I was sure the man was not happy with his termination at the magazine by Sonny. I could well imagine he was downright angry, maybe even livid, at her for not giving him another chance at the magazine. How angry was he? Enough to threaten her and make good on his threat? Maybe I was wrong, but I just couldn't see it. I'd been in the business long enough to spot when most people were hiding the truth. I was comfortable in the fact that the guy was exactly who he presented himself to be...irresponsible, yes; a con artist to some degree, yes; a murderer, no. Perhaps I would see things differently as time progressed, but for now, he didn't seem to be involved.

Of course, there were many instances of a husband hiring someone to carry out the dirty deed of getting rid of an unwanted wife. Victor Girard had a rock-solid alibi with his being in Washington D. C. at the time of her death. But that didn't mean anything. The question was, why hire me if that was the case? And I, as of yet, hadn't come across any reason for his wanting to get her out of the way. The senator's children...now there were a couple of screwballs if I'd ever seen any. Neither of his daughters had cared for their stepmother, and it didn't appear that Victoria's husband, Neil Chelton, had either. If I could pin this murder—if it *was* murder—on insanity, my choice of trigger person would be the eldest daughter, Victoria. She sure was one for the books, and I didn't care for the woman at all. But the big question mark in my mind was why. *Why* would someone want to get rid of Sonny permanently? When I found that out, then I could—

"Sam! Sam, are you listening?"

My thoughts were interrupted by my grandmother's voice and I looked up, focusing first on Gran and then on Bernie.

"What?" I asked.

"Dear, Bernie just asked you what she could do to help you in your investigation. She wants to help you find out what happened to Sonny. We've been talking, and we think we can do some undercover work for you."

I eyed my grandmother with a look of incredulity on my face. "Undercover work? Are you *serious*? Neither one of you are going to do anything, you got it? So, get that through your heads."

"And why not?" Bernie protested. "Why can't we help out? I'm at the office almost every day. I could be your inside gal."

"Forget it! I don't even know what I'm dealing with here yet. You could be putting yourself in a dangerous position if it was—"

"Murder?" my grandmother interjected. "If she was murdered, maybe you'll need our help, dear."

"Gran, I said *forget it!*"

"Okay, okay," Bernie said...but I didn't fail to notice her sly wink at my grandmother. I gave her a hard stare and she shrugged. Then she looked at my grandmother once again and said, "Ruby, did I ever tell you that my great granddaddy was a second cousin to Jefferson Davis, President of the Confederacy?"

As the two women cleaned the kitchen after dinner, I was

in my bedroom going over some notes I'd made when I heard Bernie's voice.

"Who's playing Monopoly?" she asked.

"Oh, Sam and I started that game a couple of nights ago."

"I wouldn't mind playing," Bernie said. "Unless you don't want me to join the two of you, and in that case, I'll just watch."

Oh, no! I wasn't sitting around here tonight playing a game with these two women. I never wanted to play the game with Gran in the first place, and I wasn't going to be in their company while they pestered me into giving them some sort of covert mission in helping me with this case. I graciously offered my place in the game to Bernie, saying I had to go out anyway. Neither one of the ladies asked where I had to go, which was a good thing, because I didn't have an answer for them. But once they sat down at the dining room table to play, I hightailed it out of there. The last thing I heard before closing the door behind me was Bernie's voice saying, "Gee, Ruby, it seems he stinks at playing Monopoly, too."

Now just what did she mean by that? What else did I stink at?

***

The Double Shot had a fair number of customers for a Thursday night. I was headed toward the bar where Neamon, the owner, stood on the other side of it when I heard a sharp whistle pierce the atmosphere. I looked to my right. There, at a table and sitting by himself, was Pete "Bulldog" Dixon. He waved me over.

"What are you drinking?" I asked as I eased myself into the chair opposite him.

"Bourbon."

"I thought that stuff did a number on you at your poker party?"

"It did, but I'm not guzzling tonight. I'm nursing it," he said.

"Ah...." I muttered, nodding.

84

Neamon approached the table wearing a stained, worn white apron tied around his ever-growing middle, and a damp rag draped across his left shoulder. After I gave him my order of a scotch on the rocks, he left us, returning a moment later with my drink.

"I'm glad you're here. You're just the guy I want to see," Bulldog said. "Now I know this will be confidential between us. I won't do anything with the information until you give me the clearance. So, what's up? What's going on? Why is J. Edgar in town?"

"Hoover? He's in town?" I asked.

"Oh, come on!" he protested. "You're not going to start holding out on me at this point in time, are you? After all we've been through together? I'll find out sooner or later, so you might as well tell me. I won't rat you out."

I laughed. "No, seriously. I don't know anything about it. What makes you think he's in town?"

"Okay, if we're going to play games, I'll bite. Stanley Kopp—a kid I know who's a bellhop there—well, he says he saw J. Edgar with two of his men, the chief, and your former partner from the department walking into the Book Cadillac Hotel this afternoon. He says they had coffee in the restaurant and had their heads together in a hushed conversation. He says all the hotel's employees were whispering to each other about it. Now, what are you trying to pull? What's the story?"

"I'm not trying to pull anything. I have no story to tell you. I haven't heard a thing."

"Oh, right! Detective McPherson is playing ball with the Feds and you know nothing about it."

"I'm telling you, I don't. Mac doesn't tell me everything. I saw him a couple of days ago, but he never mentioned any of this."

"You being straight with me?" Bulldog asked. "He didn't mention what it was that could bring J. Edgar and his boys to Detroit?"

"I'm being straight with you. We talked about a case that I'm working on."

"Which is what? Or don't I get to know that, either?"

I shrugged. "Nah, I can tell you, but I don't have all the dope yet, so keep it to yourself for now. I'm looking into the death of Sondra Girard."

Bulldog's eyebrows went up. "The senator's wife? *That* Sondra Girard? How come? That was an accident."

"Well, so it would appear. He's just not sure. He paid me to nose around for a week, and that's what I'm doing."

"Find out anything yet?" he asked.

"Not much. I talked to his two daughters. Neither one liked the woman's position in their father's life, that's for sure. The people at the magazine think she was okay. The senator has a son, but he lives in Montana, so he won't know anything. No point in getting in contact with him." I shrugged again.

"Heh!" Bulldog said loudly, deliberately.

He had my complete attention. "What?"

"He wasn't in Montana when his stepmother left this earth."

My pulse quickened. I sat straighter in the chair and leaned in over the table that separated us. "Are you sure about that? How can you be so sure?"

"Because I saw him…right here in town."

"What? You know this guy?"

"Yeah, Steven Girard. Graduated from high school with him."

"Okay, so you saw him in town. How can you be sure it was around the time of Mrs. Girard's death? Maybe he returned to Detroit *after* her death, coming home for the funeral."

86

"It wasn't *around* the time of her death. It was the day *of* her death."

"Come on!" I said. "Quit pulling my leg. How do you know it was that particular day? I think you're just trying to get even with me for not telling you about Hoover."

"Aha! I *knew* you knew about his visit. Now, let me in on the dope."

I laughed. "Honest, I don't know! This is the first I've heard about him even being in town. Mac never mentioned it to me."

Bulldog took a swig of his bourbon, his eyes scrunched up, never leaving my face. I laughed again and took a hefty swallow of my own drink.

"No, seriously, how do you know it was the date she drowned?"

"In high school, I hung around with four other guys. We were pretty tight. So each year, usually in the summer, we do a get-together. Maybe we'll spend one day at Briggs Stadium watching a Tigers baseball game, and go out to dinner afterward. We might play poker way into the wee hours of the next morning. A year ago, at the beginning of July, we went up to Imlay City. One of the guys owns a cabin up there. Gee, that was a great weekend," he mused. He leaned back and sighed with fond memories.

"Hey," I said. "Is this going anywhere?"

Bulldog straightened in his chair. "Oh yeah, well, like I said, we make it a point of getting together once a year. You know, just the guys...no wives or kids allowed, although not *all* of us are married yet. Anyway, this summer we were all getting together for the first full weekend in August. That night, Friday the sixth, the guys were going to be arriving in the city. Well, a couple of them still live here, but—"

"Bulldog! Get to the point!"

"I'm coming to it. Hold your horses. So, I'm down on Grand

River that afternoon and who do I see coming out of Dittrich Furs? It's Steve Girard."

I looked at him with a blank stare. "You told me all of that just to say you'd seen him on Grand River?"

"Well, no. It all ties in, just be patient. You see, this was on Friday afternoon. As I'm walking in front of the fur store, he comes walking out carrying something on a hanger under some thick plastic. Well, I figure he just bought a fur, you know? Anyway, I stopped and said, 'Hey, there! Steve!' At first, he just stares at me. I tell him, it's me…Pete Dixon. Then—and this is kind of weird, now that I really think of it—he looks around like he's looking to see if anyone is watching us, or near enough to overhear what we're saying. Eh, I must have been in a good mood that day because I told him about the guys getting together that evening and asked him if he wanted to join us. I honestly don't know what got into me, because he and I never hung around together. Looking back, he was sort of weird in school. But he was on the basketball team with Arnie, so I figured I'd invite him."

"Arnie?" I asked.

"Yeah, one of the guys who was coming into town that evening."

"You said he was weird. Weird in what way?" I asked him. I was curious.

"Eh, you know, quiet. Not really hanging out with the other fellows on the team, or even in school in general. He kind of kept to himself. Come to think of it, even Arnie didn't care for him all that much. I don't know why I invited him." Bulldog rubbed at his chin, like he was trying to figure it all out. He took another gulp of his drink.

"Okay, so he hung out with you and the other guys that night. How does that help me with my investigation? He couldn't have done anything to her if he was with you and your buddies," I reasoned.

"Oh no, didn't I tell you? He turned me down, said he had someone to meet that night. He said he had to give them something *and ask* them something. And he couldn't keep from smiling about it, like he was excited about it but didn't want to appear that way. At the time, I figured he'd just bought a woman a fur coat, you know? I mean, he had the thing slung over his shoulder and he was wearing this big goofy smile. And what he had to ask her…well, you figure it out. Well, maybe I took it the wrong way, but if I didn't, and he wasn't going over to the senator's pool to do in his stepmother, I know who he went to meet."

Bulldog sat back in his chair and lifted his glass to his lips, looking smug and self-satisfied.

CHAPTER FOURTEEN

It was pretty early when I walked out of The Double Shot and into the mild night air. Bulldog had wanted me to stay for another drink and I would have, but Bernie had caught me right before I was to leave the house, asking me if I would be home at a decent hour. She wanted me to give her a ride back to her place so she wouldn't have to spend money on a taxicab. I had walked to Neamon's bar that night, and now I was glad I had. The stroll home would give me the opportunity to think about, and digest, what the Detroit News journalist had revealed. Apparently, word about town was that the young thirty-two-year-old Steven Girard, the senator's son, had been having an affair with a married woman for three or four years now, seeing her whenever he could on his return trips to Detroit. Obviously, I wasn't in on the scoop because I had never heard about this at all.

While it wasn't unheard of that a man would have an affair with a married woman, it was *who* he was having the affair with that shocked me. Charlotte Montgomery had to be in her mid-forties, married to a sixty-something man one didn't want to tangle with. Her husband was the Honorable Charles M. Montgomery, one of the toughest judges to ever sit on the bench in Detroit. He was immovable in his rulings, and swift and severe in his sentencing. He also had a reputation for allowing no one—absolutely no one—to get in his way about anything. I could understand completely the situation when Bulldog told me that those who knew of this refused to speak of it, and no one would write a word of it for publication. Everyone was aware that if they did, they were playing with fire and it was sure that they would get burned. He also told me that the senator knew nothing of his son's actions, and Steven had wanted to keep it that way. I could understand that, too.

What in the hell was Steven Girard doing? Certainly, *he* had to know that he, more than anyone else, was playing with that fire, didn't he? All of this left me in a pickle. I'd have to find out if he was with Mrs. Charlotte Montgomery the night that Sonny drowned. But I'd have to tread carefully.

***

Bernie and I were in the Chevy and backing out of the driveway by ten minutes after eight. She sat silently on the seat next to me until I told her that I had stopped by Senator Girard's home that afternoon, but no one had answered.

"Well, if you have to speak to him, you'd better make it quick. He's headed back to Washington D. C. tomorrow afternoon, and who knows how long he'll be there? I think his flight is at one o'clock," she said.

"Think he'll be awake when I get you home?" I asked her.

Bernie shrugged, and the rest of the trip was made without conversation. When I pulled up in front of the Victorian home, no light shone from within. It appeared that either Victor Girard was out for the evening, or else he had retired for the night already. I walked Bernie to her door, making sure she was safely tucked inside for the night. On my way back to the auto, I noticed the back of the house that the senator lived in was darkened also. I

91

would call him in the morning. Right now, I was looking forward to getting home and getting comfortable.

As I approached the Chevy, there was the elderly woman from across the street again. This was the third time I had seen her come out onto her porch to wave to me. She had done it the other night when I dropped Bernie off, and earlier today when I stopped by to talk to the senator. Now, here she was again. I waved back, to which she tapped her cane loudly a few times on the concrete and put her hands on her hips. Something seemed to be agitating her. For all I knew, she was one in a long list of lonely senior citizens that had wanted nothing more than to have some acknowledgment and attention. I decided to meander over, thinking I could ask her a question or two. When I reached the woman who lived straight across from the senator's residence, I noticed how tiny she was. She stood no taller than four feet nine or ten inches, and was a bit pudgy around the middle. Her alabaster hair was braided at the nape of her neck and ran the length of her humped back. She had delicate features, and clear, sparkling light blue eyes. Although time had carved grooves into her face, the general beauty of her youth seemed to shine through.

"Well, it's about time!" she sputtered.

"Pardon me?"

Exasperated, she asked, "Are you the detective looking into her death? The senator's wife's?"

"Yes, I am," I said, surprised by her question.

"Your boss told me he'd send someone out, but I didn't expect it would be more than a month later!" the small woman complained. "I've been watching for you every day since it happened! What kind of numbskull are you? Or don't any of you down at the precinct value the help of an old woman?"

"My boss?" I was confused. Who was she speaking of? Was she speaking of the senator?

"That police detective!" she said with impatience. "The one who came out that night they took her body away! I saw the cars pull up and kept watching out the window. Later, when they came from the rear of the property carrying someone on a stretcher, a cold jolt ran through me and I walked over. I wanted to know what had happened! He told me to get back inside, but I told him I might have some information for him. At first I thought he'd had a heart attack or something…the senator, that is. But when I found out it was *her*…well, I got to thinking. That detective with the dark curly hair told me to go back home and he'd send someone out later to speak to me. I've been waiting for over a month, young man, and I'm not happy about that!"

Lawrence Brown! That idiot, Lawrence Brown!

She eased herself down into one of two chairs that were placed on her front porch, separated by a small black wrought-iron table, and tapped the other chair with her cane. "Now, sit down and I'll tell you what I know."

I took a seat, eager to hear what she would have to say.

"Now, what's your name? I'm not letting you get away without knowing your name, in case I need to call the police department to complain about you," she said.

I chuckled and told her who I was. "And, by the way, I'm not with the department. Senator Girard hired me to nose around about his wife's death. The man you want to call and complain about is Detective Lawrence Brown. Make sure you remember the name. He's the guy with the dark curly hair, and he never had any intention of sending someone out to talk to you."

A grunt of disgust rose from deep within her throat. "Well, isn't that a swift kick in the britches? Then I'll tell *you* what I know, young man. She had a visitor that evening."

That bit of information startled me. "Are you sure it was that same night, Mrs…. Uh…."

93

"Marsh. Mrs. Lavinia Marsh." She paused and turned her head to the left to look at me. "Did you know my husband, Emmet?"

"No, I don't believe I did," I answered.

"When Emmet was alive he was a surgeon at Harper Hospital…one of the best surgeons around. But back to Mrs. Girard. She had a visitor that very night. I saw her walking up the drive about seven."

"What makes you so sure it was that night, and how can you be certain about the time? And you say it was a woman?" This morsel of news made it a whole new ballgame.

"Unless *he* likes to wear a skirt and knows how to walk pretty doggone well in a pair of pumps, I'd say it was a woman, young man! I know it was that night because, like I said, it was the same night I was watching out the window and the cars pulled up a bit after midnight. Contrary to what all of you young people think, us old ones still have our faculties. I haven't had problems with my memory, you young whippersnapper. I was sitting in the parlor in my chair by the window, like I always do. Bessie brought me my supper at the usual time, six-fifteen. Bessie is my housekeeper. She brings it to me on a tray each night while I sit in the parlor, because I like to tune into my shows. The Fred Waring Show comes on at seven, and I don't like to miss it." She paused again in her account of that night and asked, "Do you listen to that show?"

"Sometimes," I said, pulling my small notebook from my top suit coat pocket. I wanted to jot down what she was telling me.

She nodded, and then continued. "Well, anyway, I had finished with my meal and the show was just coming on. The opening music had just started and I caught movement out of my left eye. I turned to see a woman walking up the drive to the Girard home. As a matter of fact, I remember being surprised."

94

"Why were you surprised?"

"Because no one ever visited the senator or his wife. His children don't come around anymore and, unless they're having one of their parties — which isn't often — I've never been aware of anyone calling on them. I don't think she had any friends, really." Mrs. Lavinia Marsh shook her head sadly. "It's a downright shame, because I thought she was a lovely young woman."

"What did she look like? This visitor," I asked, ready to record the description in my notebook.

Lavinia Marsh shrugged. "Don't know," she said. "I was looking at the back of her."

"How about hair color?"

"Don't know that, either. She had on a big floppy hat, and if she had long hair, it was tucked up underneath."

"Okay, then what about height and weight?"

"She wasn't fat. In fact, I'd say normal, but she was real tall," the old woman offered.

"How tall?" I persisted.

"*Really* tall, but I couldn't tell you in feet and inches."

I wrote down "TALL" in capital letters and underlined it and put a question mark in parentheses in my notes, just to remind me that she was taller than average. The woman could tell me little else. Shortly after The Fred Waring Show ended, she had dozed off, not waking until just before ten that night. She noted that when she roused herself, she'd again looked out the window, but the senator's residence was shrouded in darkness until she saw that a taxicab let the senator off in his drive a couple of hours later, and then the cars from the city pulled up about half past midnight. She had missed seeing the female caller leave the premises. When the men emerged from the rear of the property, sometime later, that was when her curiosity proved to be too great and she'd thrown on her robe and walked across the street.

"So, young man, I'd say you need to find that woman who visited her that night. You need to talk to her. I bet she'd be able to tell you if Mrs. Girard had been feeling ill when she saw her. I'm sure that's what happened. She probably went in swimming after her company left, and got to feeling ill and couldn't pull herself out." Lavinia Marsh shook her head with sadness again. "That poor young woman. She was always so sweet. I hated to see something like that happen to her."

I sat in the Chevy after thanking Mrs. Lavinia Marsh for the information. Pulling out a Lucky Strike, I looked back to the old woman's home. She'd gone back inside for the night. I agreed with her that I would have to find Sonny Girard's visitor, but instead of believing the mystery woman could inform me as to the health of the senator's wife, I instead believed I would have my murderer. I was sure now that Sonny had been murdered. A big part of it was all coming together neatly in my mind. I just had to figure out the why, along with the who.

CHAPTER FIFTEEN

On Friday morning, I woke to see my bedroom window covered with droplets of drizzle. The branches on the old elm tree on the front lawn swayed in an easterly direction with the brisk breeze. It was the seventeenth day of September. Gran was still sleeping; soft snores were coming from behind her bedroom door. I made my way to the kitchen and started a pot of coffee percolating on the stove. Feeling it was too early to put in that call to the senator, I instead rescued the newspaper from the front porch, tossed it on the end table in the parlor, and headed for the bathroom to take a long hot shower.

My thoughts were spinning a tale under the spray of heat. I was starting to formulate a scenario at the senator's residence on the last night of Sonny's life, but I didn't get too far. There was a knock on the bathroom door, followed by my grandmother's voice.

"Sam? Will you be in there long?"

"Give me another minute or two and I'll be out, Gran," I yelled.

I actually would have liked to prolong my time in the shower; my muscles felt soothed under the force of the hot water.

Surrendering to my grandmother's wishes, though, I quickly shampooed my hair and lathered my body. I emerged not even five minutes later wearing my black bathrobe. Gran was pouring herself a cup of coffee from the pot.

"Oh good, dear. Helen and I are going to the five and dime. They've got a sale going on. I want to get some new crochet hooks and thread. I need to get ready."

Shortly thereafter, my grandmother descended the porch steps on her way to the waiting automobile of her friend, Helen Foster, under the protection of a large black umbrella. I watched her disappear inside the car while I stood at the picture window, still dressed in my robe. Taking another sip of my coffee while they rolled out of the drive, I thought of how nice it would be to return to my bed. It was just that kind of day. But I couldn't. There were so many people still to see concerning the case of Sonny Girard's death. Instead, I sat in the chair and continued to gaze at the lousy weather. Shamus, our cat, leapt onto my lap and I ran my fingers through his silky gray coat while I finished my morning beverage and smoked a Lucky Strike cigarette. I would give the senator fifteen or twenty minutes more before I placed that call.

The senator picked up after the second ring. It was just before nine thirty.

"Hello, Senator Girard. It's Sam Flanagan. I wanted to touch base with you about the investigation. I've talked to—"

"I *know* who you've spoken with! You've spoken with Victoria and Simone, haven't you?"

Puzzled, I was somewhat caught off guard by his interruption. He sounded angry.

"Yes, just yesterday," I responded. "You knew I'd be getting in touch with them, so what is the problem?"

"The problem, Flanagan, is that I don't like you bothering

98

my girls. I told you they wouldn't know anything about Sonny's accident. I think maybe this was a bad idea."

"Wait, you think *what* was a bad idea? I told *you*, Senator, that I would be speaking to all of the people who knew her. That's how an investigation gets off the ground. And in my initial interviews I have reason to suspect that this was no mere accident. It has come to my attention that a woman visited your wife on the day of her death, and I believe she, whoever she is, may very well be involved. I don't have a good description of her yet, but when I find this woman, I might have more to tell you."

There was five seconds of silence on the other end of the line, but I could hear the man breathing softly. I didn't say another word.

"What are you talking about? Are you saying Sonny was murdered?" Victor Girard asked with continued annoyance in his voice.

"Yes, sir; that's my gut feeling so far."

"You're off your rocker, Flanagan!" he spat more forcefully. "Sonny wasn't murdered, and I don't want you going around my daughters again, do you hear me? In fact, I want you off the case. Sonny suffered a tragic accident, and there is nothing more to it. If it was anything else, I'm sure the police would have suspected something."

"I was under the impression that you didn't like their findings," I gushed in a snide tone. "You paid me for a week," I said tautly.

To say I was perplexed by this turn-around in his attitude was putting it mildly.

"Keep the money, but you're off the case as of now! You've just been fired!"

I heard a click and knew he'd disconnected the line. I held the instrument out, staring at it. Anger rose from within me and I slammed the receiver back onto its base. *What a sap! What a knucklehead! What a fool!* He was all wet about this one, and I knew it. Who was he trying to protect by giving me the ax? One of his daughters? *Both* of his daughters? From the conversation that had just taken place, it sounded to me as if he was a man who was afraid, and it seemed to me as though he might have something to hide. But what could I do? Senator Girard had just terminated our relationship *and* our contract.

Still experiencing a heat inside, I looked down, watching Shamus rub against my bare ankles. What was I to do now? I could think of only one thing. Scooping up the kitten in my arms, I headed for my bedroom.

"Come on, little fella," I whispered in his ear. "Let's you and I go back to bed."

***

Shamus and I spent the rest of the morning in a wonderful state of oblivion. In fact, it wasn't until I heard the front door open and close that I was able to rouse myself fully. Gran had returned home. Afternoon had arrived, and it was time to get up and do something; what exactly, I didn't know. But I couldn't lie in bed all day, nor did I want to. When I emerged from my room, Gran looked surprised.

"What are you doing home?" she asked. "I thought you'd be out doing some investigating."

"Well, that had been the plan. I called Senator Girard this morning to bring him up to date on the case, but he canned me."

"Canned you?"

"Fired me, Gran. He took me off the case."

She gasped. "Oh, my goodness! Weren't you investigating fast enough for him, dear?"

"Maybe a little too fast," I replied. "He didn't like the fact that I had questioned his two daughters. So, he fired me and told

100

me to stay away from them. The senator, I'm afraid, is nothing more than jerk; a real nitwit."

The afternoon was spent lazily on St. Aubin, but not unpleasantly so. I read the newspaper; some of the articles I read aloud to Gran. We listened to the radio. My grandmother snoozed...and so did I for a second time. The weather continued to be dismal with a constant drizzle suspended in mid-air. All in all, it was a great day to stay inside. The only thing that ruined my peace of mind was the fact that Senator Victor Girard had turned out to be a jackass, and it greatly bugged me that I would never know what exactly happened to his young wife, when I *knew* that something sinister...very intentional on someone's part...had taken place! I tried several times not to think of it, but wasn't very successful.

At ten minutes to six o'clock we sat down to dinner at the kitchen table. Gran had roasted a whole chicken in the oven, fried up some potatoes, boiled some chopped carrots, and tossed a green salad. It looked delicious and I was hungry. During our meal, she brought up the subject of my current state of unemployment again.

"Bernie is going to be awfully upset, dear," she uttered.

"I know it."

"Did you call her yet?"

"Nope."

"Don't you think you should, dear?" she questioned.

"I figure I can do that tomorrow. Let her enjoy her Friday night. She can get plenty mad tomorrow," I reasoned.

But my plan wasn't to be. The telephone call came in that evening. Gran was closest to the instrument and answered it after the first ring. Within seconds I had figured out it was Bernie on the other end.

"Well, hello, dear. How are you? ... Yes, I can answer that one for you. He didn't do any detecting today. ... It's because he was fired. ... Yes, by the senator. ... Oh, I'm absolutely sure of it. Sam said he canned him. ... Well, all right, dear. I'll put him on."

My grandmother held the receiver out to me and shrugged her shoulders.

"Hello, Bernie," I said into the mouthpiece.

"What happened? Why in God's name did that man take you off the case?" she almost yelled.

"Now try to settle down a bit. I know you're angry, but it isn't going to do anyone any good if you bust a blood vessel," I warned her. "Listen, I called him early this morning. I wanted to catch him before he left for the airport. I wanted to bring him up to speed on what I've been doing and what I've been finding out. He told me he knew I'd been talking to his daughters and he didn't like that one bit. He told me to stay away from them and then he took me off the case. Hey, I don't like it, either. But there's nothing we can do."

"Oh, *can't* we? Well, you just wait and see! I *told* you I didn't want her to marry him! Do you understand now? I wasn't sure I liked him all that well back then, and now I *know* I don't! Be there tomorrow morning. I'm taking a taxicab over before I head to the office. I want to talk to you. Then you can give me a lift into the magazine. I'll see you in the morning."

Before I could object, she'd hung up.

CHAPTER SIXTEEN

Gran came into my bedroom earlier than I had wanted her to on Saturday morning. "Sam," she called while shaking my foot from on top of the covers. "Bernie is here, dear."

I propped open one eye and sighed loudly. "Aw, geez! Tell her I'll be out in a minute."

And then I smelled the bacon. As soon as my grandmother backed out of my room, shutting the door behind her, I tossed my legs over the side of the bed. I was tying the belt of my bathrobe as I entered the kitchen. I found my grandmother taking hot biscuits out of the oven, and Bernie was sitting at the table sipping on a cup of black coffee. She looked up at my appearance in the room.

"I'm sorry I woke you," she said.

I shook my head. "Don't give it a second thought. Let me just splash some water on my face and I'll be with you in a minute."

When I emerged from the bathroom, the table was being set for three by our guest. Any discussion was delayed until we all sat down to breakfast, our plates filled with biscuits, gravy, and bacon.

"Mmm mmm, Ruby; are you sure you don't have Southern blood running through those veins of yours? This milk and bacon grease gravy is delicious. I haven't eaten this in ages!"

My grandmother smiled broadly and shook her head. "No, I'm pretty sure I don't, dear."

"Well, my God, woman…it tastes just like my mama's." Bernie then took a sip of her coffee and my grandmother's grin grew even wider.

"Bernie," I said. "You don't seem to be quite as upset this morning. That's good."

"Don't you believe it, buddy boy!" she spat. "That man may not have had enough love or respect for Sonny, but I do! He's not going to sweep what happened to my little girl under the rug. I'll take things into my own hands!"

"How are you going to do that, dear?" my grandmother asked. "Are you going to take over the investigating?"

Bernie stopped chewing her food and stared at Gran as if she'd lost all her marbles. "No, I am not," she said. The one-time nanny looked my way. "I want to hire you myself."

"Uh, Bernie, now listen. My fee is twelve dollars a day, and I doubt your position at the magazine…well, I doubt you could afford that. Besides, I don't want to take your money. But I'll tell you what. I can nose around a few more days on what Senator Girard paid me."

"Don't you have to give that back to him?"

"Nope, he told me to keep it; and anyway, I'm not giving anything back to him. He hired me to do a job and then acted like an ass." I took a bite of my bacon slice.

"No, then you keep it. You deserve it, Sam. You worked hard for it and earned every bit of it. And this way, you'll be working for *me*. You won't owe him any information. Don't you worry about your fee; I've got some money of my own. When Sonny died, I was in her will. She bequeathed six thousand dollars to me that was left over from an inheritance by her granddaddy. Her

104

mama's daddy died some years back and left her a nice amount, and she willed to me what was left of that."

"You don't want to spend it this way, Bernie," I argued. "I'm pretty sure Sonny would have wanted you to do something nice for yourself with that."

"You just never mind. This *will* be doing something nice for me. You either take me up on my offer, or I'll find another private detective who will. This city must be full of them."

I eyed her as she took a huge bite of her biscuit and gravy. What could it hurt if I continued nosing around for a few more days on her dime? She needed to know the truth, and I was extremely curious myself. I agreed to do it. If the senator caught wind of my arrangement with Bernie and objected…well tough! I'd no longer be working for him. Hell, I was no longer working for him at this very minute! To hell with him!

Bernie bent over, picking up her purse that had been placed on the floor by her chair. She unlatched it and drew out some bills. The woman handed me two twenties and two tens.

"There," she said. "That should cover five days of detective work. And if you don't have the answer in five days, I'll pay you for another five days."

I placed the money to the side of my plate and took a last bite of biscuit. "Okay, since you've officially hired me, I'll tell you what I have found out. Thursday night, right after I dropped you off at your place, I found out that Sonny had a visitor on the very evening she died."

That got her attention. Her eyes widened. She hurriedly swallowed the food she had in her mouth, almost choking on it. Bernie coughed a couple of times and then said, "No; who?"

"Now that I don't know yet. But she wasn't alone that night, and if I'm right, she wasn't alive when her guest left."

"How did you find all this out, Sam?" Bernie asked.

"A little old lady that lives in the neighborhood…Mrs. Lavinia Marsh."

"Oh yes; she lives right across the street. What did she say he looked like?"

"She," I corrected her.

"What?"

"Not he, but she," I stated. "And she doesn't know what she looked like, but she was very tall. Mrs. Marsh only saw her from the back and the woman was wearing a hat big enough to cover her hair. This mystery woman walked up the senator's driveway at about seven that evening."

Tears were forming in the eyes of the woman who sat directly across from me at the kitchen table. She didn't say a word for several seconds, and then she turned to my grandmother, putting her hand on Gran's forearm.

"My God, Ruby," she said in an unsteady half whisper. "My baby was murdered."

***

During the drive to The Monthly Patriot, I revealed to Bernie the idea that had been formulating in my mind for more than a day. I described what I thought had happened on that tragic night…or what I thought might come close to the actual events leading up to Sonny's death. I figured it this way; Sonny had gone home from the office, made the call to her husband in Washington D.C., and then had gotten into her bathing suit, wanting to take her nightly swim before dinner. Afterward, maybe she had poured herself a glass of wine, or just maybe she received this visitor and *then* poured each of them a glass of wine to enjoy while sitting out by the pool. This visitor had changed into a swimming suit, too. After all, it was a scorcher of a summer this year, and the initial days of August were no different. While in the house changing clothes, this woman noticed the sleeping pills somewhere…maybe on a bedside table, or maybe in the bathroom. She took some of them, six to be exact, and found an opportunity to add them to Sonny's wine. If that was truly the case—and, at this point, I was just theorizing—had this woman who had gone to see Sonny done so with the intention of killing her? If she had, she may not have formulated *how* to kill Sondra Girard until she spied the sleeping draft.

After the deed was done, she took the glasses and washed them, and placed them in the cupboard. She couldn't have any evidence of her presence, or evidence that a sleeping draft had been added to Sonny's wine, now could she? And what she didn't realize in doing that was that the two wine glasses used were not kept in the cupboard, but behind the bar. Then she stopped and thought—Sonny had wine in her system. Shouldn't there be a wine glass out on the patio next to where Sonny had lain on the chaise lounge? So, she reached in the cupboard once again, grabbing one of the gold etched glasses, and poured a small amount of wine into it. And again, she was unaware of the fact that the gold etched wine glasses were only used when Sonny was with her husband, the senator. The woman then returned upstairs to change back into her street clothes. That would explain the damp spot on the senator's bed and the damp towel thrown into the bathtub, along with the water on the bathroom floor. I may have been wrong in some of my reconstruction of that night, but it all seemed to make perfect sense to me.

"Did Sonny have visitors often?" I asked Bernie.

"No, not at all. She really didn't have any close friends here. I mean, most people liked her and got on well with her, but she didn't have what you might call a close friend or a best friend. Sonny didn't agree with mixing business and pleasure. She was particular about that. She wouldn't even let Ty or myself call her 'Sonny' when others were in the office. Only people who were close to her could call her that. And she really didn't take the opportunity to meet many outside the office. She had her work, and she had the senator when he was back in town. And, of course, she had me." She hesitated a second or two. "In fact, I can't think of anyone outside of the senator's friends that ever visited, and they only came to the house when they threw their parties, which wasn't too often. And I don't believe she was close to any of them, because she would have told me if she was. You know, they were mainly people he knew from being in politics."

I pulled up in front of our destination. She sat there while I was lost in thought.

"What are you thinking, Sam?"

"Bernie, have you ever seen the senator's daughters?"

"Only one of them once or twice, I think," she answered. "His oldest girl was at the house right after we arrived here following the wedding in North Carolina. I moved up here with Sonny at the time."

"Victoria?"

"Yes, that's her," she confirmed.

"How tall would you say she is? When I was at her place, she was lying on the sofa and never stood, but she appeared as though she was rather tall to me."

"She is," Bernie agreed. "I'd say maybe five foot eight or nine; somewhere around there. I couldn't say for sure. I just figured she took after her daddy in that department. His other daughter I've never seen. He's got a boy, too, but I've never seen him, either. He lives out west somewhere. For days the senator couldn't get in touch with him to tell the boy that she had died."

I bet he couldn't, I thought. "The girls didn't attend the funeral?" I asked.

"Victoria and her husband did for all of ten minutes. That's the only other time I saw her," she said with distaste. "They came to the showing, and then Sonny's parents had her body shipped back down to North Carolina for another service and burial. The youngest girl didn't show at all; that little brat! Sonny had said all along that they weren't happy about their father marrying again, but that she was going to try to win them over."

I put my hand on Bernie's arm before she exited the Chevy. "Listen to me. It's very important that you don't go in there and talk about any of this, understand? Don't talk about any of this at all. I mean it. We don't know who or what we're really dealing with here. They don't need to know that you've hired me, either."

Wide-eyed, she nodded her head in agreement, and then got out of the car and walked into the building that housed the magazine.

CHAPTER SEVENTEEN

Bernie's mention of the senator's friends put a bit of fear into me. What if this had nothing to do with Victor Girard's children, or the people who worked for Sonny at the magazine? What if one of *his* political associates had had it in for the young reporter for some reason? Anyone could have murdered the senator's wife, and for any reason. At this point, I felt as though I was searching for the proverbial needle in a haystack.

As long as I was out and about already, I decided to see if I could get in contact with Hildie King, Sonny Girard's assistant at the magazine. Of course, she could be in the office already, but she hadn't been showing up for work lately and I thought I would try to reach her at her home. She was the only one employed at the monthly periodical who I hadn't spoken with yet.

Hildie King's apartment was located on Woodward Avenue, several blocks from my office. I climbed the three flights of stairs to get to the fourth floor, knocking on the door of apartment 417 when I located it. I was taken aback when a man answered my knock, standing about five feet ten or eleven inches and weighing maybe one hundred and eighty pounds. I assumed this was her husband. His hair was straw-colored, cropped a bit too high above his ears, and parted neatly to one side. The man's face was clean-shaven. He wasn't bad looking, but not strikingly handsome, either. He had blue eyes, nicely shaped brows, and a long, angular nose. I was betting he was in his early thirties.

"Yes?"

"I'm looking for Hildie King. Does she happen to be at home?"

He shook his head. "And you are?" he inquired.

"The name is Sam Flanagan. Can you tell me when she's expected in? I'd like to ask her about her former employer, a Mrs. Sondra Girard."

Something flickered in his eyes. His expression would have matched an audible gasp, but he didn't gasp. Instead he said, "She died."

"Yes, I know. I just wanted to ask Hildie a few questions about Mrs. Girard." I extended my hand to shake his. "And your name?" I asked

He hesitantly accepted my handshake and said, "Mark King. She's at work right now. She'll be home this evening, but I'm not sure what time. She doesn't keep regular hours."

"Well, if you could just tell your wife I stopped by, I would appreciate it. I'll try to catch her at another time."

He nodded, told me he would, and then closed the door. Hildie King was turning out to be very elusive.

It was going on ten, and I decided to make an appearance at the office. Rounding the corner, I stopped to buy a paper from the kid who tried to sell them daily. I didn't really need one because we had one delivered each day to the house, but I liked to try to help him out. His name was Hooch Beasle—Christian name, Wallace—and he was attempting to earn money to help support the family since his father was deceased. I flipped him a quarter, told him to keep the change, and wished him a happy Saturday. I

111

must have been feeling particularly generous that day.

"Jeepers! Thanks, Mr. Flanagan!" he called as I walked away.

When I entered my hallway, I spied Russell Harwood leaning against the wall near the door to my office. I passed him and inserted my key.

"I've been waiting for you," he said in an agitated tone.

"So it would appear," I replied. "What can I do for you, Mr. Harwood?"

I sat behind my desk after tossing the newspaper on the top of my filing cabinet along with my hat.

"You can tell me why you lied to me the other day," he demanded.

"Lied to you? What are you talking about?"

"You know exactly what I'm talking about! After you left, I got to wondering why the Detroit Police Department would be sending out a detective to speak to me. The more I thought about it, the more it bothered me. I wanted to know what was up with Sondra's death. I remembered your name, so all I had to do this morning was to go and ask. Guess what I found out? You're not even employed there! Why did you tell me you were a cop?"

"I didn't," I said.

He leaned closer to me over the desk, placing the palms of his hands on it. "You did, too. I got to thinking later on that maybe there was more to her accident, like it wasn't an accident at all and I might be suspected of something. You had me scared out of my mind. Now what gives? Why did you misrepresent yourself?"

"I didn't," I said.

He stood erect, but continued to glare at me.

"Hey, nice suit," I complimented him. "You look rather spiffy."

"Are you going to answer me?"

"Look, Russell, I did not misrepresent myself. You opened the door and I introduced myself as Detective Flanagan." I pointed to the upper portion of my door. "Now read what that says." I then gestured with a thumb behind me to the window. "It says the same thing here."

"Yeah, I see. Flanagan Investigations. I still say you tried to mislead me. You might want to think about how people are going to react when you try to grill them under false pretenses."

I threw up my hands in resignation. "Okay, I'm sorry. I didn't mean to make you nervous. I was just doing my job, and I didn't mean to make you think the police had you under surveillance. Let's be friends," I said with a bit of sarcasm. "Deal?"

"I just wanted you to know that you got caught and it wasn't funny. But I guess I can let bygones be bygones *this* time." He tugged at the lapels on his navy suit coat, and then brushed imaginary lint from them. "You really like the suit? It looks okay on me? I borrowed it from a friend. I have an interview today with the Detroit Times."

I whistled. "Hey, congratulations. You'll be working for Hearst, huh?"

He nodded and a slight smile formed on his lips. "Yeah, wish me luck." He paused, gingerly touching his colorful and still swollen eyelid with his fingertips. "How does the eye look?"

"Looks like it's healing," I lied. "I wish you all the luck in the world."

"Thanks! Well, see you around maybe…and remember what I said."

I gave him a mock salute and he turned around to leave. When he did, a jolt ran through me. From one shoulder to the other, across the top of the suit jacket, was fresh beige paint. As I'd approached him in the hall not ten minutes ago, I'd found him leaning against the wall; the wall that the superintendent had painted just yesterday morning. I could have run out after him and told him, but I didn't. Why ruin his good mood? I'd let him walk into that interview feeling just as confident as he was feeling now. The superintendent was going to be ticked when he saw the wall outside of my door. But I could only shake my head, not being able to prevent my lips from curling into a wee smile. And I wondered if Russel's friend—the one who owned the suit—would find it just as amusing as I did.

I then got down to business by dialing the number for The Monthly Patriot.

"Hi, Bernie," I said when she answered. "Does Hildie King happen to be in the office right now?"

"Hi, Sam. Yes, she's in today…well, that is she *was* here until about five or ten minutes ago. She went out to check on our sponsors and to try to get more people to place ads. I'm not sure when she'll be back. Do you want me to give her a message?"

"No, that's all right. I swung by her place after I dropped you off and her husband said she was at work. Maybe I'll try to catch up with her later this evening."

"Her husband? Hildie isn't married. You must have spoken to her brother. She lives with her brother. He's come in here a couple of times to pick her up after work."

"Oh, well I guess I'd just assumed it was her husband. Okay, thanks, Bernie. I'll talk to you later."

I hung up, thinking it was strange that Mark King hadn't corrected me when I called Hildie his wife. Shrugging, I knew of another person I wanted to talk to.

Asking for the operator's assistance, I obtained the number to the residence of Judge Charles M. Montgomery, and then dialed it. I was hoping his wife would answer, but I got just as lucky when a housekeeper did. The woman promptly put her employer on the line. I told Charlotte Montgomery who I was, stating detective…and then crumpling a piece of paper near the mouthpiece of the telephone to mask the name Flanagan. She asked, "Detective who?" but I plowed right on, asking if she'd been in the company of Senator Girard's son on the evening of Friday, August 6 of this year. Of course, she denied even knowing him, but when I told her this was in connection with the investigation of a crime, she suddenly asked if Steven was in any kind of trouble. Funny how things work out, isn't it? I hadn't used the young man's first name, but she did. I thought she didn't know him? She was aware of her mistake a second or two after I was. She hemmed and hawed, and finally admitted that she was, indeed, with him that night. She nervously poured forth a whole lot of information that I really had no intention of asking.

They'd met at a rather seedy hotel about twenty-five miles outside of the Detroit city limits, and the couple had remained there until Sunday morning. Her husband had left late Friday morning and would be out of town that weekend at some law symposium. Steven had given her the gift of a mink jacket and had asked her to marry him. She didn't accept the fur or the proposal. In fact, she admitted to breaking it off once and for all with her long-time paramour. It was becoming too dangerous—*he* was becoming too dangerous. Toward the end of our conversation, she turned a little nasty.

"Who did you say you are? Because if my husband ever gets wind of the fact that you've called me, it won't be good for you!"

"Mrs. Montgomery, if your husband ever gets wind of *why* I called you, it won't be good for *you*."

She didn't reply to that. The fear in her silence was unmistakable. I saw no reason to continue our little chat. I'd found out what I had needed to know, so I terminated the telephone call.

CHAPTER EIGHTEEN

The city was no longer wet, but gray clouds hovered overhead, threatening to deliver another downpour. The temperature on this Saturday afternoon was a mild sixty-eight degrees. Locking the door to my office, I headed out onto Woodward Avenue. I would walk the three blocks to J. L. Hudson's, the department store. My reason for going there was to speak with Mary Sue Easley, the roommate of Kay Rewis. Once there, I headed straight to the accessories counter, but didn't see the young lady standing behind it. Instead, a nice-looking woman of about fifty was there.

"Can I help you, sir?"

"I was looking for Mary Sue Easley, but I see she isn't here. Is she still out sick?" I asked.

"No, she's here today. You just missed her. She's on her lunch break. You can go back if you'd like," she said. The woman pointed off to her left. "See that door? She's in there."

I thanked her and headed for the employee lunchroom. Mary Sue was sitting alone at a small table at the back of the room. Only one other table was occupied. An older woman with gray hair done up in a mass of curls was sitting quietly sipping on a cup of coffee while her nose was buried in a novel.

"Oh, it's you!" Mary Sue uttered when I took the chair opposite her. She was surprised to see me. The young woman had a thermos in front of her, and she had filled the top of it with the soup she was now eating. A few celery sticks stuffed with peanut butter were sitting on a small sheet of wax paper to her right.

"Ah, so you remember me," I said.

"Of course, I do. How are you, Detective Flanagan?"

"I'm doing just fine, Mary Sue, and I hope you are, too. I was worried that I caused a little rift between you and Kay the other day. I wanted to stop by and see if everything was all right now."

She smiled. "She wasn't angry after you left. In fact, she apologized to me. Kay just gets stressed out at times."

"Have you known her long?" I asked.

"Oh, yes. We've been friends for ages. I went to school with Kay. She's really a great gal once you get to know her. She's just had a few bad breaks, and I think that is why she comes across as hard at times." She took a spoonful of her soup and sighed. "Gee, I'm sick of chicken noodle soup! But you know what they say... chicken broth is good for you when you have a cold."

I nodded.

"I'd offer you some, but I don't have anything else to put it in," she continued.

"That's very nice of you, but I just ate," I lied. "So, did you and Kay move in together right after high school?"

"No, I got the job here at Hudson's and she'd gotten a scholarship and went away to school for journalism. We would see each other occasionally when she returned home on the weekends. She met a man here in Detroit after she had graduated and moved back to the city. They were going to get married, but he was drafted into the army. While Jerry was away, Kay was planning their wedding. Then one day she got a Dear Jane letter

117

from him, the rat! It seems he'd met some British woman and that was that. Kay had a real hard time of it…I can tell you that. In dealing with it, I guess she decided she needed to have a change of scenery, so she moved to Philadelphia for almost a year. When she came back she got the apartment and the job at the magazine. She asked me to move in with her, so I did. That was about a year and a half ago."

"Mary Sue, you told me that the night of Sondra Girard's death, your roommate, Kay, returned home and was quite emotional. Had she somehow heard about her boss's death?"

"No. Neither of us heard about that until the next day," she answered.

I knew Kay could not have heard about Sondra's death that soon unless she was somehow involved. But I was trying to find out *why* she was emotional from Mary Sue, and Mary Sue wasn't biting. I'd have to ask her outright.

"You told me she came back to the apartment about nine thirty that night and that she was upset. What was she upset about?"

Mary Sue Easley hesitated and looked uncomfortable, as if it suddenly dawned on her that maybe she had been revealing too much personal information about her roommate.

"Detective Flanagan, I don't feel that I should be talking about Kay. She's a very private person, and she would be really angry if she knew I was discussing this with you."

I nodded and said, "I can understand that, but there's been a change in the investigation. We have reason to suspect that Mrs. Girard may not have suffered an accident. There may be more to it, although we aren't really sure yet. So, I need to know where Kay was that night."

The young lady's eyes grew wide. "You don't mean that she was murdered?"

"We don't know, but there is the possibility of it."

"But Kay couldn't have had anything to do with that. She was at...."

She suddenly stopped talking. I waited several seconds, but she didn't continue.

"She was where?" I finally asked.

"Well, she does volunteer work," she said in a small voice.

"Where? Where does she volunteer?"

Mary Sue Easley bent her head and put another spoonful of soup into her mouth. "I don't know. She volunteers at a few different places," she said.

The girl was lying. I waited until she looked back up at me.

"You don't know where she does this volunteer work?"

She averted her gaze again and shook her head. "I only know a taxicab picks her up each Monday and Friday and takes her to her volunteer work, but she never talks about it."

"Kay doesn't own a car?" I inquired.

Mary Sue shook her head. "Neither of us do. We take the bus to work each day."

"When does she leave to do her volunteer work?"

She hesitated. I could see a look of slight panic on her face. The young woman tried to hide it, but it was there just the same. "Usually the taxicab picks her up in the early evening, maybe around four or five. I can't really remember." She was lying again. She did know where she went, and she knew when she left the apartment. I didn't call her on it. "But, Detective Flanagan, if you need to know anything else, I would appreciate it if you would speak to Kay herself."

I rose from my seat, thanked Mary Sue for speaking with me, and told her that she shouldn't mention to Kay that we had talked. I told her it didn't sound like her roommate was involved in any way, and therefore, couldn't be useful in the investigation.

119

Mentioning it to her would only put Mary Sue in the difficult position of having to explain to her roommate what we had discussed. A look of relief washed over her.

Of course, Kay Rewis could very well be involved. I only said what I had to Mary Sue to put her at ease. And you could bet your life that prior to four o'clock on Monday evening, I'd be parked outside of Kay's apartment ready to follow that taxicab.

Back in the office, I pulled out a new package of folders from the bottom drawer of my filing cabinet. While I had my spiral notebooks in which I kept jottings of current cases at home, I'd gotten into the habit of typing more professional accounts here at the office. I'd started doing this a couple of weeks ago, when I'd purchased a second-hand typewriter. One of the problems I faced when using the machine was that I didn't really know how to type, but I was learning. I was now transferring the highlights of my talk with Mary Sue Easley to paper, pecking the appropriate keys with an index finger once I located them. When I'd finished, I looked at my watch. Only mid-afternoon, it was growing darker outside, but I wanted to swing by The Monthly Patriot to see if I could catch Hildie King before I headed for home. I wasn't going to just chance it, though. I'd call to find out if she had returned.

"She still isn't back, Sam," Bernie told me. "But hey, I just thought of something. If you can't catch her at home tonight, it's because she was telling Kay this morning that she was going out with her brother this evening. Some place called The Bowery. I'm assuming that's a supper club. Do you know it?"

"Yeah, it's over in Hamtramck," I said. "Thanks, Bernie. I'll talk to you later."

After disconnecting, I grabbed my hat and made my way down to the parking lot. I'd be glad to get home. Visions of a soft bed and a short nap danced in my head.

***

120

By nine o'clock that evening, I had paid my dollar and six bits for the cover charge and found a table to sit at in The Bowery. It was a Saturday night and the place was packed...no surprise there. The joint usually did a hefty business, especially on weekends. I'd ordered my scotch on the rocks. While I took a sip, I scanned the crowd. Of course, I wasn't looking for Hildie...I didn't know what the woman looked like. But I did know what her brother, Mark, looked like. I felt confident I could pick him out in this crowd. When I found him, I would find her. So far, I was having no luck.

At nine-fifteen, Frank Barbaro, the owner of the posh nightclub, mounted the stage and announced, "Good evening ladies and gentlemen. It's showtime at the Bowery."

The club was touted as being *the* place to see "your favorite radio and movie stars, direct from Hollywood," and it was no exaggeration. When the curtain rose, the audience applauded, seeing Jimmy Durante—the Schnozzola—as his fingers slid across the ivory keys at the piano. He sang his signature song, "Inka Dinka Doo." Gran would have loved being here, and I made a mental note to bring her along some night.

It wasn't until there was a break in Jimmy's act and a local orchestra was playing dance music that I saw Mark King rise from his sitting position at a high-backed booth. He was holding the hand of a young woman that I assumed was his sister, Hildie. From my vantage point, I liked what I saw. She stood maybe five feet five, and her light brown hair was rolled away from her face and up in the back. She had red lips and curves in all the right places. The attractive woman was wearing a close-fitting, long-sleeved white evening gown with pearl beading along the side slit at her left leg, and it was plunged just enough at the neckline to view a portion of her ample cleavage. I continued to enjoy my drink as I watched the young couple dance. Mark King and his

121

sister remained on the floor for three songs, returning to their booth only when Jimmy Durante came back on stage. I sauntered over with my drink in hand.

"Mr. King," I said, while standing at the end of their booth. His expression told me he'd recognized me, but I couldn't tell if my presence made him happy or not. Hildie gave her brother a questioning look. I turned my gaze upon her. She was even more striking up close. Her clear blue eyes were mesmerizing. "The name is Flanagan," I said to her. "I called at your apartment this morning in hopes of speaking with you; *if* you're Hildie King, that is. Did your brother tell you?"

She glanced at her companion for the evening again. "Why no, he didn't mention it. You wanted to speak to me, Mr. Flanagan? May I ask what about?"

I gestured to the booth and said, "Mind if I join you for a moment? I don't want to intrude if it's a special night, but I wanted to ask you about the death of Sondra Girard."

I thought I saw Miss King's brother roll his eyes, or at least make a similar gesture, but I ignored him and kept my focus on the lady.

Her expression was one of surprise. She followed the curve of the circular booth, inching closer to her brother. Hildie King then patted the area she'd been sitting in. "Not at all; please do," she offered.

No sooner had I lowered myself into the booth when one of the two Bowery photographers made her way to us. She was a cute little gal with a nice smile and a short gold skirt, probably no more than twenty-five years of age.

"How about I take a photo as a memento of the evening?" she asked.

"Oh, yes, let's," an excited Hildie responded.

"Uh, Hildie—" Mark began to object.

"Oh, come on, Mark! Why not?"

Edging my way out of the booth again, I felt the woman's hand on my forearm, stopping me.

"You don't want me in the picture," I protested. "I'd only ruin it," and I smiled.

"You're wrong," the woman shot back. "I *do* want you in it, Mr. Flanagan. Now slide over closer to me."

In the end, we ordered two copies of the photo — well, I wanted one, too — where Hildie sat between us with her arms around our shoulders. After the club photographer left to develop the shot, I ordered another round of drinks for us. Hildie was drinking a red wine, while her brother was sipping schnapps over ice.

"Uh, Hildie," Mark began. "It's getting rather late."

"Why, it's only ten thirty, Mark," she countered.

His eyes darted to mine, and then back to hers. "Don't you think we've been here long enough? I think we should go," he persisted.

"Stay for one more," I encouraged him. "The drinks have already been ordered. Stay and relax awhile." The man gave me a look that told me to butt out. That was fine, because I was beginning to not like him any more than he did me. In fact, I rather enjoyed taunting him. So, I continued. "Besides, it's a free drink. No one turns down a free drink."

"Yes, Mark, stop being such a stuffed shirt!" Hildie added. "And anyhow, it's Saturday and the night is young."

Before he could argue the point, the waiter returned with his tray carrying our drink order. When the young man departed from the table, Mark King stood up. His face was coloring with anger.

"Let's go, Hildie. The night is over!"

Apparently he thought she would follow suit. She did not. Instead, she slid his glass over to me and said, "Then Mr. Flanagan will enjoy your Kirschwasser."

"His what?" I asked.

"Kirschwasser," she answered. "I just learned that word this week. It means cherry schnapps. Isn't it a funny word?" Her eyes locked with mine and her lips curled into a seductive smile as she lifted her wine glass to take a sip.

"The word sounds German," I replied with disgust.

"Funny how they speak," she said, not averting her gaze. Tearing herself away to say something to her brother, she offered up an idea. "Why don't you go home, Mark? You look tired. I'm sure Mr. Flanagan won't mind giving me a ride at the end of the evening." She then put her hand, with the expertly painted red fingernails, on my arm. "You won't, will you?"

"It would be my pleasure," I said, and smiled at her.

After Mark left the club in a huff, I was having the time of my life. Hildie and I danced to quite a few current songs. In the moments when we would return to the booth, we discussed her relationship with her former employer.

"I loved Sondra, Sam," she revealed. "We were quite close. She was only a few years older than me, and we had so much in common. Sondra was like a sister to me...*more* than a sister to me. I miss her so much."

"I'm trying to figure out what happened that night. How could a woman so experienced in swimming have had such an accident?"

"That's been bothering me, too. And I don't like where my thoughts lead me."

She lowered her eyes and lifted her wine glass to her lips.

"Where do they take you?" I asked.

"To nowhere pleasant," she responded. Hildie didn't continue.

"Tell me about the unpleasantness," I coaxed.

The remarkably beautiful woman hedged answering and I waited patiently.

"I don't have all the answers, but something was bothering her. She'd been down for days over something. Sondra just wasn't herself in the office. She was unusually quiet," she finally revealed.

"You don't know what that something was?"

"No. She didn't tell me and I didn't push. But that wasn't like her. We were very close and she usually confided in me. She may not have told me what was wrong, but she couldn't hide from me that something was."

"Bernie says she wasn't really close to anyone," I told her.

She waved her hand through the air dismissively. "That woman! She would have *liked* it to be that way, but she was wrong. Maybe Sondra never let on about our friendship for fear the woman would get jealous. Bernie was like that with Sondra; so possessive. But Sondra told me everything. Bernie just didn't know it. I spent so much time with her, inside and outside of work. I'd meet her when Victor was in Washington D. C. I love Victorian homes and Sondra's was beautiful." She stopped briefly while taking a sip of her wine. "You know what we used to tell each other?" she asked.

I shook my head.

"We used to tell each other that we were the sisters neither of us had ever had. Anyway, I just knew something was off when she returned to the office that day. She came in from her interview and she was different. Don't ask me how I knew, I just did. It was like she was terribly agitated. Something was weighing heavily on her mind, but I didn't know exactly what. I remember wondering if it had something to do with *him*...her husband. I can tell you that that marriage was not made in heaven. And I asked her if the appointment went all right. She told me it had. She said she'd gotten enough information to write the story, but didn't elaborate. Anyway, I couldn't get her to open up. I went home but couldn't get her off my mind, so I called her that evening. I was worried about her, but there was no answer."

"What time was that, Hildie?"

"About nine, maybe a few moments before. I knew her husband was taking a nighttime flight out of Washington D. C., so I figured it would be all right to telephone her. I knew he wouldn't be home yet," she sighed. "Maybe if I had just made that call a bit earlier…well, who knows?"

I took a sip of my scotch before asking, "Do you think someone could have done this to her?"

Hildie's flawless face wore a look of astonishment. "No, no, not at all! She was amazing. Everyone thought so; or at least I did. I can't believe anyone would have wanted to hurt her, Sam. I'm more afraid that she did this to herself!" She lowered her gaze, and her words became fainter. "But I don't want to know if that's true," she said with sadness. "Because you see, if that was the case…well, was there something that I could have done to prevent all of this? Had I known how truly desperate Sondra was, and had actually *done* something about it, maybe she would be here with us right now."

CHAPTER NINETEEN

I'd only had a few short hours of fitful sleep when I finally surrendered and left my bedroom. Now, at ten minutes after five on Sunday morning, I was sitting in the parlor, smoking a cigarette. The only illumination in the room was from the tip of my Lucky Strike. After my evening at The Bowery with Hildie, I had more questions than I had answers.

Why hadn't Bernie known of the close friendship between Sondra and her assistant at the magazine? Or did she just *choose* to discount the relationship? Was it true that the one-time nanny would have preferred that no one else get close to the senator's wife? In considering Bernice Dayle's love and protective nature toward the deceased young woman...yes, I could see where she would downgrade any other meaningful bond Sondra had formed. And what the hell was bothering Sondra Girard? If I could only find that out, I could probably put this case to rest. Could the female visitor, seen by Lavinia Marsh, be just that... an innocent, well-meaning visitor? Maybe the woman arrived, stayed briefly, and after she took her leave, Sonny did herself in. Maybe after her guest had gone, the troubled senator's wife poured a glass of wine, swallowed six sleeping pills with it,

127

and dove into the pool to wait on the effects of the medication. Maybe Mrs. Marsh just hadn't seen the woman's departure. The possibility certainly existed. Too many possibilities existed.

My brain was hurting. I'd much rather think of the pleasant aspects of my night out. It had been a great evening…well, up until we started to leave, that is.

We had stayed at the club until twelve forty-five, when we decided to call it a night. The woman and I slid out of the booth and headed for the exit. Before we could reach it, Mark King re-entered in an angry state. With swift, determined steps, he was heading straight for us. Hildie sighed heavily when she caught sight of him. She stopped dead in her tracks and turned to me.

"Sam, call me, all right? I really enjoyed this evening."

She touched me lovingly on my right cheek, and then left with her brother. Now *there* was a puzzle! What in the hell was up with that man? No wonder the gorgeous lady wasn't married at the age of thirty—she had a brother who wouldn't let her out of his sight! Shaking my head, I took another drag on my smoke.

As hard as I tried to avoid it, my mind kept wandering back to the image I had created of Sondra Girard submerged in that backyard pool. My image was that of a woman, face down, because I'd never seen a photo of Mrs. Girard. I sat there for two hours, trying to figure out what could've been mentally tormenting her, and couldn't come up with a thing. Finally, I dozed right where I was with Shamus, our kitten, curled up on my lap. I had closed my eyes and entered a bizarre world of nightmares, frightening situations that I couldn't recall when I woke up a couple of hours later.

***

Someone was gently jostling my knee. "Sam? I'm leaving now."

I opened one eye as Shamus dove off my lap, hit the floor, and disappeared around the corner and into the dining room. Gran was wearing her dark green dress with the white cuffs on its short sleeves. It was her Sunday best. The pearls my grandfather had given her as a gift for Christmas day twenty years ago hung from around her neck. She was undoubtedly attending the Baptist church this morning with her friend, Helen Foster.

Rising from my sleeping position in the chair, I felt a few bones crack. I was stiff. Bending down to kiss her, I told her I would see her later.

"There are a couple of hard boiled eggs in a bowl on the counter, and I made some coffee, dear."

She walked out the door to the waiting automobile in our driveway, and I headed into the kitchen to grab my first cup of java for the day. The sun blazed through the side window, enveloping the room in a comforting warmth. It was going to be a gorgeous Sunday. What were my plans for it? I didn't know. Quite possibly, I would do as little as I could. Stepping back from this investigation might be a beneficial thing today. I needed, and wanted, time in which to just think about what everyone I'd talked to had told me. Total quiet in the relaxation of home would suit me just fine. But that wasn't going to happen. And I found that out when Gran arrived home a few hours later and announced that Helen, her best friend, and a woman who loved to irritate me for some reason, had gone home to change her clothes, and would be right back. She was going to visit during the day and then be our guest for Sunday dinner. *Oh, that's just great!*

***

Finally I could feel myself begin to unwind. Sitting in the cream-colored chair in the parlor, I had my smokes on the end table, a short glass with three fingers of my premium scotch in it in my left hand, while today's newspaper was in my right. I'd tried to find out the current happenings in Detroit earlier, but with Helen sitting on the couch across from me, her eyes boring in my direction while my grandmother was preparing the evening meal, there was little chance of that. Now that dinner had been eaten and the kitchen cleaned, I was able to get away from the two ladies. Gran and her friend were in the kitchen, sitting at the table playing a friendly game of cards. Apparently they would not be going to the evening service at church.

A half an hour into my peace and quiet, the card game of War that the ladies were playing erupted into an actual battle.

"You can't do that!" I heard my grandmother's raised voice saying.

"What do you mean I can't do that? I did it, didn't I?"

"But that's cheating!"

"This is War, isn't it? There are no rules in war. Haven't you ever heard the saying 'all's fair in love and war'?" Helen shot back.

"That's cheating!"

"Is not!"

Next, it sounded as if someone had thrown the whole deck of cards across the table. There was no way that I was leaving my seat to get involved in this one.

"Now look at what you've done," Helen shouted. "I'm not picking them up, either! In fact, I think I'll just head for home."

"Well, you just do that!" Gran replied.

I lowered the paper as Helen passed me on her way to the front door. Gran was following her. Before my grandmother's friend walked out, she stopped to say something.

"You going to church Wednesday night, Ruby?" she asked in a completely normal voice.

"Well, of course," Gran answered sweetly.

"Okay, I'll be here to pick you up at six sharp." Helen Foster then leaned in and kissed my grandmother on the cheek, thanked her for the supper, and said goodnight to her.

"What in the world was that?" I asked, knitting my eyebrows together as Gran passed in front of me on her way back into the kitchen.

"What, dear?" She had a blank look on her face.

"Never mind," I said.

She shrugged and disappeared around the corner.

Gran was in the kitchen—undoubtedly picking up the cards off the floor—while I enjoyed another fifteen minutes of sweet peace and solitude. At the end of that fifteen minutes, the telephone rang. I tried to ignore it.

"Sam," my grandmother said in a loud whisper while sticking her head into the parlor. "It's Bernie. She wants to talk to you, dear, and she seems upset."

"Why are you whispering?" I asked, but she didn't answer.

After placing the receiver to my ear from the telephone on the rear wall in the kitchen, I greeted Bernie.

"Sam," she was whispering, too. "Get over here right away! Someone's broken in!"

"Broken in? Where? The guesthouse?"

"Yes," she cried frantically. "The place is a mess! I'm scared. Get here as soon as you can!"

***

Bernie was right. Her place was a mess. Papers were strewn across her small living room, the sofa cushions were slit, and two end tables were overturned. In the kitchen, several pieces of china lay shattered on the floor and counter. I whistled in disbelief when I saw it.

"Do you know if they took anything?" I asked.

She shook her head. "Not that I can figure out. I looked, but nothing seems to be missing. They just roughed the place up but good."

"Pack whatever you'll need. You can't stay here," I told her while still surveying the damage.

She ran into the bedroom and carried out an already stuffed suitcase. "I was hoping you'd say that," she said.

I took the suitcase from her and we were almost out the door when she suddenly stopped and gasped. Then she ran toward her bedroom and disappeared inside. After a moment, she returned to me holding a thick stack of bills in her right hand.

"What on earth...? Don't you believe in banks?"

"No! Now let's go!"

She rushed past me in her hurry to get to the auto parked at the curb. Once she was sitting beside me, she started to count her money, but I wanted some answers.

"All right, tell me what happened," I demanded.

"Shh! I'm counting," she replied.

"Bernie, I want to know why someone felt the need to break into your home," I pushed on. "Do you think this was just a random break-in, or —?"

"Oh dagnabit! Now you made me lose count!"

I let it go. There would be plenty of time to grill her once we reached the house on St. Aubin. A loud sigh escaped my lips at the realization that I would be sleeping on the sofa tonight, and very possibly for many nights.

CHAPTER TWENTY

After my grandmother had changed the bedding in my room, and after Bernie had found a hiding spot for her almost six-thousand dollars, we all three sat around the kitchen table with cups of freshly brewed tea. I'd asked Bernie about the break-in, but so far, she was ignoring me. Instead, she was conversing with my grandmother.

"I can't thank you enough, Ruby, for allowing me to stay here for a bit. It would have been too creepy to stay by myself in the guesthouse."

"Oh, that's no problem, dear. Sam enjoys sleeping on the sofa," my grandmother replied.

I rolled my eyes.

"Ooh, that's good tea, Ruby," Bernice Dayle said, in an attempt to delay answering my question.

Finally, I broke into this nice, friendly chatter.

"Okay, I love sleeping on the sofa and the tea is just terrific! Now let's stop horsing around and get down to business here. Tell me why someone would want to break into your home, Bernie. Tell me everything that happened."

The woman responded by taking another sip of her hot

beverage and asking Gran if she had any peanut butter cookies left in the house. I'd had it! I got the attention of both of the women by smacking the tabletop with my opened palm.

Bernie jumped in her seat, spilling a bit of tea from the cup she held. "Lordy!" she exclaimed.

"I think you'd better tell him what he wants to know, Bernie. It looks like he's getting angry," Gran interjected.

"You bet I am!" My face was stone, staring at the woman who was to be our overnight guest. I never wavered in my gaze or expression. *Her* face, on the other hand, displayed her great unease.

"All right! All right!" Bernie relinquished. "What is it you want to know?"

I sighed long and loud. "Were you home when this person broke in?"

"Oh no! Are you joking? If I *had* been, I would have had a heart attack." She paused, taking another drink of her tea.

At this point frustration overcame me, and I had to stop myself from throttling the woman. I inhaled deeply and said, "All right, then where were you? Tell me all about your day. What did you do?"

"Well, I woke up this morning, fixed myself some toast and tea, and then went outside on the patio for a breath of fresh air. I just love this time of year, don't you, Ruby?"

My palm met the surface of the kitchen table once again and I called out the woman's name in a raised voice through clenched teeth. She gave me a dirty look, but continued.

"I wasn't out there ten minutes when I heard the phone ringing inside. It was Nola Carver. Ty's wife? Well, she wanted to know if I wanted to come to their place for an early Sunday supper. I jumped at it. I never quite know what to do with myself on the weekends. With Sonny gone, it gets so lonely. Nola picked me up around two." Bernie creased her brows. "No, it was more like two-thirty."

I sighed audibly and looked at my watch. "Will this take until midnight?"

"I sure hope not," Gran muttered. "I have to work in the morning."

"When I got to Nola and Ty's, we sat for a bit, just talking. And then I helped Nola with fixing dinner. We had trout that Ty had caught late yesterday afternoon. Anyway, while we were working in the kitchen to get dinner on the table, Ty went to the cemetery to visit his mama and daddy's graves. After he got back, we ate. Then I helped her clean the kitchen and we sat around listening to the radio."

"When did you get home?" I asked.

"Nola was tired, so Ty dropped me off at home about seven tonight," Bernie replied. "But I didn't go into the guesthouse right away. You know, it's been bothering me that a lot of Sonny's personal things were still in that house, and why should *he* have them? So, seeing as how the senator was in Washington, I just let myself in with the key I had. Sonny gave me a key when we first moved up here, and I wanted to get in there before he realized I still had it and took it away from me. I took a bunch of photographs that were in a box in her closet. You know, pictures of Sonny when she was a young girl. I also grabbed some of her jewelry, like the sapphire ring her mama and daddy gave her as a high school graduation present."

"I'm not sure that was so wise, Bernie," I said.

"You just let him say something to me," Bernie said defiantly. "He'd better not! What would *he* want with her things anyway? In fact, I wonder if he's starting to get rid of her clothes already. She always had three bathing suits, but I only saw one hanging in her closet. She must have been wearing one of them when they

135

found her, but only the blue bathing suit was hanging up."

"Bernie," I said, apprehension climbing up the back of my neck. "What did you, Nola, and Ty talk about when you were visiting with them this afternoon?"

She shrugged. "Oh, lots of things. The magazine, Sonny, how mild the weather had been. Why?"

"Did you mention anything about this investigation?"

"Only that the senator called you off the case, so I decided to hire you myself," the woman answered.

I groaned, showing my disappointment. "Didn't I tell you *not* to say anything about that to anyone?"

"But it was Nola and Ty!" she exclaimed. "What harm was there in telling *them*?"

"Because we don't know what, or who, is behind her death," I calmly explained. "How do you know they aren't involved? I mean look at it this way...don't you find it funny that you tell them you hired me, and then you just happen to have a break-in at your place where nothing of value was taken? Don't you find it rather odd? I think this break-in was meant to scare you off. You *did* say that Ty went to the cemetery. How long was he gone?"

"About an hour or a little more. But Ty wouldn't do something like that! Why would he?"

"I don't know, but we can't rule out anything or anyone just yet."

I watched as Bernice Dayle looked past me and focused on the wall behind me. Her face was suffusing with color. She was considering something...something that might be important. She was holding back on something.

"What?"

"What?" she mimicked me.

"Out with it, Bernie. What are you thinking?"

"Well, uh, it's just that, um...."

She squirmed for about three minutes before she told me the rest of the story, fighting me all the while I finally dragged it out of her. *Oh brother! What in the world has she done?*

Bernice Dayle, being the pig-headed woman that she was, felt that maybe I was moving too slowly on this case, and that maybe *she* could be of some help. She had wanted an answer to the reason for Sonny's death, and she had wanted it *now*...even though she'd only hired me two days ago. The best way to get that answer to the puzzle of what happened to Sonny was to aid me in sleuthing. Last night she'd been restless. She couldn't sleep; her mind wouldn't let her. Instead, she came up with a cockamamie plan and she put it into motion. Bernie had called all of those who could be suspect in the death of her one-time ward and, trying to lower her voice to sound like that of a man, she had said one sentence and one sentence only..."I know what you did to my baby, Mrs. Girard." After uttering that one phrase, she waited for their response and then hung up, saying nothing more. She had made the calls sometime after ten o'clock last night, but couldn't be too sure of the exact time.

Now I had a boatload of people to suspect of the intrusion into her guesthouse. She claimed that Russell Harwood had not answered, and I knew *I* had been with Hildie King. But it left everyone else; the senator's two daughters, Kay Rewis, and no, it didn't eliminate Ty Carver as a possible suspect, even though she claimed not to have even called him. In her own words, "Why would I call Ty? He had nothing to do with it." But how could anyone really know that at this point?

Feeling a tension headache coming on, I rubbed at my temples and sighed. "Bernie, did it ever occur to you that no matter how hard you try to lower your voice to sound like a man, you still have that Southern drawl? And, don't you think they all know that it is only *you* who would consider Sonny to be *your baby*?"

137

She didn't say a word in response, but had the decency to blush and look regretful.

CHAPTER TWENTY-ONE

Waking on Monday morning, I felt as though I'd hardly slept at all through the night. My back was sore from laying in an awkward position on the sofa, and I still had that headache. Mentally, I felt sick about what Bernie had done in her attempt to do some undercover work while "assisting" me in this investigation. I still felt as though I could have throttled her, but that wasn't going to rectify the situation. The damage had been done. The main thing now was to find out who had broken into her home before any more damage could occur and before anyone got hurt. By finding out the identity of the intruder, I was sure the killer of Sondra Girard would be exposed, too.

The twentieth day of September was going to be gorgeous, if only weather wise. The sun was radiant, and a soft breeze moved refreshingly throughout the city. It was early when I maneuvered my body out of my prone position in the parlor. Gran sat at the kitchen table, ready for work, drinking a cup of coffee while staring out the side window.

"Good morning, Gran," I muttered as I passed her, heading into the bathroom.

"Hello, dear," she replied.

Bernie joined us fifteen minutes later, still dressed in her multi-colored floral nightgown and brown bathrobe. She voiced her opposition to going into work for the day.

"How can I sit behind that desk knowing that it could have been one of them who broke into my home? If I had been there at the time, would they have killed me?" She shook her head and took a sip of coffee.

"I need you to get dressed, regardless. After I drop Gran off at work, I want to swing by The Monthly Patriot. I need you to get that ledger that tells where Sonny had her last appointment that day. I want to know who she had the interview with. You have a key to the office, don't you? You don't have to stay there, Bernie," I said. "I can bring you right back here. No one gets there until nine, right?"

She nodded.

"Then you can get the appointment book and get out of there before anyone knows it. We'll come back here and you can call off sick, but don't you dare say a word as to where you are staying. Got it?"

***

Bernice Dayle and I made our drive to the office on Michigan Avenue in silence after dropping Gran off at Augie's Cuchina for her shift. I parked out front and waited for her to return with the ledger. She was gone only moments, wanting to leave before any of the employees began arriving for the day. We returned to the house on St. Aubin and, after feigning illness on the telephone to Editor in Chief Ty Carver, Bernie promptly went back to bed in my room.

I sat at the kitchen table, and while eating an apple, I began to read. According to what was written in the book, Sondra Girard was to meet General Foreman Floyd Killebrew at Chrysler's Highland Park facility between eleven thirty and noon on the morning of August 6. Instead of making the trip out there, I thought I would put in a call to him to see if the man would have time to meet with me...if not today, then soon. After assistance from an operator, I heard the general foreman's personal line ring in my ear. It rang four times.

"Hello, Floyd Killebrew speaking," the deep voice sounded in my ear.

"Hello," I responded. "Mr. Killebrew, my name is Sam Flanagan, and I'm a private detective. I'd like to meet with you sometime today, if you can manage it. It involves a case I'm working on."

"Private detective? Well...um...I guess I would have time. Say late this afternoon?"

"Sure, I can make it then."

"Mr. Flanagan, may I know what the nature of the case is? What kind of information are you seeking? Maybe I can be better prepared to tell you what you need to know if I know what this is all about."

"Of course. I wanted to ask you about your interview with Mrs. Sondra Girard on the morning of her fatal accident back in the early part of August. I'm looking into the tragedy a bit more closely, and wanted to know how she appeared to you. You know, her mood, et cetera," I explained.

"Hmm," he muttered. "I sure was shocked to hear of her death, I can tell you that. But Mr. Flanagan, I think I can save you a trip out here. I didn't see her for any interview in August."

"You mean the interview was conducted with someone else at the plant?"

"No," Floyd Killebrew replied. "She didn't come out here at all. She never interviewed anyone here."

"She didn't?" This information took me by surprise. "I'm looking at her appointment book right now, Mr. Killebrew,

141

and it's written down that she had scheduled an appointment to speak to you sometime around eleven thirty on the morning of August 6. Now you're telling me she didn't show up for that appointment?"

"Well, not quite. Let me back up a bit. She *did* schedule the appointment and we agreed to meet at that time and on that day, but something came up where I couldn't follow through with it. You see, my wife was expecting our first child. She was due to have the baby around the sixteenth of August, but little Floyd Jr. decided to arrive more than a week early. So, there I was that morning, sitting in the waiting room at Harper Hospital while my wife was down the hall in labor. All of a sudden, I remembered our appointment. I panicked. I found a pay telephone in the hospital and called Mrs. Girard at her office. I prayed I could catch her before she started out to come to the plant. She answered and I explained the situation. She was very understanding, and I promised her I would make it up to her at a later date. Sadly, that's never going to happen now." He paused and I heard him try to muffle a cough. "So you see, I didn't see her that morning."

I had to pull myself out of the moment of abstraction I was in after hearing this news.

"Mr. Killebrew, did she happen to mention going somewhere else? You know, somewhere she could try obtaining information for her magazine instead of interviewing you that morning?"

"No, I can't recall that she did. She congratulated me about the baby, and said she would call at a later date. That's the last I spoke with her. And as far as that conversation goes, she seemed fine as I recall. She was very polite and cordial. I wish I could have been a bit more help to you."

"That's quite all right. Thank you very much for taking the time to speak to me."

We disconnected the call, and I sat with my brows knit

together wondering where the senator's wife had gone that morning. If she hadn't gone to the Chrysler Highland Park plant that morning, where had she gone and who had she interviewed? She certainly had kept a date with someone. But her intended interview with the plant's general foreman was the last entry in her appointment book. And I wondered why Sondra, herself, had answered the phone instead of Bernie. Wasn't that her job at the magazine? Why hadn't Bernie been aware of a change in plans that morning? I decided to ask her.

When I got to my bedroom door, I heard the snoring that was coming from behind it and thought twice about knocking. I'd wait for a while and see if Bernie would soon wake on her own. In the meantime, I'd do a bit of housework. I gathered a pail, the bleach, and a rag and took them into the bathroom.

***

After lighting a Lucky Strike cigarette, I then looked at my watch. It was Monday afternoon. I was sitting in the '38 burgundy Chevy, parked about four car lengths from the apartment building that Kay Rewis lived in. I'd arrived twenty minutes ago, and had secured an excellent parking location in which to watch the front entrance. Hoping she would keep to her schedule, I slumped down in the seat and leaned back against the headrest. My driver's side window was down six inches to allow the smoke from my cigarette to exit the automobile, and the peals of the neighborhood children's laughter during play to enter. It had been a beautiful day, with the temperature hitting seventy-four degrees.

Five minutes later, a mangy looking dog stopped by the maple tree next to my car. He lifted his right hind leg and began to urinate on the bark at its base. Then the canine looked up and noticed me. His yelp was high-pitched and constant.

"Hey, mister, I think he likes you," the boy who was holding

143

his leash said.

"Yeah? Well, I don't want him to like me, so beat it with your dog, kid," I demanded.

All I needed was for Kay to emerge from her residence, look toward the barking animal, and see me. The kid gave me a dirty look and yanked on the leash.

"Come on, Chief!" I heard him say. "He's mean!"

Until I could see the young journalist from the magazine come out of her building, I was using the time to ponder the question of where Sondra Girard had gone on that Friday morning in the first week of August. She'd made the appointment to see Floyd Killebrew at the Chrysler plant and noted it in her appointment book, but circumstances had changed, and she'd never gone. But she'd gone somewhere instead—*but where*? Bernie didn't know. When I had questioned her earlier, she was just as confused about it as I was. She said she didn't remember any calls coming into the office before Sonny had left that morning. Now that was odd, because I certainly didn't believe that Mr. Killebrew was lying. Why would he? I'd somehow have to figure how Sonny Girard had changed her plans without Bernie's knowledge, and I had a sneaking suspicion that it wasn't going to be an easy thing to do.

At three fifty-eight a yellow cab passed by the door to my own auto and pulled up directly in front of the apartment building in which Kay Rewis lived with her roommate, Mary Sue Easley. Kay came trotting out and climbed into its back seat. I turned the key in the ignition to start my own car, waited a few seconds, and then pulled out behind them. I continued to follow them through the city until the taxicab stopped at the curb in front of the Beloved Brethren Orphanage, which was connected to St. Timothy's Catholic Church located on West Grand Boulevard. Kay exited, stuck her head back in the window again, undoubtedly to pay her fare, and then walked into the building. The yellow cab pulled away and drove out of sight. I made a note of her destination in my pocket notebook and pulled away from the curb. I'd return tomorrow while she was at work.

I thought of going home, but I didn't think sitting around in the company of my grandmother and Bernie Dayle for the entire evening sounded like much fun. What *did* sound like fun was stopping by The Double Shot for a bite to eat and a couple of drinks. I headed in the direction of the bar.

CHAPTER TWENTY-TWO

The Double Shot was located only a few short blocks from the house on St. Aubin. Whenever I was in the mood for a drink, or just wanted to get away from Gran, this was where I would come most evenings. The food was good, the prices were cheap, and I liked Neamon Riley, the owner. It was a little hole in the wall, really, but I felt comfortable there. Neamon and his wife, Lena, had purchased the place about eight years ago, with the financial help of Lena's cousin, Finney. So technically, Finney was part owner, although he rarely stepped foot into the joint. Business was usually pretty slow on Mondays, and this Monday was no different. Normally I would have headed for a stool at the bar, but I wanted to be alone with my thoughts so I chose a table to sit at.

"Hey, Sam," Neamon said when he had shuffled over to stand beside me. "What can I get ya tonight?"

I nodded to behind the bar. "What's Lena stirring in that pot?"

"Chili. She made it fresh today. Want a bowl of it?"

"Yeah, that sounds good. How about an order of toast to go with it? And bring me lots of crackers, too."

"You got it. You want your scotch on the rocks, too, tonight?" he asked.

I nodded.

Lena was Neamon's wife of twenty-some years. She didn't make an appearance in the bar very often, but when she did, she usually prepared the specials for the day. I'd eaten her chili before and I could find nothing to complain about. Neamon went to get my order, and I looked around. Most times I knew someone in attendance, but tonight I didn't recognize either of the other customers. Two men, older than myself, sat stools apart from each other at the bar, each of them silently sipping on their beers.

I jumped in my seat when three high school aged boys banged repeatedly on the plate glass window, looking into the establishment from out on the sidewalk. Lena yelled out in a loud voice, "Get outta here!" and they laughed as they ran away. "Damn kids!" we all heard her say.

I was served my chili, toast, and scotch by Neamon's wife. When she sat down opposite me at my table, I knew I wasn't going to get in much time contemplating the case I was currently working on.

"So how is Ruby doing, Sam?" she asked.

I answered her cordial questions and listened to her fears about her son, Neamon Jr., in between bites of chili and toast. Apparently the young man's draft number had been chosen as of a couple of days ago. Naturally, she was filled with anxiety. Actually, I didn't mind the diversion of this conversation. It was good to focus on something else for a change.

When she excused herself a half an hour later to return to her work behind the bar, my eyes followed the woman. A slight jolt of surprise ran through me as I saw none other than Mr. Wesley Barnard, the husband of the senator's youngest daughter,

Simone, sitting on the stool nearest the cash register. When had he entered the bar? I hadn't even noticed. The man was dressed in a casual brown suit. His dark wavy hair was combed directly back from his face. After visiting the bathroom, I thought I would take the rest of my drink to the stool next to him and engage him in conversation.

I was probably in there a whole three minutes. Returning to my table, I picked up the glass containing the small remnant of my scotch and carried it to the bar. I sat on the stool next to the one that had been occupied by Mr. Barnard, but his stool was vacant now. I thought that maybe he had rounded the corner to use the pay phone, because his mug still contained half of his beer. I decided to ask to make sure.

"Hey, where did he go?" I nodded toward the empty seat next to mine.

"Who? Wes?" Neamon questioned me.

"Yeah," I answered.

"You just missed him." Neamon then nodded toward the huge glass window that looked out onto Dequindre Street. "He headed out with some guy."

I turned, following his gaze. I was just in time to make out the figures of two men wearing fedoras entering the alley between The La Salle and Easy Step Shoe Repair. The shoe repair shop was closed for the day. The La Salle had been a cinema showing the silents in its heyday, but now sat vacant and lifeless. Back in 1928, in the wee hours of the morning, a fire had ignited in its offices, causing major damage to the back of the building. Miraculously, it hadn't had the chance to spread to the area where moviegoers would sit in the theater. There had been talk among the people of Detroit that the owner had started the fire himself, wanting to claim the insurance money. Even though there wasn't enough evidence to support that theory, the harm to his reputation had been done. He closed the theater and moved his family out of state. No one had ever purchased the property, so the ornate building existed only as a reminder of its former self.

"Where they going? There's nothing behind there."

"Now, how in the hell should I know?" Neamon asked, without really expecting an answer.

I turned around in my seat and held my glass up, indicating I wanted another scotch on the rocks.

"So, how do you know Wesley Barnard?" I asked the bar owner while he poured my drink.

"How do you think? He's been coming in here two or three times a week for the past couple of years or more. He usually comes in after he gets off work, but lately he comes in once a week about this time, also. That guy he walked out with...he met him in here I'd say about two or three months ago. I guess they got to talkin', and now they meet and go somewhere together. But it's none of my business what they do. Why all the questions, anyway?"

"Just curious," I said. "His father-in-law hired me about a week ago to look into something, and I'd just met Wesley recently because of it."

"Well, I'll be!" Neamon exclaimed. "Did ya hear that, Lena? Sam's gettin' hoity-toity in the world. He's workin' for Senator Girard."

Lena came to stand in front of me and smiled. "Is that right, Sam? Gee, what an honor. So, what's he like? The senator...is he as handsome in person as he looks in the newspaper?"

"I'd say he's distinguished looking," I offered. Taking a swig of my scotch, I didn't think it was necessary to reveal that the senator was a total jerk who had fired me.

149

CHAPTER TWENTY-THREE

Tuesday was going to be another gorgeous day. I woke on the twenty-first day of September with the sun streaming in through the picture window and warming the entire parlor. Outside the trees were leaning toward the east with a wind that was a bit fiercer than it was yesterday.

Bernie insisted upon me taking her to the market as soon as I had dressed. She wanted to cook breakfast for Gran and myself as a way of "earning her stay" as she put it. The result was a bowl of white mush with crumbled bacon mixed throughout and a clump of butter melting on top. I'd never eaten grits before, and I wasn't looking forward to it now. Washing half of my portion down with my black coffee, I lied, saying I was stuffed to avoid eating the rest. I had noticed that Gran left quite a bit of hers untouched, too. But none of it went to waste. Bernie reached over and grabbed our bowls, scraping what was left in them into her own bowl. She continued to eat while telling me what had occurred to her last night as she lay sleepless in my bed.

"Laying there, I realized something, Sam. It may just be of some help to you; I don't really know."

Yes, what she had remembered the last day of Sondra Girard's life was going to be very helpful to me; well, at least I *hoped* it would be. Since they had taken an early bus into the office on Michigan Avenue that last Friday morning, Bernie hadn't had time for breakfast. Soon after unlocking the door at The Monthly Patriot, she had felt a great emptiness in her stomach. She dug on the bottom of her pocket book for any loose change to go with the two dollars she had in her wallet, then headed over to The Boxcar Café, where she had ordered a breakfast to go. She had ordered two scrambled eggs, hash brown potatoes, ham, two slices of toast, and two coffees to bring back with her to her place of work, one of the coffees being for Sonny.

"So, you see," she continued with her account of that morning. "Sonny must have gotten that call while I was gone. *That's* why I didn't answer the phone about the cancellation! And there's another thing. Oh, I'd say about a week after she died, there was a note of condolence from some man. It arrived at the office. In it this man said he was so sorry to have heard about Sonny...only he called her 'Mrs. Girard.' He said he was fortunate to have met her, and he was grateful that Mrs. Girard took an interest in their effort to assist in supporting this great nation and our allies. The thing is, I didn't recognize the name. And whoever it was, I am sure I didn't have him down in her appointment book at any time. But I remember there was a company logo on the letterhead. Last night, I thought that she might have possibly gone to interview him, instead. What do you think?"

"Well, who was it?" I asked. "What was on the letterhead?"

Bernie shrugged while buttering a slice of toast. "I couldn't tell you. I don't remember."

"Do you still have the letter? Is it in your desk at the magazine?"

She shook her head. "Nope."

I sighed, feeling deflated. What was I going to have to do...

151

search out each and every business or factory in the city and surrounding area?

"Well, then that's no good. It could be anyone, and any business in the city or outside its limits. How am I going to hunt down *that* information?"

Bernie shrugged as she took a bite of the toast. "How should I know? *You're* the detective. But you can always ask Ty," she said in a matter-of-fact tone.

"Ty?"

She nodded her head. "Well, I gave the letter to him. I didn't know what it was all about. I thought maybe he might."

"And did he?" I asked her. A spark of hope was beginning to ignite within me.

She shrugged again. "He never really said, but I got the idea he was confused by it, too."

Quite possibly, Ty Carver would still have the letter; or at the very least, I was praying he would remember it. I would swing by the office of The Monthly Patriot sometime today under the pretense of wanting to speak to Bernie. Hopefully, that would nix anyone's idea that the woman was in residence at Gran's house. At the same time, I could talk to Ty Carver about this letter of condolence. It might just lead me to the alternate destination Sonny had traveled to that last morning of her life.

***

The office of The Monthly Patriot almost seemed deserted when I walked in, but I could see Kay Rewis sitting at her desk in an inner office through her slightly opened door. She had her head down, reading something that lay in front of her. I didn't draw attention to myself, but entered and shut the door behind me quietly. I then veered to the right, toward the opened door to the office of the editor in chief. He, too, had his head bent in reading. Softly, I rapped on his door. When he looked up, he smiled.

"Mr. Flanagan, right?"

"That's right," I said. "I'm flattered you remembered."

"Well, don't give me too much credit. Eons ago I went to school with a boy named Ridley Flanagan. Wouldn't happen to be a relative, would he?"

I shook my head and said, "Not that I know of."

The editor leaned back in his chair, bringing his hands together in front of him with his fingertips touching each other. "Okay, so how can I help you today?"

I sat down in one of the leather chairs facing his desk and removed my hat. "I was really here to see Bernie. She's not at her desk. Will she be back soon?" I asked.

"No, I'm afraid Bernie is feeling under the weather. She's been out yesterday and today."

"Oh, that's too bad. I wanted to ask her about something. She'd mentioned in passing that someone had sent a letter of condolence about Mrs. Girard's death. In investigating, I found out that the interview that she had scheduled for that Friday morning back in August had been cancelled by the general foreman out at the Chrysler plant. I was wondering if maybe this other gentleman had spoken to her at some point."

Ty Carver's eyebrows went up. "Well, that's news to me… about the cancellation, I mean. I'd just assumed she had gone out there."

"Nope, I talked to the man yesterday and he told me he had to cancel the appointment for the interview. I know she went somewhere, but I just don't know where. Would you have any ideas?"

Ty Carver shook his head.

"Did Bernie ever tell you about the condolence letter that was sent to the office here?"

He shook his head again. Now *that* surprised me. What was this man trying to hide? And *why* was he trying to hide anything at all? Bernie told me she had handed the letter over to Ty Carver and he had seemed confused by it, too. Something wasn't right here. I said nothing, but continued to stare at the man. Finally, he spoke.

"What's your interest in speaking to the person she interviewed?" he asked.

"It may lead to nowhere, but just possibly, if I could find out who she went and saw that morning, I might find out if something was bothering her. Maybe I could get a handle on her mood. I really don't know, but it's worth a try."

"I wish I could help you, Mr. Flanagan. I just can't come up with anything that would shed any light on the subject."

I thanked him for his time and left his office. Once in the Chevy, I headed in the direction of the Beloved Brethren Orphanage, still perplexed about why Ty Carver would lie to me.

***

When I entered the orphanage, my eyes landed on a nun sitting behind a beaten and battered desk that desperately needed a fresh coat of stain. The chair she'd been sitting in was in no better condition. When she rose from it at the sight of me, it wobbled. She stood facing me now.

"Hello," she said while walking toward me with her right hand extended. "I'm Sister Thomas Benedict. How may I be of service to you?"

The nun was a tiny woman in her robe and habit, and even though her eyebrows were a bit thick and unruly, she had a lovely face. Deep brown eyes stared at me from behind gold wire-rimmed glasses. I took her hand and shook it gently.

"Hello, Sister," I said. "I'm actually here to find out if my cousin is here. I know she volunteers at the orphanage, and—"

Before I could go on, the nun interrupted me by asking, "And your cousin is?"

"Kay Rewis," I responded.

Sister Thomas Benedict smiled widely. "Ah, yes. Kay is a godsend to us. But she isn't here right now, Mr...."

"Johnson," I said, thinking quickly.

"Well, Mr. Johnson, Kay does volunteer with us. We are so lucky to have her, but she only comes to us on Mondays and Fridays. It has been very rare that she has come to the orphanage on a different day of the week."

"She must be at work then. I checked the apartment, but no one answered," I lied. "I'm only in town for a short time, and I thought I would look her up. I knew she volunteered here, but I'm not sure exactly what she does."

"Ah, well, I can tell you that," said Sister Thomas Benedict. "But only if you join me in a cup of tea. I was just going to brew one for myself and I would love the company. Maybe I can make you a cup, also, Mr. Johnson?"

I smiled, nodded, and thanked her. As I followed her into the kitchen at the Beloved Brethren Orphanage, I sent a message heavenward, hoping the Lord would understand the reason for my falsehoods.

***

I re-entered the Chevy, extracted a Lucky Strike cigarette from my top pocket, and lit it. Whistling audibly, my mind was running at top speed, and the beats of my heart rendered me a bit out of breath. I'd been working on the puzzle of Mrs. Sondra Girard's death for exactly one whole week and one whole day. Could it be that the solution was right at my fingertips? It all seemed to make perfect sense, but I needed to slow down and thoroughly examine what I had found out. The examination of it all would come this evening. Right now, I wanted to return home and spend a bit of time there before I paid a visit to Miss Kay Rewis later tonight. What I needed to do was calm my mind and proceed with caution.

CHAPTER TWENTY-FOUR

My plans didn't quite work out the way I had wanted them to. I pulled into the drive and parked the auto in the garage. Heading toward the back door, my attention was drawn to Mrs. Sarah Petrovich, who was running as fast as she could from across the street to our home while calling out my grandmother's name in a loud, emotional voice. Clearly, something was wrong. Startled, I entered through the rear and ran through the kitchen and dining room, and once in the parlor, I headed straight for the front door to meet the upset woman. My heart began beating too fast, because I saw that the plumpish woman held an official looking envelope in her hand, and she was beginning to cry. My God! I dreaded to think what this meant. I was praying that she hadn't received bad news about her son, Tommy. Tommy had disappeared while in the Netherlands six months ago. He'd parachuted out of his Army Air Corps plane, and he and another soldier hadn't been seen by their unit since then. I was so afraid that the communication she now held in her hand was from the authorities telling her and her husband that they had located his body.

My grandmother and Bernie had been sitting at the kitchen

157

table when I first entered the house, but now they stood behind me as I opened the front screen door and ushered Mrs. Petrovich inside. Once inside, the ladies put their arms around her and led her to the sofa, encouraging her to sit down. The woman who lived across from us put her hand to her chest and her breathing became unnatural. While Bernie rubbed her back, Gran was holding her hand and speaking to her in a soothing voice.

"Sarah, breathe, dear. Breathe in slowly."

Bernie turned to look at me as I stood in the middle of the parlor. "Do you have anything strong to drink in the house? I think she might need a sip of it to calm down."

Without hesitation, I ran into the kitchen to retrieve my bottle of scotch. I heard Bernie's call to bring enough glasses for everyone, so I did. I certainly could do with a sip of something strong myself. Our glasses holding the scotch now, Mrs. Petrovich raised hers to her lips with encouragement from my grandmother.

"Take a swig of this, dear," my grandmother urged her.

But the woman took a much larger swig than she should have. She coughed violently as her face showed her dislike for the sting of the alcohol.

My grandmother gently plucked the envelope from the hand of our neighbor and held it out to me. "Here, Sam. Read this to her, dear," she told me.

I took the letter into my own hands, which were now shaking. I knew Sarah Petrovich couldn't read. Anything she wanted to know, her husband read to her. Hesitantly, I removed the contents of the envelope. Staring at the folded sheet of paper, I found myself not wanting to be the first one to find out its contents. I didn't want to be the one to tell this woman that her son wasn't coming home…that he would never be coming home. To the ladies, it must have seemed like an eternity before I fully opened the communication, but they didn't rush me. Maybe they didn't want to hear the inevitable, either.

Finally unfolding the letter, I held my breath while I scanned what was written. My expression was stone when I looked across the room at the women.

"Mrs. Petrovich…." My voice came out in a hoarse whisper. I cleared my throat and continued. "He's alive! He's coming home! Tommy's coming home!"

Sarah Petrovich fell sideways into the arms of my grandmother, sobbing loudly, while Bernie slapped her own knee and let out a piercing "Woo Hoo! Well, hot damn! This calls for another bit of scotch," as she reached for the bottle that rested on the coffee table. And I had to laugh aloud when she asked, "Who's Tommy?"

***

My plan was to visit Kay Rewis at her apartment, but I didn't dare leave the ladies until Mr. Vasily Petrovich, Tommy's father and Sarah's husband, returned home from work. When I saw him pull up in his auto, I crossed the street to talk to him before he could enter his own home.

"Your wife is at our house," I told him.

He nodded.

"I don't think she can make it back home without some assistance," I said further.

"What happened? Is she sick? Did she fall or something?"

Shaking my head, I told him it was nothing like that. I told him that she had been drinking.

"*Drinking*? Drinking *what*?" he asked in a voice showing great surprise.

"My scotch. She isn't alone. Gran and our friend, Bernie, are joining her. Don't be too hard on her, she has some news for you."

"Tommy?" he asked in a whisper that was barely audible while his face paled a bit.

159

"Yeah," I answered, and placed my hand on his shoulder. "It's going to be all right, but I will let her tell you the good news. I've got to run out for a bit, but just walk on in. They're all sitting around the kitchen table."

I now sat parked on the street on which Kay Rewis's apartment building was located. Situated a few car lengths away from the front entrance, I sat there pondering how in the hell I was going to handle this. Taking a draw on the cigarette I'd just lit, I had to admit to myself that this wasn't going to be easy, nor was I going to enjoy it. From what Sister Thomas Benedict had told me, coupled with the information I'd gotten out of Mary Sue Easley at her place of employment, I now knew why Kay felt the need to "get away" from Detroit and move to Philadelphia for almost a year after the break-up with her fiancé, Jerry. It didn't take a genius to put it all together. I also thought I now knew the origin of Kay's resentment toward her employer. Could it be that her boss had put it all together, too? Was that why Kay had come home emotionally upset that night in early August...the same night Sondra Girard had lost her life in a drowning incident? If I was right, I may have come to the end of this case. If I was right, Kay Rewis was a murderer. And that's what I was here to find out...if I was right.

From Sister Thomas Benedict, I'd learned that Kay Rewis had come to the orphanage wanting to volunteer at the end of February in 1942. She wanted to work with the children...the babies in particular. Kay's timing was very much appreciated. The nun told me the story of an infant who, just ten days earlier, had been left on their doorstep. The baby boy was in a basket with a heavy blanket covering it. Pinned to the blanket was a note, which read, "My name is Jerome David. I have no last name. My mother loves me very much, but isn't able to keep me and care for me. Will you take me in? I was born on February 3, 1942." When

160

Kay showed up, asking if they needed help, it was an answer to a prayer from the Lord above. Little Jerry, as they called him, had been a colicky baby. The nuns at Beloved Brethren could use all the help they could get. Kay Rewis stepped into the position of caring for this little one and never uttered one word of complaint. "Kay is wonderful with all of the children, but Little Jerry has a special place in her heart," Sister Thomas Benedict had told me.

Yeah, I bet he does! I thought to myself now.

Kay answered my knock. She wore a blue and white gingham apron over her dark blue slacks and light green sweater. The young woman's blonde hair was pulled back in a messy ponytail. Her eyes widened at the sight of me.

"May I come in?" I asked.

"Why…yes, I suppose so," she answered, sounding not too sure, and backed up to allow me entrance. "I was just doing the supper dishes. What is this about?"

Sitting down in the only chair in the small living area, I could hear water running from the bathroom, and I assumed Mary Sue was showering. Kay took a seat on the sofa opposite me.

"We need to talk, Miss Rewis. We need to talk about Sondra Girard."

"But I told you everything I know. I really don't know anything about her accident."

"It wasn't an accident, and I think you *do* know more."

I let that sink in, saying nothing more, but I studied her face. Her brows came together in a frown. After ten seconds, she spoke again.

"I don't understand."

"We believe she was murdered. We have evidence that points in that direction."

"*Murdered*?" she asked in bewilderment. "I don't believe it! Who would want to do something like that to her?"

161

"Maybe you?"

"*Me*? Why *me*?" she asked me, sounding alarmed.

"Because we think Mrs. Girard found out the same thing that we found out, and it's something you wanted to keep secret at all costs."

"Found out? Found out *what*?"

"We know about little Jerry."

Kay's mouth dropped open, but her face froze before any words could spill forth. Her coloring paled, and I turned when a gasp came from the open doorway of the bathroom. Mary Sue stood there in a bathrobe and a towel wrapped turban-like around her freshly shampooed hair. She moved forward quickly, sitting down next to her roommate, and put an arm around the woman who was now on the verge of tears.

Kay's voice cracked when she finally asked, "How did you find out?"

"The question is, how did Sondra Girard find out? And more importantly, what happened when she did? Did she threaten you with going public with the information? Did that anger you? Did you try to reason with her? Or did you just want to shut her up permanently?"

The young woman placed both hands to the side of her face and shook her head violently. "No, no, no, no! What are you *saying*? She never found out, and even if she had, she never said anything to me. I wouldn't *kill* someone for that! Yes, I was jealous of her. I'll admit that! Everything came too easy to her, it seemed. I resented that I couldn't keep little Jerry, yet she had everything in life. She had everything handed to her, it seemed. I wanted my baby. I wanted him with *me*, but I didn't have the means to support him...and the shame it would bring, well.... Detective Flanagan, it broke my heart to leave him on that doorstep. I wanted to bring my baby home and raise him. But

162

how? How could I do that? How was I supposed to do that as a single woman? I couldn't tell my parents. I could tell no one. Mary Sue is the *only* one who knows, and she's been wonderful to me. She's the best friend I've ever had, and is so supportive. No one else knows. *No one!*"

Mary Sue looked at me straight on with ice cold eyes.

"Then if you weren't upset at knowing your boss held this information over you, why did you come home the evening she had been killed in an emotional state?" I demanded.

Kay inhaled deeply and slowly, trying to calm herself. "You're right. I *did* come home that evening beside myself with worry and anguish. I came home upset because there was a young couple who had come to the orphanage that day. They were very interested in adopting little Jerry, and I panicked. Even though I want him to have a good home and a good life, I panicked that I would never see my boy again. I wasn't ready for that. I don't know if I will *ever* be ready for that. I needn't have worried, though. Two weeks later they came back and said they'd found a newborn they were interested in adopting. It's easy enough to check out. Go to the Beloved Brethren Orphanage and ask the sisters there. They'll tell you."

Not able to hold back any longer, Kay Rewis now released her tears while falling sideways into the arms of her friend and confidante. I rose, holding my fedora in my hands, and headed for the door.

"Wait," Kay said. "What are you going to do with the information you have on little Jerry? Detective Flanagan, please, I can't have the orphanage finding out I'm little Jerry's mother! *Please!*"

"As long as what you've told me is the truth, I'm not going to do a damn thing, Miss Rewis. Not one damn thing. If what you've told me is true, and you're not involved in your employer's death,

I don't know anything at all about your situation."

Once outside in the hall, I heard Kay's sobs. I also heard Mary Sue say in a soothing voice, "There, there; everything is going to be all right, Kay. I told you I would always be here for you, and I will."

I believed Mary Sue. She would always be supportive of her friend, of that I had no doubt. Did I feel like a heel? Sure, I did… to a certain extent. But this was a murder investigation and I had to have answers, no matter what it took to get them. I placed my hat on my head and slowly walked toward the exit that led to the street. I wouldn't be visiting Mary Sue at her place of employment again, and I wouldn't be coming back here, either. Everything Kay had told me tonight…well, I believed her, too. She wasn't the killer of Sondra Girard. I knew that now. Or, at least, I thought I did at this point. Time would tell.

Getting into the '38 Chevy, I realized I knew something else. I realized I didn't want to go back to the home on St. Aubin Street. Not yet, anyway. The women had probably passed out from drinking what was left of my bottle of premium scotch. I was antsy, restless; I wanted to have someone to talk to. And even if the two women were wide awake, I didn't want to have Bernie and my grandmother to talk to. Checking the time on my watch, I noted that it was a few minutes before seven. Starting the engine, I pulled away from the curb and went in search of a pay telephone.

CHAPTER TWENTY-FIVE

As soon as I exited the auto, a chilled wind attempted to carry my hat into the parking lot at The Grind, a small coffee shop situated some blocks from my office down on Woodward Avenue. More importantly, it was located only a few doors from the apartment building where Hildie King lived with her brother, Mark. It was Hildie I had called from the pay phone. She had agreed to meet me at the small neighborhood eatery, saying she would rather I didn't pick her up at her residence because her brother was in a foul mood this evening. When *wasn't* he? She would see me there as soon as she could get away.

"Are you sure you don't want anything but coffee, Sam?"

I looked up into the face of Birdie, the waitress who had worked at The Grind for what seemed like forever.

"Nah, this coffee will do for right now. I'm expecting someone, Birdie."

The seventyish woman sighed and stuck her pencil above her right ear. "I sure hope it's not a woman, Sam."

"Well, I didn't know that you cared, Birdie," I said with exaggerated sweetness.

"I don't," she said as if she was bored. She gestured with her

165

head to the right, and behind the counter. "But every time you are in the company of a woman in here, those two get their hearts broken."

My eyes traveled to the two young waitresses who had their heads together, whispering. They had their eyes on me, so I waved. They waved back and turned abruptly, snickering.

"How old are they? All of twenty?" I asked.

"Yeah, about that. You ought to be ashamed of yourself."

"Why? What did *I* do?"

But Birdie just turned and walked away without giving me an answer. I was nearing the end of my first refill on the coffee when I spied Hildie. She hurried over to the booth I was sitting in and sat opposite me. She removed her babushka and light coat, setting them beside her. Her soft fawn-colored hair was beautiful, done up in a braid that outlined the sides and back of her head. The indigo suit jacket and skirt she wore complimented her eyes. She truly was an attractive woman.

"I'm sorry I made you wait. It was a bit hard getting away."

"Your brother?" I asked. When she nodded, I said, "I don't understand. What is he, your watch dog?"

She laughed softly. "Yes, something like that. He feels he has to *protect* me for some reason. What are you drinking? Coffee? I'd love a cup. It's getting a bit chilly out there tonight."

I signaled to Birdie, who responded by bringing the pot and another cup and saucer with her. After asking if we'd like to order anything else, to which we declined, she moved away from the booth. Hildie lifted the coffee to her lips and took a sip. She then placed the palms of her hands around the cup in an attempt to warm them.

"How was your day?" I asked her.

She shrugged. "Nothing special," she replied. "The usual; work, then home, then dinner, that sort of thing. How about yours? Are you still trying to find out what happened to Sondra?"

"Sure. I haven't given up yet."

"Getting anywhere?" Hildie lifted her cup again.

"Now that you ask, the answer is not really. I still say there is something more to this. It wasn't just an accident, but whatever actually happened, and why, I may never find out. At this point, I still don't know what was bothering her. I may never know, but I think that holds the key to that night."

"I really miss her. It just isn't the same without her there in the office every day. Ty Carver is such a sweet man, and I hate to put even more stress on him, but I've been considering looking for work elsewhere. You know, he hired a new reporter today. Some man; I don't know his name yet. Ty is trying to save the magazine, but I'm not sure I want to be a part of it without Sondra." She hesitated for a few seconds, and then reached across the table to cover my hand with hers. "I'm really glad you called me tonight, Sam. I've been thinking of you."

"I'm glad I called, too, Hildie. It's nice to get away from what I've been working on for a bit. And I thought of you right away."

She smiled and her eyes bore into mine. "And here I am asking you about it. You want a night away from it, and I bring it up."

"No, no that's all right. I don't really mind. In fact, tell me what you think of Russell Harwood. I know he was let go from the magazine a couple of weeks before Sonny's tragedy, but did she ever say anything to you about him? How do *you* feel about him?"

"Sonny?" she asked with a faraway look on her face.

"Yes," I replied. "Did she ever explain how she felt in letting him go?

She then seemed to consider before answering. Shrugging, she said, "He was an okay guy. He was always clowning around in the office. If he had put half as much energy into doing his work, he still might be employed at the magazine. I know Sondra didn't think one way or the other about him. I mean they were civil to one another, but that was it. Why do you ask, Sam?"

"Oh, just curious I suppose. Did she ever tell you *why* he was fired?" I asked.

"One day we had sandwiches ordered into the office. We were all sitting in the reception room; Kay, Bernie, Ty, and me, and she just said she had to let him go. She didn't explain and we didn't ask her to. At the time we were all surprised, but I just figured she'd had enough of his antics. He wasn't really productive enough."

"And none of the others ever said anything about it?"

Hildie shook her head. "No. I knew that Sondra would let me in on the whole story when she was ready." Her lips formed a beautiful smile and then suddenly the smile erupted into laughter. "You know, Russell could be quite humorous at times. One time he...."

She was laughing too hard to continue now. I waited, but her laughter was contagious and I, too, began to laugh along with her. In the next instant, he was there, standing at the end of the booth. Neither of us had been aware of his approach.

"Hildie! What are you doing here? You said you wanted a hot bath and then to get into bed. I ran your water and when I came out of the bathroom, you were gone!" Mark King blurted.

I looked up at him, all traces of gaiety gone from my expression. "Hey pal, I have a great idea. Why don't you get a bell to wear around your neck so we'll be warned when you're coming?"

He turned a taut face toward me as he clenched his fists at his side. "You try to be a smart man, eh, Flanagan?" he spit.

Nodding, I said, "Yeah, I'd like to think so."

168

He made a move, his desire being to have his right fist meet my face, but Hildie jumped up and grabbed his forearm.

"Stop it! Just stop it, Mark! You're acting like a fool!" She sighed in resignation and bent down to scoop up her coat and scarf from the seat. "I'm sorry about this, Sam. Thanks for the coffee, but maybe another time. I'll call you."

As brother and sister passed by The Grind's window looking out onto Woodward Avenue, I could see they were arguing. Hildie was giving him hell, and Mark was looking sheepish. If the woman ever wanted to meet with me again, it would *have* to be she who called me, because I was just about done with this little cat and mouse game. I was beginning to feel that it just might not be worth it to play.

My gaze traveled back inside to the opposite side of the diner, where my intent was to locate Birdie. She stood behind the counter, filling sugar containers.

"Hey, Birdie," I called out to her. "I changed my mind. I think I will have something to eat after all. Could you please bring me a menu?"

CHAPTER TWENTY-SIX

I was the first one to rise on Wednesday morning. The sun was bright and the air was on the cooler side. I doubted the temperature would climb above the low sixties. That was just fine with me...autumn was my favorite time of year. Enjoying the solitude, I had a glorious hour and twenty minutes to read the morning paper and sip on my coffee without interruption from the two ladies in the house. Once Bernie emerged from behind my bedroom door, I was going to ask her again about the mysterious letter of condolence that she claimed she had given to Ty Carver. Either she had gotten the story wrong, or the editor of the magazine was lying to me for some reason. And if the man was lying, I wanted to find out why. I heard her rise and enter the bathroom. Two seconds later, the telephone rang.

"Hello?" I said into the mouthpiece.

"Mr. Flanagan?"

"Yes?"

"This is Ty Carver over at The Monthly Patriot," the caller identified himself. "I hope you don't mind me phoning your home, but have you been in contact with Bernie in the last day or two?"

"Uh...no, why?"

"Well, I haven't heard from her since Monday. She called then to say she was feeling ill, and I've called there but she doesn't answer. I called yesterday afternoon and I called this morning just before ringing you. I guess I'll just swing by her place around lunchtime to check on her," he said.

I had to think quickly. "Hey, I'll be in that area this morning. I can stop by and see if she's okay if you'd like."

"Oh, I would appreciate that," he said, and I breathed easier. "But that's not the only reason I wanted to talk to you. Yesterday you asked me if I knew of any letter that had arrived after Sonny's death. I don't know how I didn't remember it, but it slipped my mind. When you asked me about it, it just didn't ring a bell for some reason. I wouldn't have remembered it still if I hadn't been looking for something else in my desk drawer here at the office. I came across it this morning. Do you have something to write with? I can tell you who the gentleman was who sent it and where he works."

My heart picked up speed and I frantically looked through a kitchen drawer for a piece of paper and a pencil. *This was terrific!* "Okay, go ahead, Mr. Carver."

"The man is a Mr. Gilbert Pittman. It says he's plant manager out at the Ford Motor's Willow Run Bomber facility. You know where that's at?"

"Yes," I answered. "Mr. Carver, does there happen to be a phone number attached to that letter head?"

He rattled off the number while I quickly recorded it on the paper. If I was in luck, I could obtain an appointment to see this Gilbert Pittman sometime today, and if not, maybe I could ask him some questions by telephone instead of making the trip out there.

"Now if you could do me a favor, Mr. Flanagan, I'd like you

171

to ask Bernie to call the office if you get in contact with her this morning. I should be here until four thirty at least. Can you do that?"

"I certainly will, and thanks for calling."

We hung up and I felt like grabbing Bernie as soon as she appeared from the bathroom, taking her in my arms, and dancing around the room with her. Before Ty Carver called, I had no idea where to turn to next in this investigation. Maybe my luck was changing. There was always the chance that my call out to the bomber plant would net me nothing, but my gut told me that quite possibly this was the alternate appointment Sonny had set up for that last Friday morning of her life. Saying a little prayer that that was the case certainly couldn't hurt, either.

At breakfast, I told Bernie of Ty Carver's phone call and told her that maybe she'd better think about returning to work.

"I don't want to," she said nervously. "I'd be afraid, Sam. Sitting in that office would give me the heebie-jeebies. One of *them* could have broken into the guesthouse. And how can I go back home? I'd be scared to death to stay alone."

"I think you'll be fine at the office. And no, you're not going to go back to the guesthouse. You'll come back here after work. But either way you decide, you'll have to call Ty this morning."

Bernie finally made that call to Ty Carver after the kitchen was cleaned from breakfast. She told him she had a bad case of the stomach flu and thought it would be best if she took the rest of the week off. She would see him Monday morning.

I made my call to Mr. Gilbert Pittman after that. I had to go through two other gentlemen before I was connected with the plant manager. Explaining who I was and what I was working on, I asked if I could possibly see him later this afternoon.

"I'm sorry," he said. "*Who* is it that you want to know about?"

"Mrs. Sondra Girard. She was the owner of The Monthly

172

Patriot, a local monthly magazine. I'm trying to figure out if she came out to the plant to interview you on the day of her death. That would have been on August 6 of this year. She was a reporter."

There was silence on the other end for a few short seconds.

"*Oh!* Oh, yes, I think I know who you're talking about now. Yes, I don't honestly remember the exact date, but she did come out here in the beginning of August, I think. In fact, I received a call from her on that same morning, asking if she could come out to interview me on our operations for her magazine. I saw she had died when I read the next day's paper, and I was flabbergasted. Wasn't it a drowning?"

"Yes, it was. Do you think you'd have some time to give me this afternoon? If not today, maybe tomorrow?"

"What did you say your name was again?"

"Flanagan."

He cleared his throat. "Uh, Mr. Flanagan, I'd like to help you out, truly, but this is such a bad time. We've got some real problems down here that need to be solved pronto. I don't think I'll have time for you today *or* tomorrow, and I don't know when."

"Then if I could keep you on the phone maybe five or ten minutes to ask a few questions, it would really be helpful to me," I pleaded.

He sighed and said, "Okay, but no more than five minutes. We really do have a crisis down here."

"So, Sondra Girard actually did see you on that morning after her phone call to you?" I asked.

"Oh, yes. She got here around twelve-thirty or a quarter to one, as I recall. The thing is, after I agreed to see her, we had a bit of an emergency at the plant; the same problem we're having now. I didn't have the chance to call her back to cancel."

"How did she seem? What were your first impressions of

her, Mr. Pittman?"

"As soon as I saw her, I remember thinking she was a lovely young woman. She was neat, professional looking. She had a pretty smile. In fact, she reminded me of my daughter. Same color hair…auburn. The young lady was very attractive, but don't get me wrong. I'm not being disrespectful when I say that. Hell, I'm sixty-four years old. What was she? In her late twenties?"

"Early thirties," I said. "How about her mood?"

"She seemed fine. Mrs. Girard was very cordial and seemed excited to be here. The sad part was, I couldn't grant her the interview. That day one of our machines broke down. In fact, same as today. Same machine, same problem. It wasn't calibrating correctly. And the machine I'm talking about has been malfunctioning off and on for the last six months. When something like that happens, we go into a bit of a panic and have to get on it right away. We can't send our military pilots up in unsafe bombers. And we have a certain contract to fill, and a certain timeline to stick to. It's been messing with our schedule."

I interrupted him. "If she didn't interview you, then what happened? She just left?"

"No, now I threw out a suggestion. I felt bad that she'd made the long trip out here, you know? With many of the men overseas, most of our employees are women who work on the line. I suggested that she go into the employee cafeteria and talk to some of the gals. After all, it was lunchtime, and she could find many of them in there, and it wouldn't interrupt their work schedules. She was very understanding about the change in plans, and even seemed pleased about the idea."

"Ah, okay. Would it be possible for me to talk to the women she spoke with? I could come out there tomorrow around lunchtime," I offered.

"I can save you the time and trouble," he responded. "She

didn't end up interviewing any of the ladies here." I furrowed my eyebrows in confusion, and he continued. "You see, Mr. Flanagan, I showed her the main part of the factory while I was suggesting my alternate idea to her. We couldn't go too far onto the floor because it was roped off around the defective machine. She'd just agreed to seeing the women when she stopped and kind of got a funny look on her face. Then she turned to me and said, 'What's *he* doing here?' Quite honestly, that threw me for a loop. I didn't know what the hell she was talking about. I turned to look in the direction she'd been staring right before she'd asked that, but *I* didn't see anyone. And then, all of a sudden, she says to me that she didn't feel all that well. She asked if she could call back at some other time to set up another appointment. I told her sure. I guess some sort of bug hit her real fast."

Now this was interesting! Who had she seen? Who could have possibly been in the plant that she would not have expected to be there? I felt a surge go through my body. This was very key to the investigation, I was sure. It was important. And I didn't have a clue as to what it meant!

"Before I let you go, is there anything else you can tell me, sir?"

"Nope, not that I can think of," he said. "You know it's funny, though. I remember being confused after her initial phone call that morning."

"Why is that?" I asked.

"Well…and I doubt this will help you in your investigation… but she went on about how terrific it was to finally get in to see me. She told me that after trying to make the appointment for an interview for months, she'd hit the jackpot that day. The strange thing is, we had never had a call from her magazine to request an interview. At least, not that I know of. Now, if that's all, I really need to end this call," he said.

175

I thanked him for his time and we disconnected. Lighting a cigarette, I sat down at the kitchen table and wondered what it all meant.

CHAPTER TWENTY-SEVEN

Things began to unravel rather quickly after that call, but the early part of the day passed with little significance to the current case I was working on. First of all, Gran and Bernie wanted me to take them to do a bit of grocery shopping. It was true that we were running low on most items. We left the house a little past noon. After our trip into town and our arrival back home, I decided to rake up the few leaves that had fallen from our elm tree in the front yard while the ladies put the newly bought food items away and started to prepare an early supper. The two of them had plans to attend the Wednesday evening service at the First Baptist Church along with Gran's friend, Helen Foster. By the time I re-entered the house, my grandmother was placing a meatloaf in the oven while Bernie stood at the kitchen sink, peeling potatoes and washing a head of fresh broccoli in preparation for the meal.

Deciding to get out from under foot, I grabbed my Lucky Strikes and a pack of matches and went to sit on the top step of the front porch. I wasn't having much luck figuring out who Sonny had seen at the Ford Motor Company's Willow Run Bomber Plant. It was obviously someone who she didn't

177

believe belonged there. And it was obviously a *he* and not a *she*. Mrs. Lavinia Marsh swore that Sonny's visitor the night of her drowning was a woman. Could she have been mistaken? Could it be that a man was dressed as a woman and had great success in pulling it off? The elderly woman *did* say that the visitor was very tall. I wondered as I puffed on my smoke.

I hadn't noticed his approach, but now Albie Randle stood before me with his hands on his hips. Albie, age twelve, lived next door with his parents and younger brother, Bobby.

"Gee, Mr. Flanagan, ya sure look like you're lost in thought," he said.

"I guess I was. What's up, Albie?"

"I sorta need to talk to ya, kinda like man to man. Can ya spare a few minutes?"

Inside I was chuckling, but I didn't dare let it show on my face. According to Albie, this was going to be serious business. I slid over to the right and patted the step, indicating that he should sit next to me. He did.

"I gotta problem, Mr. Flanagan."

"What is it?" I asked.

"Well, this Friday there's a dance at the school." He sighed and placed his chin in the palms of his hands as his elbows rested on his knees.

"Why does that have to be a problem?"

"I don't wanna go," he said with a slight whine.

"Simple, don't go. I don't see where that's a problem," I told him.

"Too late," he moaned. "I already asked Betty Ann Moore to go with me."

I looked at him as he buried his face in his hands. Not being able to stop myself, I began to laugh.

"Okay, so I'm assuming she said yes, right? What could be

upsetting about that?"

He raised his head and began ticking off reasons on his fingers. "Number one, I don't know how to dance. Number two, I figure I should get her a corsage, or something like that, and I'd like to be able to take her out for a Coca-Cola or a sundae afterward, but I have no money. Pa says I should get a job. But even if I could start a job tomorrow, I won't be able to earn enough money by Friday. Shoot, it's already Wednesday. Number three, some of the guys were teasing me because Betty Ann is a bit taller than I am." He then hid his face again.

"Is Betty Ann a pretty girl?"

He nodded. "Prettiest girl I know," he moaned through his fingers.

"Well, forget the guys who tease you. They're just jealous. And besides, some of my best dates were with girls who were taller than I was."

"Taller than *you*, Mr. Flanagan?" he asked in disbelief while he pivoted his head to face me.

"Yeah, I wasn't always this tall. Now, learning to dance… well, that's an easy one. Ask your mother to show you a few steps. If she won't, or doesn't have the time, come on over tomorrow after school and Gran will help you out."

"*Mrs. Flanagan*? I don't think she'd know any of the popular steps," he argued. "I don't mean to be disrespectful, but she's kinda old."

I rubbed at my chin. "Eh, you might have a point there. But you could always ask Bernie," I offered.

"Who's Bernie?" Albie asked while scrunching up his nose.

"A lady who is staying with us. Now, she's a bit older than your ma, but I bet she knows some good moves. And you should call her Miss Dayle."

I said nothing more. I knew he wanted me to be the solution to

179

his monetary problem, too, but I purposely kept quiet. Realizing I wasn't going to go on, he began to get nervous and squirm a little. Finally, he brought the subject up again.

"Well, what about the money? Do ya have any suggestions, Mr. Flanagan?"

I rubbed at my chin again, looking straight ahead. "Gee, Albie, I sure don't. Now that one is a bit more difficult to solve."

He was quiet for a few moments and then, hesitantly, he began to carefully ask me for the money, something I knew he would do.

"Ya know," he began. "I might have an idea. You just tell me what ya think, okay?"

"Okay," I agreed.

"Well, what if *you* had enough money for me to borrow?"

"Me?" I asked.

"Well, yeah. I figure you always have money, being as you're a famous detective and all. Ya might even be loaded," the boy said, giving me a sheepish stare.

I reached deep into my pocket and brought out all the money I had in it. It amounted to one dollar and fourteen cents, my change from paying today's grocery bill. He looked at it and frowned.

"Not enough, huh?"

He shook his head and sighed with resignation.

"Well, I figure it's enough to buy each of you a Coca-Cola, and it might be enough to get a small corsage or maybe even one flower. But I agree that it won't be enough for both. You think about it and I'll be right back." I rose and walked into the house. When I came back outside I held up a bill and said, "Or will this do?"

His head turned to look up at me. "Sure! Wow, Mr. Flanagan!" He jumped to his feet and grabbed the five-dollar bill I held in my

180

hand. "Gee, thanks!"

"You know what I just paid for, don't you?"

"What?" he asked.

"A whole lot of snow shoveling this winter."

"Sure," he willingly agreed. "Anything you say!"

***

My belly was full, Gran and Bernie were gone to the evening church service, and I was finally able to have a wonderful couple of hours of needed solitude. I sat in the beige chair in the parlor, puffed on a Lucky Strike cigarette, and listened to a war update broadcast by Edward R. Murrow. Our military troops, and those of our allies, were making headway into Europe. Life was good, at least for the moment. But my rosy outlook didn't last very long. The ringing of the telephone pulled me away from my comfortable position.

Was that whimpering I heard in response to my greeting? Instead of hanging up, I decided to repeat what I'd just said.

"Hello?" More sniffling sounded on the other end. I waited. Something told me this was no prank. "Can I help you?" I tried one more time.

"Yesh," came a low and unsteady reply.

"Who *is* this?"

"Weshley Barnard."

A jolt ran through me. "Wes? Wes, what's wrong?"

"Oh God," he said loudly and more forcefully into my ear. He was slurring his words. He'd definitely been drinking…and it sounded as though he'd been drinking a lot. "I din't know! I din't know! You gotsa beliebe me," he pleaded.

"Okay, back up a minute." He sniffed loudly into the receiver. "You didn't know *what*?" I asked.

And that's when his whines became all out sobs. He tried to talk through his tears but I couldn't make out a single thing he

181

was saying. The man was crying too hard and he was slurring too much.

"Hey, buddy, just take a few deep breaths and tell me what's happened. Take your time and then tell me what this is all about. I'm not going anywhere."

"Yeah," I heard him mutter.

His dramatic inhales were traveling through the airwaves to my ear. He was still whimpering softly. I patiently waited until fifteen seconds of silence passed. Immediately following, I heard soft snores and heavy breathing.

"Wes! Wesley! Are you with me? Don't go to sleep. Where *are* you?" I raised my voice.

"Huh?" he whispered.

"Where are you?"

The moans and faint cries started again. "In the hallway...on the tele.... But I din't know," he repeated himself. "I only went becaush I was curioush, ya know? My grampa came over from there. I wanted out. I din't ...gree with any of that...."

My brows furrowed. What in the hell was he talking about? I tried to hang on to every word.

"I din't know...were...to kill her."

I stiffened. He was fading fast. Because of his weeping and slurring, I couldn't make out all of what he had just said. I needed to find out exactly where he was before he passed out on me.

"Wesley, where in the hell *are* you?" I shouted into the phone.

"I gotta room. Shimone and I argued," he mumbled. "... Rega...need to go sit down...."

A thud sounded in my ear, and I figured he had passed out and dropped the receiver. If I was right in my assumption, he had just told me that he had gotten a room at The Regal Hotel, situated near the docks on the waterfront. The Regal was a fleabag of a hotel, where someone could purchase a room for the

182

afternoon or a whole night at the cost of a buck and four bits. There was nothing *regal* about the joint.

Considering his condition, I wasn't going to get any information out of him unless I did something to rectify the situation. He would need to sober up. I eyed the coffee pot on the stove, holding our dinner's leftover java. It wouldn't be hot now, but lukewarm would do. I walked into the pantry and got the old thermos down from the top shelf. After I filled it with coffee, I pulled out the chunk of meatloaf from the icebox. A quickly thrown together sandwich would hopefully fill his stomach and soak up the liquor. I bagged the sandwich and I was out the back door.

Almost twenty minutes later, I was passing through the front entrance of the shabby hotel. A wall of musty odor smacked me in the face as I stepped inside its dingy interior. The deep red carpet was covered in some spots with oily black stains that had no chance in hell of ever being lifted from its fibers. Approximately twenty feet ahead and to the right was a reception desk. The old man standing behind it had a cigarette dangling from between his lips while he chuckled. Gray whiskers covered his upper lip and jaw line. On closer inspection, I noted that he could have been forty or he could have been sixty. It was hard to tell in his scruffy condition. A battered radio sat on the counter off to the left and behind him. He was listening to an argument between John and Blanche from an episode of The Bickersons. The long ash from his smoke fell to the counter as his slender frame quaked with amusement at the comedy show. When I came to stand directly in front of him, I asked him what room Wesley Barnard was in.

"What?" he yelled over the boom of volume coming out of the radio.

I repeated my question and he repeated his in the same deafening tone. Calmly, I laid down my thermos and bag. I then

183

grabbed him by his mis-buttoned graying short-sleeved shirt and brought his face close to mine.

"Turn the damn radio off, pops!" I said through clenched teeth.

He pulled away from me, shooing at my hands. He then moved to turn the volume down.

"What the hell is your problem, pal?" he asked with contempt.

"I need the room number of Wesley Barnard. He checked in today."

With a sugary insincerity, he answered me. "Well, I don't think he did."

Our eyes bored into one another's and we were silent for about ten seconds. I broke the silence.

"How would you like to swallow a few teeth? Now to avoid that, maybe you should check your registry just to be sure."

Before reaching under the counter for the check-in book, he held out his hand, palm up.

My eyebrows lifted.

"I think I'll need a little compensation to do ya that favor. Don't you think so, too?" he asked, and then smirked.

That wasn't what I thought he really needed, but I didn't want to waste any more time on this creep. What I wanted to do was to get to Wesley Barnard's room and sober him up. I needed to hear his story. Reaching into my pocket, I realized I still only had that dollar and fourteen cents on me. Crumpling the bill into a ball as I withdrew it from my pocket, I grabbed the man's wrist, shoved the bill in his hand, and curled his fingers around it. I kept my hand covering his. He smiled.

"Ah," he said. "I think I remember that a Mr. Barnard is registered in room 27."

I grabbed my package and thermos and headed down the only hallway in sight. I wasn't too far down it when I heard him yell, "Hey! What kind of crap is *this*? I got a ten spot...."

But I'd turned the corner toward room 27 by then and had stopped listening to him. I rapped on the door when I reached it. Not hearing any movement, I didn't hesitate to try the knob. I was in luck; the door to the room was unlocked. Slowly, I opened it and spied Wesley Barnard sprawled across the single bed, lying face down on top of a red sheet.

Immediately, I proceeded to enter while calling his name. "C'mon, Wes. Get up."

And that's when I heard a thunderous crack. Suddenly, a pain shot through me from head to foot and I lost my balance. Unfortunately, the crack was the sound that my skull had made when I was slammed from behind. I was out before I even hit the floor.

CHAPTER TWENTY-EIGHT

When I woke, it was almost an hour later and someone was shaking my shoulder.

"Sam? Sam, I need you to come to."

The voice was one I had recognized. My ex-partner at the precinct, Mac McPherson, was looming above me. I struggled to get into a sitting position, but with the slightest movement my head throbbed as if a twenty-pound lead weight was bouncing around inside of it. As I rose, my vision seemed to blur for a few seconds. Sitting on the floor, I gingerly scooted back to lean against the wall. I touched the back of my head and felt something damp. When I put my hand in front of my face, I noted the blood covering my fingertips.

"Whoa," I said audibly.

"You all right?" Mac asked.

"Maybe," I replied, because I really wasn't sure if I was or not. His voice seemed to be far off and surrounded by an echo.

Another voice, one I found to be much more irritating, sounded from my right. "*Now* what mess have you gotten yourself into, Flanagan?"

I refused to look in the direction that bothersome voice was

186

coming from. Instead, I slowly lifted my face to tell Mac, "Get him out of here, will you?"

My old partner spoke to his current partner. "Larry, why don't you go question the dame again?"

"I already questioned her thoroughly," Larry Brown said.

"Well, do it again. Make sure we got it all." Brown chuckled as he left the room. Once he was gone, Mac turned his attention on me again. "Tell me what happened here, Sam."

I told him about the phone call I'd received that night, and how Wesley Barnard had been crying and slurring his words.

"That's his name? Wesley Barnard?"

"Yep. He's the son-in-law of Senator Victor Girard," I told him.

Mac whistled softly. "Is that right?"

I nodded, but immediately winced with the pain. "Anyway, he was blubbering and I could hardly make out what he was saying. I figured I would need to sober him up quick." I gestured to the thermos and bag that someone had placed on the windowsill. "I brought the coffee and a sandwich for him in hopes of doing just that. When I opened the door, he was laying on the bed, passed out. I called out his name as I stepped in, and that's when someone belted me from behind."

"You sure he was just passed out when you got here?" Mac asked.

I nodded again, and instantly regretted it. "What brought you here, Mac?" I asked.

"A woman passed by this room. The door was open and she saw you lying on the floor. She ran to the telephone in the hall and called us. She said the receiver was dangling off the hook when she reached it. He must have called you from there, huh?"

"I guess," I replied, cradling the back of my head with the palm of my hand.

187

"Well," Mac said. "Doc Macgregor will be here any minute. Maybe he can look at your head."

"*Fergus*? Why Fergus Macgregor?" I asked, confused as to the reason the Wayne County coroner had been called for my head wound.

"Because in between the time you got knocked out and us being called, your friend lying on the bed over there got himself killed. You're lucky you didn't end up the same way."

"*What*?" I struggled to rise from my sitting position on the floor. Feeling a bit dizzy, I reached out for the single chair in the corner of the room. After sitting in it, my eyes traveled to the lifeless body of Wesley Barnard, his eyes partly opened in a blank stare and his throat slashed from ear to ear. The sight of the gaping wound sent a jolt through my system and I jerked my face away, giving no thought to the shift of the lead weight in my head. "*My God!*" I whispered.

"Yep, this is a nasty one, isn't it?"

"Mac, he was dead by the time I entered this room," I said.

"How do you know?"

"Because at the time, I thought he had passed out on top of a red sheet. Now I know that his throat had already been cut and he'd been bleeding out. It didn't register before the lights in my own head went off."

***

Doc Macgregor examined my wound, telling me I needed a few stitches. So, there I sat at Harper Hospital waiting for the emergency room doctor to enter the tiny cubicle. Only a drab, solid green curtain hanging on hooks that extended from a metal bar shielded me from the eyes of passersby. Forty minutes passed before a nurse slid the curtain part way across and stuck her head in.

"He's not been in yet?" she asked.

"No."

"Well, sit tight. He will be."

Before she could leave, I caught her attention.

"Listen, nurse, I'm worried about my grandmother."

"Is she here, too?" she asked.

"No, no nothing like that. But she doesn't know where I am."

"Like I said, sit tight and you can make a call to her after the doctor has seen you."

And then she was gone. Another thirty-five minutes passed before a tall, lanky man wearing a white coat entered. He had wavy jet-black hair — mounds of it — and olive skin coloring. His nametag read something I couldn't pronounce. He spoke perfect English, minus any accent, as he addressed me.

"Mr. Flanagan? You've gotten hit on the head, I see," he muttered while reading a sheet of paper attached to a clipboard.

"Yes," I responded.

"Let's take a look, shall we?" He gently guided my head downward as far as it could bend. His fingers gingerly located my wound and I winced. "Sorry," he said. "My goodness, how did you get this? You're already forming a huge lump."

"Let's just say someone didn't like me very much."

"Well, let's get this cleaned up and stitched before we do anything else."

He proceeded to use a moist towelette to wipe the drying blood away from the injury. The man was as gentle as he could be, but it still hurt like hell. It didn't bother me half as much when he was sewing me up. Once that was done, he asked me some questions while his pencil was poised over his clipboard.

"Now, do you have any dizziness?"

"No, only when I first came to."

He looked up. "Then you lost consciousness when you were hit?"

189

"Yeah, for about an hour."

"Hmm," he uttered. "That's not good. How about your vision? Any blurriness?"

Again, I told him only when I had first come to. He reached into a deep pocket attached to the side of his white lab coat and pulled out a pen-like instrument. He held it up to my face and shined the light streaming from it into each eye. The doctor then placed it back into his pocket.

"Your pupils aren't dilated," he reported. "And that's a good thing. Now, I'm going to read off a few things and you just tell me if you're experiencing any of this with a simple yes or no, okay?"

I nodded, and he began checking off my answers on the sheet.

"Severe headache?"

"Yes."

"Nausea?"

"No."

"Difficulty with memory?"

"No."

"Lack of coordination?"

"No."

"Okay, now repeat after me. Mary had a little lamb, its fleece was white as snow; and everywhere that Mary went, the lamb was sure to go."

I repeated after him and then asked, "What was that for?"

He chuckled. "Just to see if you're slurring your words. You didn't seem to be having any problems, but I wanted to make sure. That hit on the head could be very serious. I was checking to make sure you didn't suffer a concussion, but some of these symptoms may still show up. I'd like to keep you overnight, if you don't mind."

I groaned. "Is that really necessary, Doc? I've got a

grandmother to care for, and I certainly don't want to leave her alone for that length of time."

Okay, so Bernie was there and I wasn't as worried as I let on. But spending the night in a hospital bed wasn't appealing to me at all. I stared at him, trying to read his expression while he contemplated.

"Mr. Flanagan, if you promise to follow my instructions to the letter, I'll let you leave. First of all, don't go right to sleep when you get home." He looked at his watch. "It's ten-fifty right now. See if you can stay up for a few more hours. Take ordinary aspirin as needed for the headache. Keep an ice pack on the wound for as long as you can stand it, and then periodically throughout the next few days. That will help the swelling to go down. I'm not sure what you do for a living, but I'd like you to see if you can take a couple of days off work. If you can't, I want you specifically to take it easy tomorrow, at least." He stuck his hand back into his pocket again and pulled out a business card. "Here," he said, handing it to me. "Call me immediately, no matter what hour, if you experience any of those symptoms in the next day or two. You'll find my office number on there, as well as that of the hospital. Make an appointment to get those stitches out in a week."

I hopped off the table, thanked him, and went to the reception desk to check out. Since they had already obtained my home phone number and address, there was very little to do. Walking through the hospital parking lot to the car, the wind vigorously whipped against my face. The biting air felt refreshing.

191

CHAPTER TWENTY-NINE

Waking the next morning, I dragged myself off the couch, still feeling incredibly groggy. I made my way to the bathroom to relieve myself and splash cold water on my face in an attempt to clear the cobwebs from my head. Last night I'd come home, and finding the women in bed, had wrapped some cubes of ice in a clean dish towel and applied it to the area I'd just had stitched up. It stung. Then I grabbed that day's newspaper and tried to occupy my time with reading about the happenings in and around Detroit. I don't know exactly when, but I dozed in the chair. At some point during the wee hours of the morning, I roused myself to undress and settle under a blanket on the couch. Somehow, in rising this morning, I felt as though I'd only been asleep for an hour or two. But when I emerged from the bathroom, I glanced at the wall clock in the kitchen. I panicked. Today was Thursday and Gran had to be at work at eight, but it was well beyond her start time. My head pounded with the stress that I suddenly felt. The house was shrouded in silence, with Gran and Bernie nowhere in sight. My eyes caught movement outside of the window looking toward the Randle home. There was Bernie standing at the fence talking to Mae, Albie's mother. I crossed the room and raised the window about six inches.

"Bernie, where is Gran?" I asked in alarm.

She pivoted to look behind her. Catching sight of me at the window, she said, "She's at work."

"How did she get there?" I questioned.

"Some big fella came and picked her up. We couldn't wake you. What'd you do? Stay out all night?"

"I'll just talk to you when you get inside." Then I turned my attention to the woman standing on the other side of the fence. "Hello, Mae," I said, and waved my hand.

Closing the window, I crossed to the pot of coffee sitting on the stove. I smiled when I found it was still hot. While pouring myself a cup, I could feel that my stress level was beginning to subside. Obviously, Gran had called Augie this morning to ask if he could pick her up for work. Thankfully, her employer had come to the rescue.

Bernie joined me at the kitchen table with a cup of coffee of her own when she came back inside the house.

"Did you come in late last night, Sam?"

"Not really all that late," I answered her. "I guess it was around eleven-thirty or so."

"Your grandmother was tired and went to bed early last night. I stayed up for a bit, but there was nothing to do and I was bored. So, after a while I hit the hay myself. Musta been out like a light as soon as my head hit the pillow. It was that woman what tuckered me out."

"What woman?" I asked.

"Oh, that friend of Ruby's. She talked non-stop in the car, going to the church and then again coming home after the service. But hey, different strokes for different folks. If your grandmother likes her...well...."

I chuckled and had to agree with her. Gran's best friend,

193

Helen Foster, was only tolerable in small doses, at least in *my* opinion. After taking a sip of coffee, I began to tell Bernie of the telephone call I had received in their absence. I told her of my little trip over near the docks to the Regal Hotel. She got a look of fear in her eyes when I was finished with my tale.

"Sam," she whispered. "*He's dead*? Simone's husband is *dead*?"

I nodded, but said nothing else. My mind's eye flashed back to the vision of Wesley Barnard laying with an unseeing stare and a wide-open gash across his throat. Inwardly, I shuddered. Maybe if I hadn't taken the time to pack that sandwich and pour that coffee in hopes of sobering Wes up…maybe if I had gotten there a bit sooner…well, maybe he'd be breathing right now. The what-ifs were haunting me.

"Land sakes!" She was still whispering. "That could have been *me*!"

"*You*?" I asked.

"Yes," she replied. "What about Sunday when someone broke into the guesthouse? What if the person who broke in was the same person who killed Simone's husband? He could have done that to *me*!"

"Or me," I added. "Who do you think slugged me over the head last night?"

Bernie rose from her chair and walked behind mine to examine my wound. She touched the injury gently enough with her fingertips, but still, it made me wince.

"Hey," I jumped. "That's tender."

"Sorry about that. It looks kinda bad, Sam. You got a purple knot like you wouldn't believe back here. They did a good job shaving around it, though."

She sat back down across from me.

"Sam, maybe we had just better forget the whole thing.

194

People are getting killed. You've been hurt. Nothing we can ever find out can bring my Sonny back home to me. It's not worth having someone else get hurt or killed. I want no more deaths. You're off the case as of now. I want to go home, anyway."

"Back to the guesthouse?"

"Mercy me, no! There's no reason to go back there. I brought everything I own here with me. I don't ever need to go back there again, and I won't. I mean back home to North Carolina. I don't belong here. There's nothing in Detroit for me. I suppose I would miss Ty and Nola, and now Ruby, of course, but I miss being in Asheville more."

"Bernie, listen. You're not responsible for what's happening, and neither am I. We're getting close. Sonny was murdered; that much we know. If I could just find out what was bothering her, what she saw, what she knew, what she wanted to discuss with the senator. And I *do* know that she saw someone at her last appointment for an interview; someone she wasn't expecting to see there. But I need to know who it was and *why* it disturbed her so much. Well, that would tie it all together and lead me to the one who killed her, the one who's been doing this. Let's give it a couple of more days. Right now, I want you to talk to me. Tell me everything again. No matter how small you think a detail is, tell me. I just want you to talk to me about Sonny. For instance, how did she get her nickname? Start from the beginning. Start anywhere, just tell me about her again."

Bernice Dayle sighed and drained her coffee cup. "Okay, but first let's go into the parlor and get comfortable," she said.

The rest of the day I was ordered to stay put. Gran and Bernie pampered me and treated me like a king. I didn't resist as much as I could have. For lunch, Bernie served me Campbell's Chicken Noodle soup, crackers, and a cup of hot tea on a tray while I sat in the chair in the parlor. When Gran arrived home from work and heard my story of the night before, she brought me an ice pack, not once, not twice, but three times throughout the remainder of the day. The ladies worked together, fixing liver and onions, mashed potatoes with gravy, brussel sprouts, and coleslaw for supper. They once again served it to me on a tray at my chair, where I had been occasionally snoozing while holding Shamus in my lap. When my meal arrived, the cat bolted off me with a meow, and went to hide behind the sofa. I was physically relaxed and my headache was only a quarter of the strength it had been last night.

After supper, the ladies sat down at the dining room table to continue their game of Monopoly. The radio was on and I was half listening to an episode of "Duffy's Tavern." I didn't seem to be able to concentrate fully on the show. Even though my body was in a carefree state, my mind would not let me rest completely. It raced with thoughts of last night. Who could have overpowered Wesley Barnard enough to be able to slit his throat? Lavinia Marsh thought Sondra Girard's visitor was a woman… she was pretty definite about that. But a *woman* slitting someone's throat? I wasn't comfortable with the thought that that would be the method a female would use to snuff out the life of another. Yet, in the state that Mr. Barnard had been last night, a child probably could have done it. I doubt he'd had much strength or coordination in him to fight off anyone who would be attacking him. But still, it seemed to me it was probably a man who had committed the ugly deed. And I *knew* the hit to the back of my head was very forceful. Yep, I was betting on it being a man who had been in that room at the Regal. And why was it that he hadn't slit *my* throat, too? Once I was down and out, it would have been a quick and easy job. The only reason I could think of was that the woman at the hotel had appeared in the hall very shortly after the blow to the back of my head, and had spied my prone body

196

on the floor. I had to give thanks to God for my undoubtedly narrow escape with death.

Apparently I had ceased my analyzing of the situation to give into the need to doze once again. The ringing of the phone later that evening sent a jolt through me, waking me with a start. Gran answered it.

"Oh, how are you, dear?" she asked. "And how are Betty and the girls?"

I rose from the chair with the knowledge that it must be Mac on the line. Maybe he had further information about Wes's murder.

"Oh, I know," Gran continued. "You should see the lump on the back of his head, but he seems to be doing all right. He's being well taken care of."

Gran said her goodbye to my ex-partner when she saw me enter the kitchen, then handed the receiver out to me.

"Hey, Mac,"

"How you feeling, Sam?" he asked.

"Eh, doing all right. The headache is finally going away."

"That's good. I don't want to keep you, but I was wondering if you could come on down to the precinct tomorrow morning. And don't make it too late, we need to talk."

"Yeah, I can do that. Did you find out more about what happened last night?" I inquired.

"Oh, you could say that, but I'd rather discuss it when I see you tomorrow. See you then, Sam."

We ended the connection. I wondered what he had found out. As curious as I was, I was going to have to wait until tomorrow morning for the answer.

My last thought for the day before falling asleep was the realization that Albie Randle hadn't come over for a bit of dance instruction. I was hoping that his mother had shown him the

197

basic steps to the Fox Trot or Lindy Hop.

CHAPTER THIRTY

Well, gee, isn't this nice? My day was starting off just grand by seeing the one person I'd rather not ever see. I caught sight of Lawrence Brown as soon as I entered the police station on Friday morning.

"What are *you* doing here, Flanagan?" he asked me.

"None of your business," I shot back.

"Aw, now c'mon! Just because you're failing at solving the mystery of the *accidental* drowning woman, you don't have to take it out on me," he said, his words dripping with sarcasm.

As I passed him on my way to Mac's personal office, I muttered, "Your fly is open."

He undoubtedly checked to see if it was by looking at his crotch, because it took him a whole ten seconds to come out with, "You're a smart ass, Flanagan!"

Okay, I'd wanted to bite my fingernails for the last thirty minutes. That's how long I'd been sitting in Mac's office, waiting for him to make an appearance. What new information that I hadn't had was he now willing to make me aware of? Would it push me further along in solving the case I was working on? When in the hell would he get in here? I was told to take one

199

of the seats facing his desk and he would be in soon. Not soon enough for me. It was another fifteen minutes before he walked in with a man I'd never seen before. Mac introduced him to me.

"Sam, thanks for waiting. This is Agent George Foyle, FBI. We'd like to speak with you."

I nodded in greeting to the tall, wiry man who was lowering himself into the seat behind the desk. Mac balanced himself on the edge of that desk after closing the door to his office. George Foyle had a pencil-thin dark brown mustache sitting under his rather long, narrow nose. His hair, parted in the middle and pomaded flat to his head, matched the color of the 'stache. The man's mouth was partly opened, and I could see that his bottom teeth were horribly crooked. I pegged him to be somewhere in his early thirties. My eyes narrowed.

"FBI? What's this all about, Mac?"

My thoughts immediately returned to the night that I'd had a drink with Bulldog Dixon down at The Double Shot. As we sat there, he had asked if I had any knowledge of why J. Edgar Hoover and a couple of his G-men were in Detroit. He wanted to know what could have been happening in the city to bring them here. Quite possibly, I was going to find out the answer to that question right now. However, it wasn't Mac who answered me.

"What do you know about Mr. Wesley Barnard?" Agent Foyle demanded to know.

My eyes directly met his. I raised my right ankle to rest on my left knee, and I brought my fingertips together while my elbows rested on the arms of the chair. "Not much of anything," I said.

"Not much of anything? Then how do you know *of* him?"

"His father-in-law, Senator Girard, hired me to do a job. I went to question the senator's daughter. It was then that I met her husband, Wesley."

"You don't call him a *friend*? You don't *go* places with him?"

I shook my head. "No, I only talked to him briefly the one time. He seemed like a rather nice man. What's this all about?"

"You only talked to him *once*, yet the man called you on Wednesday evening," he spewed.

I didn't like this guy's tone. It was accusatory. "That's right," I shot back.

Next, he threw a photograph across the desk to me. "Take a look at this!"

I leaned forward to get a better look. The photo was of a group of people, mostly men, standing with their backs to me. Their gaze was on a man who was up on a stage facing them. I focused on that man. My eyebrows rose with a start. The man on stage, making some sort of speech at a podium, wore a light-colored outfit with a darker band around his upper left arm. That armband had the Nazi swastika insignia on it. I leaned back in the chair.

"All right, what does this have to do with me?"

"Take another look," Agent George Foyle ordered. "What does this look like to you?"

Without looking at the photo again, I said, "Yeah, I get it. It looks some type of meeting with a Nazi speaking. But again… what does this have to do with me?"

"Take a good, hard look at it," he ordered. I leaned forward again, closely studying the picture. Agent Foyle then pointed with the eraser end of a pencil he was holding to someone in the crowd. "What do you see?"

Picking up the photograph, I brought it in closer to my face and honed in on the man he had indicated. The fellow was turned slightly to a gentleman on his right, and I could make out his face. I squinted. The man I was concentrating on now, I recognized. It was Wesley Barnard. Setting the photograph on the desk once again, I repeated my question. "Okay, so it's Wesley Barnard.

Now, what does this have to do with me? What is it you think I can tell you?"

"The man who took this photograph was an undercover agent of ours. This was taken a couple of weeks ago. Our man had infiltrated the group. He came out of that meeting and, shortly after, met with a go-between. He handed his contact this film, they parted ways, and he hasn't been seen since. Our operative was supposed to have gotten in touch with me and given me further information, but it appears someone got to him first. That photo was taken in this city, and we want to know where. We think you can tell us."

"Well, you're wrong."

"I'm asking you where your friend goes to these meetings! He called you on Wednesday evening. What did he say? What has he told you? Why did he call you at all if you're in no way connected to him? I'm asking you these things, and I want some answers," he said more forcefully.

"And you can keep asking, buddy! I don't have any answers for you! Wednesday night he was drunk out of his mind. He was crying and slurring so much that I couldn't understand him. I put two and two together to find out where he was. I got there too late to listen to what he had wanted to say." I turned to Mac. "What in the hell *is* this?"

"Uh, listen Foyle," Mac directed his comment to the agent. "Like I told you before, Sam here is the good guy."

"Maybe," George Foyle said with his eyes on my face. "And maybe not."

That's when I rose from my chair. "I'm out of here, unless you think you can hold me on anything, Mac."

Mac shook his head, but Foyle got one last word in.

"Don't leave town. It wouldn't make me very happy if you left town."

"Oh, I'm not going anywhere. But it wouldn't hurt me one bit if you did."

Passing through the squad room Lawrence Brown called out a jab, but I wasn't listening. Instead, I heard Mac tell him to shut up as his footsteps sounded behind me. He caught up with me in the hall leading to the exit.

"Sam! Sam, wait!"

I stopped and turned to face him. I was angry.

"What in the hell *was* that in there, Mac?"

He rubbed the back of his neck. "The hell if I know. It wasn't supposed to go down like that. Between you and me, I don't care for the guy, but I gotta work with him on this."

Then he proceeded to tell me that over a week ago, J. Edgar Hoover and two of his agents—George Foyle, and a guy named Walter North—had flown into Detroit. Mac, the chief, and the FBI agents met to discuss the subversive activity going on in the city. No one else in the department knew about any of this, although many gathered at the water fountain to discuss their theories as to what the FBI would be doing at the precinct. It was all very hush-hush. Hoover and North had returned to D.C. on Saturday, September 18, but left Foyle behind to continue working on the case. When Wesley Barnard was murdered, and I was found in his hotel room, they wanted to bring me in to see if I could be of any help. Mac had been surprised and disappointed to see how Foyle had handled our meeting of just a few moments ago.

"So, Sam, if you do remember anything, or come across anything that can help us find out who some of the other people are who attend those meetings—or if you find out *where* they are meeting—can you let us know? I know you're working on the senator's case, but it might intersect with what Barnard was into."

"If I find anything out, I'll contact you, and you alone. I'm not talking to that jackass again. If I hear anything, I'll let you know."

Mac patted my arm. "Thanks, Sam."

As soon as I hit the parking lot, I pulled out a Lucky Strike. After lighting it, I inhaled deeply. I needed a drink, but I didn't need any company while I drank it. Once inside the auto, I started the engine and headed for my office on Woodward Avenue, where I could shut the door, lock it, and pull out the filing cabinet drawer that held my bottle of Jack Daniels. If I was lucky, no one would knock and the telephone wouldn't ring. I needed to do some thinking.

CHAPTER THIRTY-ONE

To be honest, that drink turned into several. A lot of things were beginning to make sense, also…that is, up until my head hit the desk and I passed out from too much cheer. When I woke, it was dark outside and the time on my watch told me it was way past time to go home. There wasn't a sound coming from any of the other offices on my floor, or in any other portion of the building. I stood, stretched, and headed for the door. Emerging out onto the street below, a gentle breeze engulfed me, carrying a mild temperature throughout the city. When I reached the '38 Chevy I leaned against it, not wanting to leave the refreshing feeling of the night air. I reached in my pocket for a Lucky Strike and smoked it right where I stood.

As soon as I had entered the house back at home, I headed straight for the icebox and pulled out the last of the meatloaf. I made myself a sandwich, slathering a generous amount of mustard on it. Carrying it with a glass of milk to the parlor, I sat down in the chair across from the sofa where Gran was sitting looking at that day's newspaper. She wasn't actually reading anything…her eyes weren't good enough for her to make out the words. At the other end of the sofa sat Bernie, crocheting a doily.

Ballroom music was softly playing from the radio.

"Hello, dear. We missed you at supper," Gran said.

"I put some time in at the office," I replied, making it sound as though I had actually done some work there.

"Are you making any progress, Sam?" Bernie was now staring at me, awaiting my answer.

"Yes," I answered her with a mouthful of meatloaf and bread. "I think I am. What's occurred to me might be related to Sonny's death, but I'm not sure yet."

"Well, what is it that has occurred to you?"

"I don't want to say just yet, Bernie. Let me think this over. I'm not really sure how it all fits."

The woman exhaled a long and loud sigh and then she returned to her hooks and thread. Thinking on what I had learned at the precinct that morning, I thought I now knew where the city's traitorous Nazi meetings were taking place. From Neamon Riley, owner of The Double Shot, I'd learned that Wesley Barnard would meet some unknown man in the bar once a week and they would leave to go somewhere together. I had watched the back of the two men from my stool as they walked in between the shoe repair shop and the old movie theater the last time I had been in Neamon's place. Nothing was behind those buildings except for an alleyway, and then some houses on the other side of it. I hadn't thought of it while I was in Mac's office, but it occurred to me while I was in my own that the perfect meeting place for that type of activity would be the inside of the now vacant theater. If the group had gathered where the movies had been shown in the past, there were no windows for light to escape onto the street outside of the structure. No one would know they were using the joint to assemble. And there was a door leading into the theater at the back of the building. If I could just find out *who* the man was that Wesley had been meeting, maybe more of this would make

206

sense. I had a strong feeling that it all tied to Sonny's murder.

And another thing I'd began to ponder this afternoon was what Gilbert Pittman, the general manager at the bomber plant, had told me. A certain machine at the factory was messing up. It wasn't calibrating properly. They had been having trouble with it for months. But what if it wasn't the fault of the machine? What if someone had been tampering with it, and Sonny had seen that person near that same machine? What if that person was someone who was known to Sonny, but was someone she had never expected to be there? What if she had put two and two together...the man and the faulty machine? Is that what she had wanted to talk to Senator Victor Girard about? Had it bothered her to such a degree that she needed to tell someone who was in the government and would know what to do?

It all seemed to fit. Nazis in the city? Sabotage of U.S. military planes? Why not? It wasn't that huge of a stretch to me. Even though it made sense in my mind at the present, I'd have to think this through before I told Bernie my theory.

What perplexed me was that Wesley Barnard had been involved at all. *Wesley Barnard? A Nazi?* I didn't want to believe it! And I wasn't going to believe it at this point in time unless something convinced me of it. Yet it definitely was Wesley in that photograph that the FBI agent, George Foyle, had slid across the desk to me. Right now, I didn't want to think about any of it. My head was hurting too much. And I suspected that it was not hurting from the slug I had received a couple of nights ago, but rather the amount of whiskey I'd consumed throughout the day. Tomorrow I would analyze this information again.

My thoughts interrupted, my head jerked up in the direction of the ladies.

"What?"

"I asked you if you knew who this was," Gran stated. "He

207

sure looks handsome in his fancy dress.

I rose and went to Gran's side. The photo she'd been looking at was accompanied by an article about an event held at the mayor's mansion in Detroit. A fundraiser had been held a couple of nights ago to gather money for the purchase of government bonds in an attempt to aid the war effort. The mayor and his wife were pictured dressed in their finest, he in a tuxedo and his wife in an elegant gown.

"Gran, that's Mayor Edward Jeffries. I'm surprised you don't know that," I said.

My grandmother scoffed. "Oh you! Not him! I mean this man here."

She pointed to a tall gent who was standing with a tall woman off to the left of the mayor and his wife. I leaned down to get a closer look. They were in evening dress as well, and I knew who they were. I whistled.

"That, Gran, is Neil Chelton and his wife, Victoria; the senator's son-in-law and his oldest daughter."

"They're a good-looking couple, aren't they? She's very pretty," Gran said.

Bernie leaned to her right toward Gran to get a glimpse of the image of the couple, too. "Yep, that's her all right," she said.

It hit me like a ton of bricks at that moment. I straightened and stared directly in front of me, focusing on nothing. Wait a minute! What had she told me? I narrowed my eyes and thought back to everything she had said. And I knew she had basically lied about everything. For some reason, I had been all too willing to accept that Bernie was the one who had been coloring the story, but I had been wrong.

Looking at my watch, I saw that I had time enough to get to The Double Shot to ask Neamon Riley a couple of questions, and quite possibly, I would make a stop at the Regal Hotel after that. Needing to move quickly, I went into the bathroom and washed my face. On my way out the door, I grabbed my fedora and picked up the photograph. Tomorrow, I would make a call to Gilbert Pittman. If this all fell into place like I thought it was going to, I would then make my call to Mac at the precinct.

CHAPTER THIRTY-TWO

It was Friday night and The Double Shot was jam packed with area residents wanting to leave their troubles at the bottom of a frosted mug. All the stools lining the bar were filled. I scanned the area for a place to sit, and found an empty booth in the far corner of the room. Neamon caught sight of me and called out, "Be with ya in a minute, Sam." I nodded in response. Ten minutes later, he waddled over to the booth with a scotch on the rocks in his hand—even though I hadn't asked for it—set it before me, and began to walk off.

"Wait a minute," I said. "I need to talk to you."

"I'll be back in a bit. I'm kinda busy right now."

In the nearly half an hour I sat there awaiting his return, I'd pushed my scotch away, given a dollar to a guy who looked down on his luck, and watched two women dance in between the tables to a slow tune by Woody Herman. For the second time that day I was made to wait while I felt as if I had been sitting on pins and needles. Finally, the bar owner found a few moments for me.

When he reached the booth, he gestured to the glass of scotch that sat in the middle of the table. "Somethin' wrong with the drink?"

"Nope," I said, shaking my head. "Just not in the mood and I don't have the time. This isn't a social call. I've got a quick question for you." I pulled out another one-dollar bill and threw it on the table as payment for the untouched scotch, then I pulled out the photograph. "Neamon, tell me if this guy here is the one who would meet Wesley Barnard once a week. Is this guy the one who Wesley would meet and go off with?"

Neamon snatched the picture up and held it close to his face. He emitted a low whistle from between his lips. "Nice duds," he said. "Where is this that everyone would be so decked out?"

"Never mind, is that him?"

"Yeah, that's him," he said without looking again at the photo.

"You sure?"

"Of course, I'm sure. Why?"

I rose from my sitting position, took the picture from his hands, and thanked him.

"I'll tell you next time I come in," I said, and walked toward the exit.

Once in the '38 burgundy Chevy, I leaned back in the seat, exhaling loudly. I took a Lucky Strike out of my pocket, lit it, and started the engine. A surge of electricity ran the length of me. I steered the auto in the direction of The Regal Hotel.

That same thick barrier of stench hit me as soon as I entered the joint. Once again, the radio was blaring with tonight's fare. The guy behind the reception desk was dancing with himself to some ear-deafening swing music. He was the same fellow I had tangled with two nights before. When he caught sight of me walking toward him, he stopped in his tracks.

"Ah, you again," he muttered. He turned to the radio and shut it off. "What is it this time, bud?"

Reaching him, I could tell he still hadn't shaved, bathed, or

211

combed his hair, and he was wearing the same discolored shirt. "I want to ask you something."

He reacted by putting his hand out. "The lips are locked until the palm is greased."

I suppose the look on my face must have conveyed what I was about to deliver to him if he didn't comply, because he pulled his hand back and straightened. Clearing his throat, he asked, "Okay, what do you want to know?"

"The other night when I was here, you said something about a ten-spot. Did someone else come in that night and give you a Hamilton for some information?"

The man nodded his head. "Yep, and you might say *he* was a bit more grateful for my help than you were."

"Did he want the same information from you? Did he want to know what room Wesley Barnard was in?"

"Hey, listen pal, I don't want no trouble. I don't want no part of this."

"Just answer the question," I stated.

The man nodded.

I continued with my interrogation. "Do you know who the guy was?"

He shook his head. "Nah, I ain't never seen him before. He came in and asked me for the room number about ten minutes before you did. That's all I know. And I ain't seen him since. Now, I don't wanna get involved in this, ya know?"

"Did you tell the cops this?" I asked.

"Nah," he answered.

"Why not?"

"'Cuz they didn't ask me, that's why not. The guy with the curly hair just asked me what time it was that Mr. Barnard checked in, and then he asked how long you'd been here. And like I said, I don't want no trouble."

Larry Brown was a moron! "Okay, one more thing," I said, and laid the photo on the countertop directly in front of him. I pointed with my index finger to the man in question. "Is this him? Is this the guy who asked about Wesley Barnard ten minutes before I did?"

He leaned on the surface of the counter with his elbows and stared at the picture. I was quiet while he studied it. "Hot damn!" he said. "Who's the dame? She's a real looker!"

"Never mind about the dame. I'm interested in him," I said, pointing once more to the man in the photo.

I was silent while he studied the image for about ten seconds more. He raised to an upright position, handing me the photo. "It's hard to tell. When he came in the other night, he was wearing a hat."

"Look again," I told him.

He glanced at it as I held it out for him to see. "I guess so. I guess that could be him. It looks like him."

"Thanks," I said, and I headed for the door.

I smoked yet *another* Lucky Strike on my drive back to the house, and I smiled. *Gotcha*! I now thought I knew the whole story, or pretty darn close to it. It was just after midnight...too late to call General Manager Gilbert Pittman, or to try to get in contact with Mac at the precinct, but my heart was beating fast and my adrenaline was surging. I'd call them first thing in the morning, but it was going to be one helluva long night.

213

CHAPTER THIRTY-THREE

If Gilbert Pittman, the general manager at the Ford Motor Willow Run Bomber Plant, could confirm my theory, I would have this case wrapped up. I was sure of it! On the morning of Saturday, September 25, I sprang off the couch. I opened the front door to retrieve the daily newspaper and was met with a gust of chilly air. The sun was shining brightly. It was going to be a good day, weather wise. I threw the paper on the coffee table before heading toward the bathroom to take a long, hot shower. The ladies in the house hadn't come out from behind their bedroom doors yet, although I thought I had heard some movement coming from the direction of Gran's room.

Ruby Flanagan was standing at the stove, fully clothed and scrambling eggs, when I emerged from my shower dressed in my black bathrobe. Bernie was wearing her robe, too, insisting that my grandmother allow her to help with the preparing of breakfast. Sighing loudly, my grandmother told her she could make the toast. I went directly to the phone at the back of the room and dialed the number I had for the bomber facility. Getting right to the point, I asked Mr. Pittman if he employed a certain person. There was no point in driving out to the plant with the photograph of the man in question unless he replied in the negative. There was always the chance that he was not employed under his real name.

"Oh, sure," Gilbert Pittman said. "I guess he's been with us about a year now. He's one of our custodians for the maintenance of the building. But he won't be in until much later today, though. You want me to tell him he needs to get in touch with you?"

"Nope," I answered. "In fact, I don't even want you to mention that I called. I will contact him myself."

Disconnecting, I then immediately dialed the precinct and asked to talk to Mac. I was told he hadn't arrived for the day yet, but should be walking in at any moment. Leaving the message that I would call back in a bit, I hung up the receiver and sat down at the table, trying to contain myself.

"Well, look at you!" said Bernie. "You look like the cat who ate the canary."

"That's because I know who killed Sonny, and I know why."

She gasped, pulled the chair out that was situated directly across from mine, and lowered herself onto it, wearing a look of astonishment on her face. From her sitting position, she said, "Tell me who it is, Sam!"

I shook my head. "Nope, not yet."

"Why not?" Bernie demanded in a loud voice.

"Because I can't trust you with the information just yet. I'll tell you later on."

She slammed her fist down onto the tabletop with a thud that shook the piece of furniture and rattled the plates. Then, in a raised voice she asked, "And just *what* do you mean by that?"

"Just what I said. You can't be trusted. If I told you, you'd either get on the telephone and scream threats, or you would insist that I take you over there so you could do bodily harm to someone. And that would ruin everything."

215

I didn't bother looking at her; I knew her face was molded into a reddened show of anger. Instead, I picked up my slice of toast and lightly buttered it. Since I was giving Bernie no attention, she turned to my grandmother.

"Ruby, do you hear what he is saying?"

Gran nodded. "Yes, dear, and I have to agree with him. Remember how you made those telephone calls to all of the suspects, and told them you knew what they had done? Well, I think Sam is speaking about that. I think that's why he says you're not trustworthy. I honestly think you should just listen to Sam, because he usually knows what he is talking about."

"But you don't believe I'm not trustworthy, do you, Ruby?"

"Let's just eat before the eggs get cold, dear," my grandmother calmly stated, and then she took a sip of her coffee.

I smiled inside, but shoved some eggs in my mouth so it wouldn't show on my face.

***

At ten-fifteen that morning I entered the precinct. The desk sergeant told me Mac was expecting me, and I walked directly to his office. Sitting across from him at his desk, I found myself to be out of breath…not from physical exertion, but from the adrenalin that surged through my veins. Laying the photograph out in front of him, I pointed to it, saying, "Here's who you want."

"Hang on," Mac said. And then he rose from his chair and left the room. When he came back a few moments later, he said, "Follow me."

I didn't ask where we were going, but I sure as hell hoped it wouldn't be to some office where FBI agent George Foyle was sitting. That guy, and Mac's partner Larry Brown, were the two gentlemen I had no interest in being in the company of at the moment. Thankfully, we entered the chief's office. Inside, there was a small desk positioned on the far wall, but there was

216

also a table placed near the window where six people could sit comfortably. The chief was seated at that table, and Mac and I joined him. Now, the chief and I weren't the best of buddies. He usually had a snide remark to deliver whenever he saw me, but it seemed we were putting our differences aside for the time being.

"We want to hear everything you got, Flanagan," the chief said. "But hold off. I ordered some coffee for us. I don't want anyone else hearing this. Don't begin until it gets here."

Within a matter of seconds there was a soft rap on the door, followed immediately by its opening. Larry Brown carried in a tray with three Styrofoam cups on it. He set the tray on the table that we were sitting at.

"You want I should stay, Chief?" He glanced at me with a sneer.

"No, we won't need you. Thanks for the coffee, and close the door on your way out."

Brown left the room, not able to hide the look of dejection on his face.

"Okay, give it to us," the chief said.

I laid the photograph I'd brought with me on the table. "This is who killed Senator Victor Girard's wife, and this is who killed Wesley Barnard," I said, pointing to the image.

"Tell us about Barnard," the chief directed. "How do you know all of this?"

I began my story by telling them what I had been working on, and in doing so, how I'd paid a call on the senator's youngest daughter, Simone...and that's where I'd first met Wesley Barnard. From there, I told them about being in The Double Shot that past Monday, and seeing Wesley sipping on a beer while sitting at the bar, and how I'd just missed him when I came out of the bathroom. Explaining how I'd seen the backs of he and another man walking between the theater and the shoe repair shop, I informed the chief and Mac that I believed the subversive meetings were being held inside of the La Salle Theater. It was my assumption that those meetings were taking place once a week on Mondays, but they could always question Neamon Riley, the owner of The Double Shot to make sure. In fact, Neamon Riley had positively identified the man in the photo as being the guy Wesley Barnard would meet in his place each week for the past few months, and they would then leave together and disappear between the buildings across the street. The chief and Mac sat silently as I told my tale, my ex-partner occasionally jotting down notes on a piece of paper.

"I also took this picture over to the fellow who mans the reception desk at The Regal Hotel. He identified this fellow as someone who had come in asking for Wesley's room number about ten minutes before I got there. Considering the pie-eyed condition he was in, it must have been a quick and easy job to slit Wesley's throat. I honestly believe mine would have been slit, too, if it hadn't been for the dame who came along. She saw me laying there, but must have missed seeing Wesley Barnard's killer in the room for some reason."

The chief took a sip of his coffee and scratched at his head. "You sure about all this, Flanagan?"

"I'm sure. And there's more."

I then laid out the whole story of Sonny Girard's visit to the bomber plant on the morning of her death. I told them how she had set up an appointment early in the day in order to get a story for her magazine, and how she'd seen someone while there who, in her opinion, shouldn't have been there.

"The general manager, a gentleman named Gilbert Pittman, told me how a certain machine has been breaking down for months now. I believe this guy was sabotaging it, wanting to put out faulty bombers and, if nothing else, wanting to delay

218

production. Pittman verified for me this morning that this fellow works there as a janitor. I think Mrs. Girard saw him near the machine in question and put two and two together. And *he* saw that she had seen him. Right then and there, Sonny's fate was sealed. She had to be gotten rid of."

"Well, I wonder how Senator Girard will react to having had Nazis in the family," the chief said.

"Not Simone's husband. I don't think so. Wesley Barnard was no Nazi. I think he went to those meetings out of curiosity. I couldn't understand much of what he was saying in that phone call that he made to me, but there were a few things that I *could* make out. He mentioned being curious. He told me his grandfather had come over 'from there.' With a name like Barnard, I'm now assuming he meant Germany. And I think the guy was lonely. Life at home with his wife wasn't all that great, so when he sees this greaseball in the bar, it was easy to become involved in some way. And somewhere along the line, he had found out what had happened to Sonny, and he was going to spill it all to me. And he was going to bring down their meeting place, but they got to him before he could talk. I think he may have voiced his opposition to what had been done to Sondra Girard; maybe he made threats of going to the authorities. Of course, the group couldn't let him do that. I believe the night he was killed, Wesley went home, argued with Simone, then went to find a room for the night. He took a bottle of hooch with him, drank heavily, and then called me."

The chief stood, and my ex-partner and I followed suit. "Mac, make tracks and take the G-man with you. Bring 'em in," the chief ordered.

Looking at me, Mac said, "Give me the address, Sam." I told him where he needed to go. "And I suppose you'd like to be here during questioning?"

"I wouldn't miss it for the world!"

219

CHAPTER THIRTY-FOUR

As soon as Mac and Agent George Foyle left the station, I crossed the street and sat in a diner to await their return. The side of the booth I sat in was facing the large window over-looking the street. I had an excellent view of the police station and the drive Mac would pull into when he returned. I wasn't hungry and I had had enough coffee already this morning to last me for a few days, but I didn't think the owner of the diner or his staff would take very kindly to me occupying a booth just to drink a glass of water. So, I went ahead and ordered a cup of coffee. I was eager for the men's return, and the wait was hard. While sitting there, I tried to play a little game with myself. I wouldn't look at my watch until I thought ten minutes had passed. When I first noted the time, it was eleven twenty-seven. I began my wait, trying to relax. Sipping on my coffee, I watched as a mother in a nearby booth loudly and continuously urged her young son to eat all of his grilled cheese sandwich, to no avail. I didn't know who was more obnoxious, the kid who whined and stubbornly refused to do what his mother told him to do, or his mother, whose high-pitched badgering was getting on my nerves. Finally, the man who was with them—I assumed it was the boy's father—

suddenly said, "For God's sake, Delores, leave the kid alone! If he eats it, good. If he doesn't, who cares?"

She tried to express her point of view. "But look at how skinny he is! He needs to eat his food."

"And what kid at his age isn't skinny? He won't starve. I can guarantee you he'll eat when he's hungry. Now, just shut up and leave the kid alone!"

Delores's husband had a point.

Surely ten minutes had passed. I glanced at my watch and sighed. It was eleven thirty-one. Playing the game a few more times, I was always off the mark.

The waitress approached to give me a fourth refill. Middle aged, she was a bit on the pudgy side. She wore a pale-yellow uniform with a white collar and cuffs. A hair net stretched over her bleached blonde curls. Her name, which was stitched onto her uniform above her left breast with black thread, read Delphine. I placed the palm of my right hand over the top of my cup before she could pour more coffee into it. I was about to burst.

"Hey, Delphine," I said. "Let me ask you a question."

"Ask away," she replied.

"You know who Detective McPherson is? He works out of the precinct right across the street."

"Oh, sure," she answered. "I know Mac. He comes in here quite often. Why? What's up?"

"Well, I'm sitting here waiting for him to pull into that driveway, and—"

"Why? You wanna make your getaway when he goes into the station?" she asked, interrupting me. She laughed aloud, snorting in the process.

I smiled. "No, I'm not wanted by the law," I assured her. "I need to speak to him when he returns, but I need to use the restroom. I don't want to miss his arrival. If you want to make a

221

dollar tip, you'll watch for him while I'm in there."

"Sure," she said eagerly. "But make it two dollars and I promise not to take my eyes off that driveway."

"You negotiate a hard bargain, Delphine, but it's a deal," I said. Then I rose from the booth to go and take care of the little matter of emptying a very full bladder.

When I returned not even five minutes later, I spied the waitress at a booth in which an elderly woman was sitting. Still holding the coffee pot in her right hand, she was bent over viewing photographs that the woman was showing her. "Now this one is of my youngest grandson. He's my boy's son," I heard the older woman say. *Well, so much for making deals*, I thought.

Sitting back down in the booth, I noted that my coffee cup was once again filled to the brim with more of the tar-like liquid. I groaned audibly, and Delphine looked my way. I beckoned to her with the crook of my finger. She apologized to the woman with the pictures, made her excuses, and walked my way.

When she reached my booth, she said, "Yeah?"

"You must not want that two-dollar tip very badly, huh?"

"What do you mean?" she asked.

"You promised to keep your eye on the driveway across the street, but I come back here and you're fawning all over some photographs that woman is showing you."

"I kept my promise," she said in a matter-of-fact tone. "He pulled in as soon as you went to take care of your business. What did you want me to do? Come in there and get you?" She then held out her hand, palm up. "Now, are you going to keep your end of the bargain?"

I scurried out of the booth and fished for the money in my pocket. "Well, why didn't you say?"

"I just did," she said.

Handing her two dollars and a quarter, I turned to leave the diner.

"Hey," she called after me. "Don't you want your change for the coffee? It's not a whole quarter."

"No, you keep it," I shouted as I stepped out onto the street.

CHAPTER THIRTY-FIVE

When I entered the squad room back at the precinct, the chief caught sight of me and called me over to where he was standing. He leaned in close and spoke in a low tone.

"Foyle and Brown have him in interrogation room one. Mac is in room four. He's waiting for you."

"Thanks," I muttered, and headed toward the stairs to descend to the area used for questioning suspects.

As I reached the lower level of the building, a noticeable change in climate was markedly felt. The air was stagnant and cold. Conversations taking place in the squad room above were distant echoes. The rough, drab green cinder block walls were depressing down here. I followed the narrow hallway where the interrogation rooms were located. Farther ahead were the cells where the prisoners were kept, awaiting trial or prison transfers. At door number four I stopped and gave a light rap, but didn't wait for an invitation before entering. Mac was sitting directly across from her, while she wore a stiff, defiant expression. They both looked my way when I entered, but said nothing. Her lips curled into a sneer. For the first time I could see the evil in her face. Her blue eyes suddenly seemed like ice, mirroring the lack of emotion felt in her heart. She wore a taupe-colored short sleeve dress with shoulder pads and cream-colored cuffs. Her hair was styled in fawn-colored braids that framed her head, as it had been when I'd last seen her. This woman's coral lips no longer appeared seductive. I sat at the end of the table.

"Oh, Sam," she said sarcastically, dramatically. "It could have been so different, don't you think?" And then tauntingly, she laughed softly. "I thought you'd never figure it out. I enjoyed watching you try."

"The main point is it's all over, and you're going away for a very long time," Mac said.

A knock sounded on the door and then it opened. A young beat officer stood there with a sheet of paper in his hand. "The chief wanted me to give this to you, Detective McPherson."

"Thanks," Mac said as he rose from his seat, accepting the communication. He sat back down and silently read the document. The woman watched Mac as he read, and I watched her. She was detached, uncaring of her predicament, it appeared.

"Hmm, you'll find this interesting, Sam," Mac said without looking up. "Our Hildie here was born Hildegard Anika Bachmann on March 22, 1913 in Stuttgart, Germany to Gunther Bachmann and his wife, Sabine. She has three younger brothers, two of whom are fighting in the German Army. The third, and the youngest, flew for the Luftwaffe and was killed over the English Channel during a flight mission in the beginning of 1941. As a young girl, Hildegard always excelled in school, and in the fall of 1931, she enrolled in the University of Stuttgart to pursue studies in architecture. She quit her studies at the end of 1932 when she met the man who would become her husband at one of Hitler's rallies."

My eyebrows rose and I looked at Hildie, who was looking at me wearing an insincere grin. No wonder the man threw a tizzy fit every time she was out of his sight. No wonder he hadn't corrected me when I had called her his wife the first time I'd laid eyes on him. Mark wasn't her brother, but her husband. My expression went blank.

Mac continued. "Her father, Gunther, was a university professor of literature for much of his career, but in 1934 he started working for the Reich Ministry of Public Enlightenment and Propaganda in some menial position under Joseph Goebbels, where he still works today. Her husband wasn't as charmed in his own life.

"Markus Hans Klinger was born to a day laborer who worked in masonry, Dietrich Klinger, and his wife Marta on March 15, 1909 in Ludwigsburg, a smaller city just north of Stuttgart. Marta Klinger wasn't a strong woman. In her frail condition, she'd had a hard time giving birth to Markus, her first and only child, and died five days later. The boy turned out to be a handful for his father and the school system. Markus was a belligerent and rebellious child, and he became more of a problem as he moved into his teens. After getting expelled from a couple of schools, he was kicked out for a third, and last, time when he was fifteen. His father had had it and finally threw the boy out of the home, too. Little is known about where he lived or what he did with himself after that, but he would occasionally show up on his father's doorstep to ask for money. Dietrich Klinger would usually wind up giving in just to get rid of him. The last time he went to his father for a handout was in December of 1933, two months after marrying Hildegard Bachmann. He was surprised to have found that Dietrich Klinger had remarried and therefore, in his father's current situation, the older man had felt he had to lay down the law about not giving his son any more financial help. During the brief visit, Markus and his father had a violent argument over the senior Mr. Klinger's refusal to provide him with additional funds. The disagreement turned physical and, apparently, Markus tried to choke the older man. His father sent him packing, and warned the young man to never come back. Markus Klinger immediately went to the authorities and reported that his father was making anti-Hitler statements. Whether that was true or not, the Gestapo paid the older Mr. Klinger a visit and took him away for questioning. He hasn't been seen since." Mac raised his eyes and looked with disgust at Hildie. He then continued to read. "The couple never started a family of 'little Nazis' because I suppose they've been too busy acting as puppets for the Fuhrer. In 1935, Abwehr, the German military intelligence organization, recruited Markus and Hildegard Klinger. They've been in the United States since 1939, moving around to different locations."

"You married a real sweet guy, doll," I said to Hildie.

"You think you're so smart! You won't feel that way when the Fuhrer is victorious. He will rule your pathetic people with an iron fist," she spewed.

Mac laughed. "You must be punch-drunk, sister. Adolf Hitler isn't doodly-squat! Too bad you won't be around for our celebrations in the streets when we put him down."

Hildie was on her feet in a flash. With the palms of her hands on the table in front of her, she leaned forward and spit at Mac. I was half way out of my chair when she sat back down. Mac calmly brought his handkerchief out of his trouser pocket and wiped his cheek.

"I think this says it all," he said, pointing to the sheet of paper in front of him. "I think the FBI can get more information out of her concerning the network they belong to. Sam, do you have any questions for the woman?"

Have any questions? Of course, I have questions! I wanted to know how this woman had lured Sondra Girard into the pool that evening in early August…or did she have to be lured at all? I

227

wanted to know if it was her husband, Markus, who had broken into Bernie's guesthouse and trashed the place to scare her off. Too quickly I had dismissed Hildie's involvement because she was with me at The Bowery when the one-time nanny had made those threatening telephone calls to all of the people she felt were suspects in the death of Sonny. But Markus Klinger had left the dinner club earlier in a fit of anger. He'd been at home to take that call, and it was he who would have recognized the voice on the other end, having met Bernie in the office at the magazine when he picked his wife up from work on occasion. I wanted to know many things, and yet, I was extremely doubtful that I would get any of the answers. But I had to try, so I began by relating my theory that I had laid out to Bernie earlier in the week. I recounted my story of Hildie's unannounced visit, her borrowing of one of Sonny's swimsuits, their drinking a glass of wine, to which sleeping pills had been added to Sonny's without the woman's knowledge.

"How am I doing so far?" I asked.

With a smirk, Hildie said, "Not bad, Mr. Detective. I didn't think you had it in you. You know it's funny, I didn't have a plan when I first arrived there. All I knew was that she had seen Markus, and I didn't know if she was suspicious or not. When she never mentioned her change in appointment, or her seeing him to me, I knew that she was. I had to neutralize her in some way. Changing into her bathing suit and seeing the sleeping pills on the bathroom counter…well, it just came to me in a moment of brilliance. All of a sudden, I had a burst of inspiration." She emitted a soft laugh, as though she was quite proud of herself.

"And after the wine, the two of you went for your swim?" I asked.

Surprisingly, Hildie was willing to go on, explaining what had taken place in the senator's backyard that evening.

"Oh, no," she said. "Sondra had already gone for her swim, and was relaxing out in the backyard by the time I had arrived. She allowed me to go swimming because it had been so hot that day. Of course, I had to ask her if I could; she didn't offer. She let it be known that she would be eating her evening meal very soon, but I could use the pool until then. So very *gracious* of her, wasn't it? I could tell she was uncomfortable with me even being there. She would have rather that I just leave. Knowing *that* made it all the easier in getting rid of her. I don't appreciate it when people aren't cordial to me."

"Then how did she end up in the pool? Surely you didn't wait for her to fall asleep in the chaise lounge and then drag her in. There were no scrapes or injuries of any kind on her body," I questioned her.

Hildie Klinger straightened. Her demeanor was one of proud arrogance again. "No," she said. "Now that one was a real stroke of genius on my part. I waited until I noticed that she was getting very drowsy and sluggish. It didn't take long. And then...*oh, dear*...I suddenly felt a cramp coming on while swimming. It was so bad that I was starting to go *under*," she said in a dramatic display of feigned panic. "Of course, Sondra had no choice but to dive in to help me. She was so kind and caring like that," she said with exaggerated sweetness. "It was very easy to hold her under once she reached me. She barely had any fight left in her. There was no noise of any kind to alert any of the neighbors. It took no time at all. It was all so perfect." She smiled, and it took me all the self-control I could muster not to reach across the table and slap that self-satisfied grin off her face. "But tell me," she continued. "How did you know? What made you figure it all out? Where did I go wrong?"

It was my turn to smile. "You overplayed your hand, doll face. That bit about being so close to Sondra, being like a sister to her…well, you laid it on a bit too thick. Sondra was a very private person. She didn't like forming friendships with her employees. She didn't spend time with you outside of work. Sondra never received any visitors. And you didn't seem to realize that the woman's nickname was Sonny. All her closest friends called her Sonny. And then there was the fact that all the things you told me were lies. You telling me she was upset over her last interview? Hell, you weren't even there. No one was except Bernie. Bernie told me that the rest of the staff had all gone home for the day. You kept winging it, sweetheart, and the stories you were telling me weren't jiving with what others had told me. But I have to thank you. It was really *you* who, in the end, made it easy for me to solve this case."

"What do you mean?" she asked, confusion showing in her expression.

"The photo that was taken at The Bowery," I answered. "If you hadn't insisted I get in on being in that photograph, I would have never had a copy to take to a couple of people in town who knew that Markus had been associated with Mr. Wesley Barnard. That clinched the whole thing. But I have something else to ask you. Was it you or your husband who broke into the guesthouse behind Sondra Girard's home?"

Hildie smiled triumphantly. "I think I sent a definite message to that foolish woman, don't you?"

Well now, her answer certainly surprised me. I had been willing to bet that Markus had trashed Bernie's living quarters, and had I made that bet, I would have lost. I had one more question, but before I could ask it, there was a loud commotion coming from the corridor. Mac turned his head toward the door and then rose from his seat to see what was going on.

"What happened?" he asked with alarm in his voice.

"I don't know," I heard Larry Brown say in a panic. "We

230

were going to take him back to his cell, but once he got into the hallway here, he just dropped. I think he popped something into his mouth. I couldn't really tell."

I moved to the door and peered over Mac's shoulder. Markus Klinger was laying on the ground with a pained expression permanently cemented on his face. FBI agent George Foyle knelt beside him with his face hovering just above the face of the motionless man.

"Cyanide. He smells like almonds," Foyle said.

I looked back at Hildie, who appeared not to be concerned with what had just happened to her husband. Instead, she had her fingers inside the cuff of her dress. She had plucked something out of that cuff, and in an instant, it dawned on me what it was. Without delay I lurched and slid across the table top to where she sat, grabbing her wrist successfully. The small capsule she had held in her fingers catapulted from her grasp and landed on the floor in the corner of the room. The woman struggled with me while I held tight.

"Mac! Mac! Get it! It's on the floor in the corner."

Once Mac had retrieved the small pill, I released my hold on Hildie. Before I could stand, the woman spit on my face. It was my turn to pull out my handkerchief. I did so as I sat back down in my chair. Mac then called to an officer who was standing out in the hallway with Brown and Foyle. When the young man stepped inside the room, Mac ordered him to take Hildie back to her cell. Hildie Klinger's eyes were filled with venom, and as she approached to pass me, I could tell she was planning to cover me in spittle again. Before she could even take aim, I moved my right foot out from underneath the table and placed it directly in her path. She went down like dead weight, grazing her head on the coarse cement wall. When she righted herself, she placed her fingertips on her forehead, smearing the tiny pinpricks of blood that were forming.

"You dummkopf!" she spewed. Then in Mac's direction, she said, "I want to make a complaint! He tripped me deliberately!"

Mac looked at the young officer. "Did you see him trip her?"

"I didn't see it that way, Detective McPherson."

"That's what I thought," Mac said. "I didn't see it that way, either. Now get her out of here."

Hildegard Klinger moved out into the hallway with the officer without even so much as a glance at her husband's lifeless body.

CHAPTER THIRTY-SIX

Pulling into the garage at home, I saw Gran in the backyard hanging up newly washed bedding on the clothesline. I parked the car and entered the house, where I found Bernie sitting at the kitchen table, drinking a cup of tea. I sat opposite her. Before I told her the whole story, I wanted to ask her a question...it was the question I had wanted to ask Hildie out of curiosity, but was unable to do so.

"Bernie, where did Mark King work? What did he do for a living?"

"*Did*? As far as I know he still does. He's a bread delivery man. He delivers Wonder Bread to restaurants in the city."

"Ah," I said. "Well, that explains why Sonny was so surprised to see him at the bomber plant. His employment at the bomber plant also explains why Hildie was so careful not to ever obtain an appointment for Sonny for an interview there, even though she really wanted one."

"What? What are you talking about, Sam?" Bernie asked, showing confusion.

"Bernie, let's go into the parlor. I have a very long story to tell you."

233

***

Bernice Dayle didn't take the news well. She cried and cried, saying that it felt as though she had just lost Sonny all over again. I tried to comfort her and so did Gran, all to no avail. The woman was inconsolable and had locked herself and her grief behind my bedroom door for the remainder of the day and that evening. The sobbing continued well into the wee hours of the morning, preventing Gran and me from getting a good night's sleep. My grandmother emerged from her bedroom early on Sunday morning, just long enough to make a call to her best friend, Helen Foster. She told Helen she would not be accompanying her to the early morning service at the First Baptist Church. Returning to her bedroom, she then tried to make up for the lost sleep of the night before. I wasn't so lucky. Not being able to fall back to sleep, I sat in the chair and read the day's news while smoking a cigarette.

Bernie finally emerged from my room a few minutes after noon. She immediately went to the telephone located near the back door in the kitchen and made a couple of calls. When she had completed those calls, she joined me in the front parlor. Bernice Dayle looked like hell. Her eyes were red and puffy. In fact, her whole face appeared a bit swollen.

"Sam, on Monday there's a bus that goes to Cincinnati, and then I can catch a connecting bus to Asheville from there. It leaves the station at three forty in the afternoon. Will you take me? I want to go back home."

"Sure I will, Bernie, but what will you do once you get into Asheville? Will you have a place to stay?"

She shrugged. "I'll find somewhere," she answered in a weak voice. "I think I'll ask Sonny's daddy about a job at the paper. Maybe he'll hire me to do something. I was pretty good at answering the phones at the magazine. Maybe I can do that. I also just called Ty and Nola to say I wouldn't be coming back to The Monthly Patriot, and to say my goodbyes to them. I hope Ty can keep that magazine going. That was Sonny's baby."

I nodded and asked her if she would like me to fix her something to eat. She had missed supper last night. But she shook her head no. Before she headed back to my room for the day, she asked me how much she owed me.

"Nothing, Bernie. We're all set," I told her.

"Nonsense, I think I owe you for another couple of days."

"Forget it," I told her, and watched as she disappeared behind my bedroom door once again.

***

Gran worked her usual shift on Monday morning, starting at eight and ending at one thirty, so she was available to go with Bernie and me to the Greyhound Bus Depot that afternoon. The bus was on time. Before boarding, Bernie gave me a brief hug and thanked me for everything I had done in finding out what had happened to Sonny. Then she turned to my grandmother, giving her an extended hug.

"Bless your little heart, Ruby, for taking me into your home and being so kind to me," she said. "I think I'm going to miss you. You play a mean game of Monopoly. I've written down your address and I'll write to you. Let's keep in touch."

"Oh, that would be wonderful. Now, you take good care of yourself. And just remember, dear, your Sonny is in a much better place."

Bernie nodded, trying hard to form a smile on her lips. She leaned in and gave my grandmother a kiss on the cheek. We watched as the bus left the station, waving as Bernice Dayle disappeared from view. Walking back to the '38 Chevy, I put my arm around Gran. Climbing into the seat next to me, she let go of an over-exaggerated sigh.

"You feeling all right?" I asked her.

"Yes, just feeling relieved, actually. You know, Sam, Bernie is lovely and I like her. But that woman sure tuckered me out. It will be nice to have my own home back to just the two of us once more. And I *never, ever* want to eat grits again!"

I laughed and patted her on the top of her thigh. "How about this; what do you say to me taking you out for an early supper today? Pick a place. We'll go wherever you want, Gran."

"That's very nice of you, dear, but not tonight. For supper, you just find whatever you can to eat. Fix yourself a sandwich, or maybe open yourself a can of soup."

"You're not going to eat?"

"Oh, yes! I'm sure Angelo's wife will fix us some sandwiches and snacks."

I stared at her after turning the ignition in the auto. What was she talking about?

"Wait, Gran. Who in the world is Angelo?"

"Oh, my goodness. I almost forgot," she said while reaching into her dress and slipping her hand down into her brassiere. "Bernie told me to give this to you. She said she was sure she owed this to you for cracking the case." When she pulled her hand out, she brought with it three ten-dollar bills. "Can I have one of them, Sam? I'd like to take it with me to Angelo's tonight."

Shaking my head to clear the cobwebs, I asked, "But who *is* Angelo? And why do you need to take ten dollars with you tonight? Where the heck are you going, Gran?"

"Didn't I tell you?" she asked. "Augie is picking me up in a few hours and we're going to his older brother Angelo's. Of course, his other older brother Dominic will be there, too."

"Okay," I said hesitantly. "And Angelo's wife will be there too, right?"

"Oh, yes, but she isn't going to be playing with me and the

fellas. She's just there to make the snacks and keep the children away."

I was confused. "*Playing*? Playing *what* exactly?"

"Well, poker, dear. It's something the boys call five card stud; although, I think that's a silly name, don't you? Oh...," she said suddenly. "And on the way home, if you could stop at the corner store, I'd like to take two six-packs of beer with me tonight. It's only right since Angelo's wife will be giving me something to eat. But you can pay for it with one of your ten-dollar bills since you have two and I only have one."

"Gran," I sighed. "Don't you think that's a bit steep? Don't you think gambling ten dollars away is a bit foolish?"

"Not at all, dear. I won't be losing it. I feel *lucky* tonight!"

EPILOGUE

Over the next few days that followed, I'd done a lot of thinking about the case I'd just finished working on. Lavinia Marsh, the elderly woman living directly across the street from the senator, had thrown me for a loop with her description of Hildie as being an extremely tall woman. I would have said Hildie was average in height...another reason I wasn't onto her any earlier than I had been. It had suddenly dawned on me, only after the fact, that *anyone* would appear to be extremely tall when compared with the old woman. Lavinia Marsh had to be a couple of inches or so under five feet. And my disgust with Hildie and Markus Klinger had only grown stronger after I heard Tommy Petrovich's story.

Tommy Petrovich arrived home by yellow taxicab on the morning of Thursday, September 30, two days after his twenty-first birthday. After arriving back in the United States from the European conflict, he was taken to a veteran's administration hospital in Washington D. C., our nation's capital, for a few days of medical examination. There wasn't a lot of fanfare to his return to the neighborhood, but I noted that each night that followed, he and his father would sit quietly on their front porch after supper. His father, Vasily, would smoke his pipe while the younger man silently sat next to him.

The weather continued to be mild for that time of year. So it was on Tuesday, October 5, that I once again gazed out of the front window in the parlor and saw Mr. Petrovich and his son sitting on the porch of the home directly across the street from ours. The sun was still suspended up above, but wouldn't be for too much longer. I decided to meander over to where they sat. Both watched as I headed their way.

"Good evening," I said with a nod of my head when reaching the porch steps.

They nodded in return.

"It's such a beautiful night, I was thinking the two of you might like to join me in having a beer at The Double Shot. We could walk over, or I can get the Chevy out. What do you say?"

Vasily Petrovich glanced sideways at his son. "Why don't you go? It will do you good to get away for a bit, see some different scenery, see some other people."

"All right. Come with us, Dad," the young man urged.

"Nah, go on. I think I might turn in early this evening. You go and have a good time, son."

Mr. Petrovich raised his right hip and reached into his trouser pocket. He brought out two one-dollar bills and held them out to Tommy.

"No need for that, sir. Let me buy Tommy a couple of beers. I've got this."

"No, go on, take it," Vasily Petrovich insisted. "This will do the boy some good to get away, and I appreciate it." Then he turned to Tommy. "Here, take this and buy our friend, Mr. Flanagan, a beer." The boy took it, stood, and shoved it in his pocket.

During our walk to The Double Shot, it struck me that it was quite evident that this wasn't the boy who had grown up across

239

the street from my grandmother. The lad who had left over two years ago to enter a whole other world had changed. Thomas Vasily Petrovich had lost quite a few pounds, his face had taken on a more mature appearance, and he was quieter, more subdued. He'd become a man in a short period of time. I could only imagine what had happened to hasten that growth.

The Double Shot had few patrons on that Tuesday evening, and we chose a booth on the left side of the room. Our beers now before us, Tommy caught me off guard with a question.

"Do you believe in God, Mr. Flanagan?"

"Sure, I do," I answered him. "Don't you?"

"I don't know anymore," he said in a low voice. He took a long gulp of his beer and then suddenly asked, "Hey, you got any loose change for the jukebox?"

I gave him some coins and my eyes followed him as he stood in front of the machine, trying to decide what to play. "Moonlight Serenade" began to fill the room as he took his seat once again.

"You like Glenn Miller?" he asked as he lifted his mug.

"Yeah."

"I saw him, you know. Him and his band played for us when we were in England."

I nodded. And then I asked him why he was no longer sure that God existed. I don't think I was prepared for his answer. And once the young man began to talk about it, he couldn't seem to stop his flow of words. In one sitting, the dam was bursting on the story he hadn't been able to reveal to his parents.

He told me of how he and the other men in his unit had parachuted into the eastern part of the Netherlands on March 26 of this year. A friend of his from his unit had been blown farther out by high winds and gotten tangled in the branches of a tree. Tommy, having landed closer to him than anyone else, had run the thirty-five-yard distance to help him out. The rest of the men gathered their equipment and began their trek along the path into the forest that formed at the field's border.

"I'd never heard such words coming out of Ray's mouth as I did while I worked to cut him free," Tommy said with a smile. "He was a Catholic, and a good one." He patted the pocket on his shirtfront. "I got his St. Christopher's medal and his dog tags right in here."

"You do?" I asked with a sense of foreboding.

He nodded. "Even though he was older—he was twenty-seven—Ray was the first one I warmed to. He was from Kalamazoo, so I guess both of us being from Michigan made us have something in common. Anyway, he sure was mad as hell with his predicament, and all I could do was laugh at him while his feet dangled just above the ground. That made him even angrier."

Tommy told me that once free, Ray began gathering his things, and when they turned around to begin catching up to the other men, there were five Germans pointing rifles at them. The enemy then took them to a place called Westerbork.

"It's a detainment camp on the northeast border of the Netherlands," he explained. "It's kind of like a transit camp where they kept people there, mostly Dutch Jews, until they could transport them to other camps. Ray and I were probably kept there around two weeks. Time sort of gets away from you in that situation. If any of the guys from our unit doubled back to look for us the day that we landed, they were too late."

The day finally came when they, too, were transported via a crowded cattle car to a labor camp inside the borders of France, a country the Germans were occupying at present. There was a quarry located at the Natzweiler-Struthof camp, and the two young men were put to work clearing stones and boulders, along with countless others.

241

"There was one old man there who Ray thought looked an awful lot like his grandpa. Without much food for anyone to eat, the old gent was having trouble lifting the stones. Plus, if he wasn't seventy-five, he sure as hell looked all of it. He was growing weaker. He just didn't have the strength to do that kind of labor. So, Ray worked alongside him to help him out whenever the old guy started to falter. I'm telling you, Mr. Flanagan, if you don't pull your weight there, there's no reason whatsoever for the guards to keep you around. Ray was very protective of him. The old guy was falling more frequently, and those bastards noticed. So, then one day he fell one too many times. Ray was helping him up when a dirty rotten Kraut walked up behind him, and without any thought at all, put a bullet through the back of the old man's head."

A jolt of electricity shot through me. I couldn't think of a thing to say, so I kept my mouth shut.

"Ray couldn't take it. He went berserk. He began screaming and tried to rush the guard. Another guard ran over to where the scuffle was, and before Ray knew what had happened, he was on the ground. That guard rammed the butt of his rifle with such force into the side of Ray's face that he broke his jawbone. I'm not sure why they didn't kill him right then and there." Tommy took another swig of his beer and slid out of the booth. "Anything special you want to hear on the jukebox?" he asked me.

I shook my head no. While he was gone, I signaled to Neamon that we needed two more beers. Inside, I felt strange and uncomfortable. I knew what this young man was telling me was the truth, and yet, I was finding it hard to believe that something so cold and cruel could be taking place in this world. What bothered me also was the way in which my young neighbor was relaying this story. His tone was matter-of-fact, as though he was detached from the horror of it all…as though he *had* to distance

242

himself from the reality of what he had experienced, or else he wouldn't be able to cope. I suspected this was his protection mechanism, but he wasn't finished. With Benny Goodman's "Don't Be That Way" sounding in the background, he once again joined me and continued.

"Boy, what a mess!" he stated with a shake of his head. "Ray couldn't talk, he couldn't eat, and he had a helluva time swallowing. I kept telling him to hang on. We'd get out of this hell hole and get him to a doctor who could wire his jaw very soon."

"They didn't do that there?" I asked, trying to hide my astonishment.

"Hell no! They still made him work until he couldn't do it anymore. His jaw got all infected and he was in a lot of pain. The swelling in the side of his face and neck was huge! The infection must have spread throughout his body. There came a time when he had grown so weak, he couldn't even raise his head. I'd sneak into the bunker to check on him during work hours, but I could tell he was getting worse. Those bastards wouldn't even let me bring him some soup at feeding time. Huh! *Soup*," he said. "It was more like warm water with a carrot and a turnip in it. Michel would break into the mess building at night and steal some of it, along with a small piece of bread, and we would drizzle it down Ray's throat. We tried soaking tiny pieces of the bread in the liquid so it would be easier to eat, but he couldn't do it. He almost choked on the bread, so that was no good. We couldn't get enough substance into him. I watched as he got weaker by the day."

"Who is Michel?" I asked.

He chuckled. "A kid, and I mean *a kid*. He was part of the French Resistance. The kid was kind of like a courier, getting messages to others in the movement, but the Nazis had grown suspicious. They were waiting for him in the shadows at the end of the street one night. That's how he ended up at Natzweiler-Struthof. He was a daring and sassy little thing, and I was so afraid it was just a matter of time before they'd catch on to what he was doing. Well, he pushed his luck one too many times. We could hear the shouts coming from outside. A guard came into the bunker and blew the whistle. That meant that everyone had to rise and go outside in uniform order. I draped Ray's arm over my shoulder and held him up. We went into the yard. Another guard was there, and Michel was taunting him, giving him lewd gestures and shouting at him. We stood, watching the scene, and that's when it happened."

"What?" I asked, afraid to hear the answer.

"The guard who Michel was arguing with smiled and unleashed his dog. It was supposed to be a lesson to all of us. He was only twelve years old, and he wasn't going to see thirteen. They're killing whole groups of people in those camps, Mr. Flanagan. And those camps are spread out all over Europe. That night I laid down on the same bunk beside Ray. He was shaking like he was cold, although I knew his tremors weren't just because of that. I put my arms around him to give him some of my body heat and to try to steady him. I had to push any thought of Michel out of my mind or else I'd start to lose it as Ray was doing. He began to cry. His tears were dropping on my hand, but he wasn't making any sound. At some point, I dozed off. When I woke, my hand was still wet and he was warm to the touch, but he was gone. His eyes were staring up above. He must have cried throughout the whole night, and died in my arms right before I woke."

We both sat in silence for what seemed to be an eternity. I was trying to process it in my mind, and I had no idea what Tommy was thinking or feeling; something much worse, I was sure.

Finally, I had to know. "How did you ever get the hell out of there?"

He gulped some of his beer, then placed the mug down on the table top before answering. "Vasha," he said.

"Vasha? What's that?"

"*Who*, you mean *who's* that," he corrected me.

Vasha was part of a group of a half a dozen or so men who belonged to the Russian Partisan. They'd been captured and brought into the Natzweiler-Struthof camp weeks after Ray had died. Vasha seemed to be their leader. What the group *didn't* know was that Tommy had a Russian father who had taught him when he was a young boy just enough of his native language to get by. So, when the young soldier had overheard them discussing a plan to escape, he told the group he wanted in. If Tommy was going to lose his life, he'd rather lose it while actually doing something in an effort to get away from that horrific imprisonment. Under the guise of asking a guard for a cigarette one night, the Russian Partisan members put their plan into action. "Vasha could snap a neck faster than it took for you to blink," Tommy told me. In a blur, the young American soldier had run. He ran and ran and ran, hearing angry German shouts and gunfire behind him. Entering the trees that surrounded the camp, he felt sure he would feel a bullet piercing his spine, but he didn't.

"I don't know who else made it," Tommy said. "I guess I'll never know." He lifted his mug and tipped it, draining it of its contents. "Hey, can we have one more beer?"

Through our third beer, Tommy Petrovich told me how, after a long searching expedition, he'd finally found out where his unit was located and had caught up with them. But because of all that had happened during his time away from them, he was then useless as a soldier. He couldn't sleep, and when he was lucky enough to doze for a few moments, he had seen the lifeless eyes of his buddy, Ray, staring at him…or the torn and mangled body of the young boy, Michel, in his unconsciousness. He would wake screaming at the top of his lungs. Because of his lack of sleep, he couldn't understand or follow orders properly. He was putting himself and the other soldiers in danger, and that couldn't be. His superiors finally decided it was time to send him home.

"I still can't sleep most nights. When you can't sleep, you feel loopy…like you're not connected in some way. Like you're hanging suspended above what's really going on in life, if that makes sense. I should be back there with them. I let them all down. I'm here with a bed to lay in, and they're over there in some foxhole. I should be back there with them. I should be doing something to help. I've failed them. And I'll go home tonight and, if I'm lucky enough to sleep, I'll have the same nightmares."

Suddenly, without any change in his demeanor, his eyes allowed all the pain and confusion he had locked away inside of himself to gush forth in the way of huge teardrops, which flowed down his cheeks. Because of his emotionless expression, I wondered if he was even aware that he was crying.

"So, you tell me, Mr. Flanagan. Is there really a God?"

Although I couldn't provide him with a concrete explanation, I said, "Yes."

"Why? How do you really know that?"

"Because who do you think it was who prevented that bullet from entering your back as you ran into that forest?"

It was just past ten o'clock when we left The Double Shot and started our walk back to St. Aubin Street. We strolled in silence. When we stood in front of Gran's house, Tommy turned to me and shook my hand.

"Thanks for everything," he said.

I pointed to his shirt pocket. "What are you going to do with the medal and dog tags?"

"Dad's going to take a day or two off of work when he can and take me out to Kalamazoo. I want to look up Ray's family. He's got a wife and kid. He was always talking about Shirlene and his little girl. I'll give the chains to them. They deserve to know what happened and that I was with him."

I nodded, then said, "I know you feel as though you let your unit down, but it isn't your fault. Things happen for a reason, Tommy. And I know of a way you can still be working in this effort."

His eyebrows drew together. "How?"

"Get your story out. People need to hear what's going on. They need to hear the truth. Tell your story and keep telling it. Don't let the old man, Michel, or your buddy, Ray, die in vain."

"How do I do that?" he asked again.

"I know some people. Let me handle that. They'll be contacting you, I'm sure. Then go to town hall meetings and tell them the story. Go anywhere and everywhere you can where people will listen."

Tommy nodded and shook my hand for a second time. "Thanks again, Mr. Flanagan," he said.

"Don't you think you should start calling me Sam? With what you've been through, you're much older than I am at this very moment in time."

That same evening, sitting on my own porch steps while smoking a cigarette, Tommy Petrovich's story kept replaying in my mind. I sat out there until the lights went off within the house and Gran had gone to bed. I had kept telling myself that I wasn't tired yet, but in reality, the fact of the matter was that I was afraid to lie on my bed and close my eyes in the darkness of my room, fearing I would have a few nightmares of my own. The world certainly was going to hell in a handbasket, and we were all drowning in a sea of deception. How many people like Hildie and Markus Klinger were among us in the United States, plotting our destruction? How many people, living in this world at this very moment, had ice running through their veins and harbored such hatred and hardness in their hearts toward other men, different from themselves? I inwardly shuddered to think of the number, fearing it would be great. Praying to God, whom I *chose* to believe existed, I asked Him for His absolute assurance that we would be victorious over the evil we were battling.

On Wednesday morning, I called the office of The Monthly Patriot. The female voice that answered my call was one I didn't recognize. Obviously, it was Bernice Dayle's replacement. I immediately asked to speak to Kay Rewis without identifying myself, and was put straight through to her.

When she greeted me on the phone, I said, "Miss Rewis? This is Detective Flanagan. Remember me?"

Hesitantly, and in a lowered and frightened voice, she said, "Yes."

"I believe I've got a story for you. In fact, you may want to write a series of articles covering this."

The young reporter appeared to be very receptive to my idea, taking down all the information she would need to get in contact with Tommy Petrovich. Next, I dialed the telephone number I had for the Detroit News. I had already given the story of the murder of Sondra Girard to Bulldog Dixon, and he had come out with a fantastic piece on it early during the previous week. Today, I had something else in mind for Tommy's story. When the daily paper's operator answered, I asked, "Yes, may I please speak to a reporter named Miss Vee Anscombe?"

***

We received our first letter from Bernie on Friday, October 8. She was happy to tell us that she had gotten a job, not at the newspaper that Sonny's father was the editor in chief of, but rather behind the candy counter at the town's local five and dime. And she was loving it.

Oh, and about Gran's night of poker with Augie Consiglio and his brothers, Angelo and Dominic...she had returned home about eleven that night and held out to me a crisp ten-dollar-bill.

"You didn't end up playing poker?" I had asked her.

Instead of answering me, she reached into her brassiere and pulled out more money. She held up some fanned-out bills... three fives and four ones. Well, doggone! Gran really *was* filled with luck that night!

Judith G. White holds a degree in secondary education with a major in history from Western Michigan University. She currently works part time at The Henry Ford, America's Greatest History Attraction, where her life has been enriched by meeting dignitaries, entertainment personalities and leaders in business and industry. She's traveled throughout the lower forty eight states and toured Great Britain. History, reading, playing word and trivia games and, of course, writing, is what she likes to do best. She makes her home in a southern suburb of Detroit along with her husband, Jim; two children, Brandon and Erin; and two dogs, Sadie and Orie.

68497625R00152

Made in the USA
Lexington, KY
13 October 2017